POHLSTARS

FREDERIK POHL

A Del Rey Book

BALLANTINE BOOKS • NEW YORK

A Del Rey Book

Published by Ballantine Books

Copyright © 1984 by Frederik Pohl

Library of Congress Catalog Card Number: 84-91034

ISBN 0-31545-6

Manufactured in the United States of America

First Edition: October 1984

Cover art by Rick Sternbach

CONTENTS

POHLSTARS

acknowledgments

INTRODUCTION

If you find an unexpectedly Oriental flavor to this collection (and to one particular story in it), it is because a couple of months ago, for the first time in my life, I was in China. What brought me there was simple curiosity, and I sated it. I did all the things tourists are supposed to do. I climbed the Great Wall and gaped at the terracotta warriors of Hsian; I cruised on the Whangpoo River and even walked the old Silk Trail at the tag end of the Gobi Desert. But that wasn't all I was curious about, so in between the bouts of tourism, I spent a lot of time with writers. Chinese writers. Chinese *science-fiction* writers in particular . . . and I tell you true, if I had read that sentence a few years ago I would have assumed it must be the beginning of a science-fiction story, and not a very plausible one, at that. But it isn't fiction. It's real. Science fiction is being read, written, and published in the People's Republic of China.

The more I talked with the people involved in science fiction there, the more I felt that curious nibble at the fringes of the memory that is called déjà vu. I had been there before! For what the Chinese science-fiction scene

reminded me of more than anything else was the way it had been in the United States when, five decades ago, I was beginning to try to be a writer of science fiction. The Chinese science-fiction people I met seemed young, energetic, idealistic, not very sophisticated— very like the young, unsophisticated Isaac Asimov, Donald Wollheim, Cyril Kornbluth, and other teenage members of the 1930s fan group, the Futurians, which launched so many of us into careers as writers and editors. The social standing of science fiction in China is very low. The literary mandarins don't think it's literature at all—any more than America's literary mandarins did in the 1930s. (It didn't become respectable in the United States until some of those bright, unsophisticated kid fans grew up to become college professors and deans.) The economic situation of science fiction in China today maps almost exactly with that of the United States in the 1930s. An average price for a science-fiction story is about a third of a cent a word (in 1939 I was lucky enough to average almost half a cent); a Chinese editor I met confided that his salary was about eleven dollars a week (my first editorial job paid ten). And almost all the science fiction being written by Chinese authors is in the form of short stories; the few novels published are importations from abroad. That, too, was true of America then. Almost the only science-fiction *books* that one could find were written by people on the other side of the ocean, such as S. Fowler Wright, Aldous Huxley, and W. Olaf Stapledon. The book publishers in America disdained science fiction—at least when it was by American writers. It was not until around 1950—and then, again, only because some fans grew up to start or join publishing companies—that American science-fiction writers could have their novels published in hard covers.

To find out that science fiction existed outside the United States was not a surprise to me—after all, I spent a couple of years as president of the international association of science-fiction professionals, World SF, with members in several dozen countries from Singapore to the U.S.S.R. and most nations in between. But it was surely a delight!

Of course, it would take a braver man than I to predict how widespread science fiction will become in China. China is an intensely politicized country. Nearly every aspect of its life has to conform with the decisions of the high Party apparatus—whatever those decisions may be at any particular moment—and so it is impossible to guess what its future will be. China is also a country that for just about a solid century has been wracked by a series of violent convulsions, almost non-stop, revolutions, wars, and internal turmoil. From the overthrow of the Manchu dynasty—through the war with Japan; the battle against Chiang Kai-shek, the "Great Leap Forward," the "Cultural Revolution," the "Rule of the Gang of Four" and their overthrow—there has hardly been a period of more than a year without devastating upheaval. The achievements of the current regime are immense in fundamental ways: They manage to feed and educate their billion people, an accomplishment no previous rulers even tried. But they are also, by Western standards, complex, unpredictable, and frequently weird. Walking the streets of Beijing or Shanghai today, it is difficult to believe that this largest nation the world has ever seen was, just a few years ago, tearing itself to shreds in the violence of the Cultural Revolution, with factions shelling each other's campuses and factories at will—and even more difficult to understand how they managed to pull themselves together afterward. So I don't know how things are going to work out for the billion Chinese people, much less for that tiny fraction of them who read and write science fiction...but I wish them well!

This is almost my first short-story collection in a decade. It isn't that I've given up writing; it's that I've been writing novels rather than short stories most of the time.

I must confess that I find this a little nettling. I don't like to think of myself as a statistic manipulated by large economic forces...but that's the way it looks, even to me. The field that used to be dominated by the magazines, and thus by short stories, is now overwhelmingly represented by novels and films. I suppose the

average readership of the science-fiction magazines of
my youth was somewhere around forty thousand copies. Now 40 *million* people flock to see a new *Star Wars*
movie in the first weekend of its release. As to books,
the *New York Times* best-seller list has been heavily
populated with science fiction for this whole year: Arthur
C. Clarke, Isaac Asimov, Joan Vinge, Anne McCaffrey,
and a dozen others have reached the heights of book-
store sales previously scaled only rarely by a Frank
Herbert or a Robert A. Heinlein. When Cyril Kornbluth
and I wrote *The Space Merchants* thirty years ago, we
were in science-fiction's transitional period from magazines to books; we expected to earn a couple of thousand dollars from having it run as a serial in *Galaxy*
magazine, and it did—but it has earned more than that
every year since as a book.

So there is an economic incentive to write longer
pieces. But it isn't all economic. It's where the audi-
ences are . . . and no writer likes to be talking to himself.

Anyway, I'm pleased to offer you this collection. With
one exception, all the stories herein are uncollected.
The one exception is "*The Wizard-Masters of Peng-
shi Angle.*" In an earlier incarnation the story appeared
in a collection of mine nearly twenty-five years ago—
but, as you will see, the present version is rather strik-
ingly different from the one I wrote in the 1950s!

I hope you'll enjoy the stories . . . and that it won't be
so long before I have another collection of new short
stories to offer!

—Frederik Pohl
New York City
November, 1983

THE SWEET, SAD QUEEN
OF THE GRAZING ISLES

At the World Science Fiction Convention in Chicago in 1982 I was part of a panel discussing the work of the late Cordwainer Smith (pseudonym of the Johns Hopkins political science professor, Paul M. A. Linebarger). Paul Linebarger was an author whom I published extensively as long as he lived while I was editing *Galaxy* in the 1960s, and one whose work I greatly admire still. He was not merely a contributor but a friend, for which reason he tolerated my practice of changing almost every title of the Cordwainer Smith stories I published. (Other writers were less forgiving.) While talking about this on the panel, it occurred to me that it was a long time since I had made up a Cordwainer Smith story title. So I amused myself (in the boring periods while other people were talking) by inventing titles for stories Paul had never written, but should have. The one I liked best was this one...and so, that afternoon, as part of my self-imposed regime of defacing four pages of clean paper with writing every day of my life, I began to write a story to go with the title. I do not think it is a "Cordwainer Smith story" by any means. But I did bor-

1

row one of his favorite devices in the writing of it—
perhaps some readers will detect which one.

I

In Twenty and Three, born at sea,
Her daddy endowed her a legacy.
In Twenty and Ten her brother Ben
Stole the inheritance back again.
She loves but she loses, she weeps as she smiles,
The sweet, sad queen of the grazing isles.

BECAUSE I DID THE OLD COMMODORE A FAVOR, HE PROM-
ised I would always have a job with the Fleet. I always
did. I always do still, because even now I have the job.
The title and the pay and the working conditions have
changed a dozen times, and these times not the best of
them. But even Jimmy Rex knows I have that right to a
job, and grants it. Meanly.

The favor I did for Commodore Mackenzie was done
long before he was a Commodore, and I could have gone
to jail for it. Jason, he said, give me a month. I need an
extension on my loans, thirty days at most, and if you
give it me, you'll never have to worry again as long as
you live. I will worry, though, I said—a boy still in his
twenties, just a keypuncher in the records section of a
bank—I'll worry about the law, at least until the statute
of limitations runs out, because buggering the records is
a penal offense. Only if they catch you, he said, laughing,
and that they can't do. For you'll be at sea, where the
land law cannot reach. It was his first oaty-boat that was
building at the time, you see, and he had used up all his
wife's money and all he could cajole out of his first two
financial backers, and the third one, the big one, was
trying to make up his mind to plunge.

He was a powerful man even then, James Mackenzie.
No older than forty, no bigger than most, but the blue

eyes flashed and the smile was sure, and he knew how to talk a person toward any place he chose. But what decided me was not Mackenzie. It was his young wife, the lady Ella. She loved him. So I worked overtime one night, and displayed his file, and changed a few dates, sweating with fear. He had his thirty days. And the backer did, at the last minute, come through with the money to finish the boat, and so James William Mackenzie became the Commodore.

He was a son of a bitch, Commodore Mackenzie, but he had style. Fifty shares of stock I got and a title: Executive Assistant to the Fleet Captain. Very grand. Even if the fleet was still only a single vessel. But even one oaty-boat is a huge and costly machine, two hundred thousand metric tons of hull and works, towing twenty kilometers of tubes and pumps, with a deck the size of a township. The Commodore did something you won't believe with that deck, or at least with the part forward of the bridge. He planted it. He pumped aboard half a million cubic meters of San Francisco Bay bottom muck while the boat was still at the builder's dock. The water ran off through the scuppers, and the soil remained. He sailed it up toward Tacoma for the deep-water fitting and steamed slowly around the wettest, stormiest part of the Pacific Coast until the rain had rinsed it clean. Seeds and slips and bulbs and saplings came aboard, and by the time we were on our first cruise there was grass there, and gardens, and the beginnings of a grove. For his dear lady Ella hated the sea. So Owner's Quarters were an apartment below deck and a terrace above, and if you looked only forward you could think you were in some fine manor house with the weather always balmy and the lawn as steady as any on Earth. The weather was always fine because oaty-boats are never in bad weather. That is why they are boats, instead of drilling platforms or moored barges, so that they can seek out the places where sea and air are best to do their work.

And for four years they were happy, and I was happy,

and the great boat steamed slowly through the fruitful
patches of the southern ocean, sucking up the cold and
pitting it against the warm, and, oh, how the money rolled
in! And we were happiest of all in the fourth year, when
Ella was pregnant. She was a tiny, frail woman, all spirit
and no stamina, and there were times when in even the
calmest seas she seemed unwell. Yet as a pregnant woman
she bloomed, prettier than ever and glowing with the child
inside. The baby was born, even prettier than her mother.
It was in the month of May, and so they called her May,
and then the happiness stopped because Ella died. It was
not childbirth alone—she had the best of doctors, flown
in from Sydney and San Francisco. It was cancer. She
had known she had it, and kept it secret, and wouldn't
let them cut it away because it would have cut away the
unborn child as well. Childbirth merely finished her off.

It was her wish to be buried on land. The Commodore
walked dry-eyed through the crew quarters and crooked
a finger at an oiler's mate named Elsie Van Dorn. A large,
plain woman, but a kind one. And when he came back
from the funeral, he took all the Fleet stock that was in
Ella's name and put it into baby May's, and gave me a
new job. "Van Dorn will be May's nursemaid," he said,
"but you'll be her godfather." That was a joke, I think,
because we had been told that money was his god. "You're
Managing Director of the May Mackenzie Trust, and if
you do anything wrong with it I'll kill you. Even if I die
for it. Even if I die first, for I'll leave a little sum of money
and some orders, and someone will be watching who has
a gun." He still owed me for the favor I had done him,
you see, but he remembered what it was.

And for seven years baby May grew, and wasn't a
baby any more.

There are little girls with a face so fine and a look so
sweet that they'll break your heart. May was one. She
was slight for her age, and all her life. Yet even when she
first toddled she would pause, and stick her thumb in her
mouth, and gaze out over the privet and the boxwood

hedges at the southern seas with an ancient mariner's look of sadness and resignation that made you forget the rumpled hair and the dragging diaper; and when she was old enough to talk and tie her shoes, I fell in love. It is not a thing I want to have laughed at and so I will say no more, but it's true. I did. I loved her truly and purely, and went on doing so. Not as a godfather.

She had a father's love for those seven years, though. She was the Commodore's only daughter and his only legitimate child—the only child of his I saw then, for the bastard was away at school and then at work in the Fleet's landside offices. He was busy every minute, the Commodore, but he always found time to see May and to play with her, and to tuck her in at night. I was less busy than that. There was not much work attached to being the Managing Director of the May Mackenzie Trust, for every penny of it was invested in the oaty fleet, two ships, and then seven, and then a dozen; the money rolled in, but every spare penny went back into building more. So I competed with Elsie Van Dorn. I became May's other nanny. They were the best years I have ever lived. I took her with me around the boat. We watched the dry ammonia powder being pumped out of our belly into the hold of a tanker, kerchiefs to our noses to keep from sneezing, and we listened to the screaming hydrogen flow as it went into the refrigeration ships, the huge red flags warning us not to light a match or scratch a spark—as though anyone in the Fleet were such a fool! We watched the huge slow spinning of the low-pressure turbines as they transformed the heat into power, and we waved good-by to the crews of the scout skimmers as they went out to seek colder depths and warmer air to steer toward. Every member of the crew knew May, and petted her when she would let them. They weren't truly a crew. They were more like a city, for we had power workers and fertilizer chemists and oceanographers and engineers and navigators and cooks and cleaning men and fire wardens and a ship's master with five assistants to guide us and half a dozen

gardeners for the greensward and the farms on the after-deck. There were more than eighteen hundred human beings on board, and I think May knew the name of every one. She knew none better than me. I was her godfather and her friend. There were a hundred other children on board, and four who were her special friends, but there was no person who was more special than I.

And then the Commodore one morning came to break-fast in May's room, as he always did when he was aboard, and looked tired, admitted he'd had a bad night's sleep, got up from the table, fell face down on his plate, and died.

I could forgive the Commodore for dying. He didn't plan to do it, and it happens to us all. But I will never forgive him for dying with his will so written that his bastardly bastard son, Ben, became May's guardian until she was thirty years old.

He was aboard before the body was cold and had moved into the Commodore's rooms before the smoke of the Commodore's cigars was aired out. The will gave him the voting rights on May's stock. I could forbid him to sell a share. I could take the dividends and invest them any-where I chose—but where was there a better investment than the oaty fleet?

I could, in fact, do nothing.

For a month, then, I looked over my shoulder every minute, expecting to see the Commodore's hired assassin, but the assassin never came. All that came was a note, one day, mailed from Papua New Guinea via the boat's air service, and all it said was, "It's not your fault, this time."

The Commodore never broke a promise to me but two. The first was that he'd have me killed if I failed to protect May's interest. I did fail her then, and knew I had, but I didn't die. The other promise was that I would never have to worry again, because after he died, for twenty years and more, I did nothing else.

II

Later on, in Twenty-three,
The queen she married, but not to me.
Later still, in Twenty-four,
A scowling imp of a son she bore.
She bore him and raised him for years and miles,
The son of the queen of the grazing isles.

When May was fifteen, Van Dorn went at last back to
the engines, and May went off to school. She took her
four friends with her, the four other Mays with whom
she'd grown up, but Ben would not allow me to join them.
"You can keep your job and your pay, Jason," he said to
me, "but leave my sister May alone, for when she's ready
to fall in love it will be with a rich boy and a sensible boy
and a handsome boy, and not with a dirty old man who
sleeps with her socks under his pillow." That was a lie.
I told him it was a lie. But what was behind it was no lie,
for the love was still there. If May had been five years
older, if she had been a year older even, I might easily
have told her what I felt before I let her go. And might
have got a good answer, perhaps. There was thirty years
between us, and I am not handsome. But she was easy
with me, and trusted me, and had good reason for trust.
So Ben the Bastard fouled Owner's Quarters with his
fat dark wife and their sallow brat, Betsy, who never liked
me. Nor I her, to be sure. That whole family was repellent.
I never knew Ben's mother, but I knew who she was. A
file clerk in a lawyer's office. The Commodore seduced
her to get a look into the lawyer's contract files, where
there was something worth money for him to see. He got
his look. She got his child. He would never marry her,
of course, for she hadn't a dime, and when she pupped
his bastard, he was long gone away. I will say for the

Commodore that he acknowledged the son. He paid the bills to bring him up, even when it was hard for him. He sent the boy through school and gave him a place with the Fleet, though not at sea, but would never give him his name.

So it was Benjamin (which means "gift of God") Zoll (for that was the woman's name) who came aboard with the will in his pocket and the resolve in his heart to reign.

Well, he had more than arrogance. He was a mean-hearted man, but a hardworking one. The first day he was over the side in a diving mask, discovering cracks in the antifouling plates and surfacing in a fury. Twenty maintenance workers lost their jobs that day, but the next crew kept the plates repaired, and we saved a thousand dollars worth of steaming fuel a week.

An ocean-thermal generating boat lives off the temperature difference between deep water and sun-warmed surface water. The top water warms the working fluid— a halocarbon with a low boiling point—and it becomes steam and goes through the low-pressure turbines to make electricity; the electricity splits water into hydrogen and fixes nitrogen from the air, and we sell what it makes. The difficulty is the halocarbon working fluid. It is too expensive to vent to the air. It must be condensed and recycled, and for that we need something cold. The sea gives us that. There is plenty of cold water in every deep sea, but it is half a kilometer down or more, and so we must pump it to the surface. Pumping and pumping. Pumping cold water up from the deep. Pumping the working fluid through the solar collectors. Pumping water past the electrodes to be split into its gases; pumping the gases into the refrigerator ships to be carried away. Out of every hundred kilowatt-hours of energy we make, ninety-seven go into running the gear itself.

But that three percent left over makes us rich, for once the boat is built it is all free.

Ben Zoll had never worked on an oaty-boat, and so he had much to learn. He learned it fast. If he did not have the Commodore's name, he had at least inherited his drive.

May had the name. And bastard Ben kept her from everything else, kept her from the presidency of the Fleet, kept her from the voting rights to her stock.

He did not begrudge her money. She had the best schools. She had horses to ride and clothes for a princess. It was no sacrifice to Ben to allow her any money she needed. The billions of land people hungered insatiably for every grain of ammonia and every wisp of hydrogen we could make. The company prospered under bastard Ben.

And so did I, for my pitiful fifty shares of stock had already made me a millionaire. I didn't need the job anymore. But I kept it, and I stayed on the O.T. Where else was there to go? No sensible person would want to live on a continent with all those writhing billions. Land people are a suing, assassinating, conniving bunch. And I had formed the habit of living under the Law of the Sea—

And, besides, every now and then May came home to visit.

She did not come often. But there were school holidays. Any time there were a few days together, she would take the long five-hour flight from Massachusetts to the Bismarcks or the Coral Sea or wherever we were grazing, and in the summers, always, for weeks on end. It was not May alone, for the four other Mays always came too, to visit their families and to get away from the stink and strife. They were beautiful girls. Girls to break a thousand hearts, and I suppose they did. There was Maisie Richardson, huge and blond and glowing with health, and May Holliston-Peirce, the hydrologist's daughter, with trusting blue eyes and a sweet, guileful tongue, and Tseling Mei, who became a movie star, and May Bancroft, black and handsome and the wisest of them all. And May herself. My May. She was always the most beautiful of them all. There are pretty babies who grow up blotchy or sullen or fat, but there was never a day in any company when May was not the most beautiful there. They were all almost of an age, May and the four other Mays, and, oh, heaven, how they brightened up the old O.T.! There

was a May for any man's taste, and all of them for every
taste, for they were kind and clever, they were lovely and
loving. They chattered and whispered among themselves,
and if ever a joke went the wrong way or a word touched
a nerve, they made it up at once with a kindness and a
kiss.

And then there was Betsy.

Betsy Zoll. Bitch child of the bastard, Ben. If you take
the raw materials for two young women and give all of
the beauty and kindness and grace to one—say, to May—
what is left over is Betsy Zoll. May was a diamond. Betsy
was flawed glass. When the Mays were not aboard, Betsy
was the princess royal, and sometimes, on a good day,
she almost looked the part. But in their shade she drooped
and sulked. The shiny glass was beside true diamonds,
and its luster was gone. They let her tag along with them,
out of kindness. Out of envy, she wished them dead. So
the holidays were no joy for Betsy Zoll, and she couldn't
wait, couldn't wait for them to be over and the Mays back
in school so she could try to reign again.

And then there was a Christmas season coming when
Betsy was all smiles and triumph.

She must have hunted all over the boat for me, for I
was down in the boiler room to see if there was a need,
as ship's gossip said there was a plan, to buy new generators. "Well, Jason," she said, beaming so fondly that
my heart sank, "getting ready for Christmas?"

The engineers and oilers watched us from a distance,
whispering to themselves, although no one needed to
whisper with the great coughing sigh of the low-pressure
turbines in every ear. I wished her a Merry Christmas
civilly and excused myself to let my office know where
I was—there was no reason not to now, you see, because
Betsy had already found me. When I finished with the
phone, she giggled. "Next week that will cost you a
quarter," she said.

I had known she would bring bad news, of course,
because that was her nature, but what she said was as-

tonishing. "It will cost money to use the ship's phone?"

She pursed her lips and inclined her head. "To use the phone, and to run your video, and to turn on a fan, yes," she said, the sallow face and the pale eyebrows twitching with pleasure. "Father says it's time we started charging for all the electricity the crew uses. Fifty cents a kilowatt-hour to start, Father says."

"It makes no sense!"

"*Dollars* and cents," she said gleefully. "That's our electricity, old man. It's worth money. Why should we give it away when we can sell it?"

I drew back from her, because she had pressed her face almost into mine and her breath was like a sewer. Betsy was fifteen years old then, but the freshness of youth had never touched her. I said, "We can't sell electricity, Betsy, only what we can make from it. If we want to produce more to sell, we'll have to devote more space to conversion processes, and where's the space to come from?"

"Good question, old man," she said triumphantly. "Father has of course thought of all that. To begin with, there's a thousand cubic meters wasted under the foredeck. We'll do our hydrogen electrolysis up there, which gives more room amidships for the ammonia and—"

"Owner's Quarters!" I said.

"Old man," she lectured, "people like us won't live on this little tub forever. We've got new boats building ten times the size of this. We're going to move the flag."

The ship's gossip was not only gossip, then, and the truth was worse than the gossip. It was worse than I knew, in fact, for Betsy had saved the worst for the last. "When May comes home for Christmas, we'll see what she has to say," I said, for it was in the Commodore's will that May's own quarters were hers forever. And I had delivered myself into Betsy's hands.

"When May comes home for Christmas," she parroted spitefully, "what we'll see, old man, is that she isn't coming home for Christmas. Why, Jason! Do you mean she never told you that she's got a boy friend? His name's

Frank Appermoy, and she's spending her Christmas with him and his mother."

And May had not written me a word! As Betsy well knew. She did not bother to disguise her triumph as she glanced at her watch and moved her lips for a moment before she spoke, that charnel breath well suited to the words she said. "Allowing for the time differences," she said, "I'd guess they're probably humping in his big water bed on Hawaii right now. Tough shit, old man," she said, and turned and left me standing.

Back in my office, the first thing I did was order up all the data we had in store on Frank Appermoy and the rest of the Appermoy clan. The second thing, while I was waiting for the readouts, was to put through a call to May at the Appermoy estate on the Big Island. It was 10 P.M. on the Kona coast, and according to the butler who answered my call, Miss May and Master Frank were at a luau and were not expected to return for at least two hours. So I asked them to call me, and got down to the hard-copy prints.

I already knew that the Appermoys were rich. I even knew that they competed with us, or wanted to, though their total production of nitrogen and hydrogen in a year was less than that of the smallest of our boats. Their process was not the same as ours, either.

The Appermoy money came, in the first place, from radioactive waste. Old Simon Appermoy had been as clever as the Commodore and as diligent. He had worked out a plan, and then had sought out and signed disposal contracts with every nuclear power plant he could find and half a dozen national defense departments, all of them so madly happy to find anyone who would take their waste radionuclides away that they paid huge amounts for every ton. Then Simon Appermoy vitrified the dirty stuff. He dissolved it in glassy chunks, and then he did the clever thing. He bought a couple of seamounts in the Pacific, the tail end of the Hawaiian chain, the volcanic islands that had risen from the sea bottom and been planed flat

by the waves over tens of millions of years. Whether the
sovereign state of Hawaii had any title to sell them was
a whole other question, but a clouded title never worried
old Appermoy—I'll say why in a minute. Then he drilled
holes in the flat summits of the seamounts and dumped
the glassy radionuclides in.

So far it was simple waste disposal. Enough to make
him rich, but only the beginning. His next step was to
become our competitor.

Some unsung genius on Appermoy's payroll had informed him that all that hot stuff a thousand fathoms down
would start a warm-water plume moving up toward the
surface; and that plume contained energy that Appermoy
could suck out with slow, huge, vertical-axis blades. And
so he did, and used that energy just as we did, to make
electricity that would fix nitrogen and split water into fuel.
But he did not suck all the energy out, because he wanted
some of that warmed plume to reach the surface so that
it could carry with it the organic detritus from the bottom
that had accumulated for tens of millions of years. If you
saw that trash in your living room, you would call it filth
and try to mop it away; but if you saw it in your garden,
it would delight your heart, for it was rich in organics.
And as it came to the surface, it fed microorganisms to
feed krill to feed fish. Any kind of fish Appermoy chose
to stock, in fact, because the steel skeletons that held his
works above the seamounts made marvelous habitats for
food fish and game fish and every fish that swam in the
sea. I don't know what reward Simon Appermoy gave
the flunky who devised this plan. Most likely Appermoy
gave him cement overshoes and a quick drop without a
face mask to the surface of the seamount, where his poor
empty-eyed skull could watch the muck swirl slowly up-
ward.

But it all worked. It was almost the opposite of our
process, you see. We pumped up cold water to condense
the warmed vapor that the sun boiled for us. Appermoy
warmed the waters of the deep with his radioactive filth—
to make much the same end products, yes, but also to

gain what we did not, several thousand tons a day of high-quality ocean fish to feed the billions on the land.

A rich family they were. A decent family they were not. Their empire was built on poisons at the base, and the money that gave Appermoy his start was more poisonous still. He got it the same way the Commodore did—he married it—but while the Commodore married a lady, what Simon Appermoy married was the spawn of four generations of Mafia chiefs. That was how they got their first contracts for disposing of radioactive waste. That was how they kept competition away. Others saw what Appermoy had done and tried to find seamounts of their own, but if strikes did not befall them, unexplained accidents did.

So the family was foul; young Frank Appermoy himself, less so. There were no great sins to his record in the datastore, unless you call polo playing a sin. He did not, however, meet Ben Zoll's specifications except for the first of them. He was rich. But you can't call someone who lives to hit a little ball from horseback sensible, and handsome he certainly was not. One of his horses had thrown him and kicked him. He was not yet fully recovered, the datastore said, and the picture confirmed it. Although the right side of his face had been very much rebuilt since the accident, he looked odd. He did not look terrifying or repulsive, but not even a mother could call him handsome—not even the mother of all lies and wickedness who had borne him, Simon Appermoy's wretched wife.

And yet my May had chosen him to wed.

The scouts had found us a nice flow of cold water in the deeps south of the Philippines, and that is always a great treasure. Every extra degree of differential between surface temperature and deep makes a great enhancement in power yield when you work with such short margins as ours. So we were thousands of kilometers west of Hawaii, and yet it was well dark before May and her gallant called me back. I was sitting on my private little

weather deck, gazing at the Southern Cross and wishing I had been born a couple of decades later than I was, when the phone rang.

There they were, the two of them. His arm was around her shoulder, and he was grinning at me with that twisted— but not evil—face, and May was looking apologetic but ecstatic. "It has all gone so very fast, Uncle Jason." She had never called me "uncle" before. "I wanted to call you a thousand times, but—"

"It doesn't matter," I said, lying.

"You will come to the wedding, though, won't you? Please?"

As though there were any doubt of that! But the boy added his pleas as well. "You're the only real family May has, sir." None of her young men had ever called me "sir" before, either. "My mother says she'll try to be her mother, too, since I never had a sister, and heaven knows, sir, I'll do all I can to make her happy! And it wouldn't be right to marry May if you weren't here."

The statute of limitations had expired long since, of course, but there was nothing I wanted on land. Even on an island. Especially an island belonging to the Apper-moys. But he added the clincher: "You really have to, sir, because we want you to give her away."

And I gave her away.

I gave her away on the steps of the mansion at South Point, with Kilauea steaming behind the house, with a lei around May's sweet neck and the priest wearing a mi-crophone in his collar so that all the fourteen hundred guests could hear, and Betsy grinning wickedly at me from the first row, and the groom white-faced and sweating, for he had had some kind of convulsion just before the ceremony. He had good enough manners, young Frank Appermoy. But I did not want to give May away to any man, with good manners or bad, rich or poor, young or old, as long as that man was not me. Especially not to one who, as I learned, every now and then had blinding headaches and convulsions. I wish that horse had kicked a little harder.

Whether they were happy or not I do not know. I
suppose they were. The next year they had a baby, James
Reginald Appermoy, and the year after that young Frank's
scrambled brain quit trying to keep him alive and my May
was a widow at twenty-two. The bitch mother-in-law said
she killed him.

At one and twenty to a husband was wed.
At two and twenty the husband was dead.
Her mother, no mother, called her no wife.
Her sister, no sister, plagued all of her life.
Her living was bounded in snares and guiles,
The sweet, luckless queen of the grazing isles.

May could not stay on the Big Island with the old
Appermoy woman spreading scandalous tales about her.
Ben the bastard invited her home. Not to the boat she
had grown up on, because her old home there had become
part of the new electrolysis plant, but to the homes on
the biggest of the new oaty-boats. Two million deadweight
tons! The oaties weren't boats anymore, they were floating islands, and there was room for a dozen large families
in owner's country on the foredeck. In spite of this, Ben
claimed at first that there was no room for me, but that
was only to make May beg. "Oh, well," he said, giving
in as he had planned to all along, "at least he can change
the baby's diapers. I'll find him quarters with the crew."

Quarters with the crew. And I custodian of May's vast
estate and a part owner in my own right, with my fifty
shares. May owned three Fleet shares to bastard Ben's
one, but they did us little good. For Ben had the will, and
control of the voting rights until she reached the age of
thirty. I could not believe the Commodore had been so
insane. Yet when I slipped away to Reykjavik and spoke
to a lawyer at the Sea court, he told me the will was firm,
and I went back to May with a shifty lie about where I
had been and watched her nurse the child. I did not know
what to say to her.

But May did not ask. In those first months she was all

for the child, singing to him, petting him, nursing him—wincing now and then, for he was a terrible biter. And a terribly ugly little brat, too. May would sit by the great oval pool among the palms on the foredeck with Jimmy Rex in her arms or whimpering in a bed beside her; and I would be there to give her company; and surely, almost every time, there would be Betsy as well, practicing her dives off the high board or sipping mai tais with one of the corrupt, pretty young men who were always her houseguests. And always with one eye on May and the child.

It was easy to know what Betsy wanted. Whatever May had, that was it. She had even wanted that sorry, spasmed Frank Appermoy—and had got him, at least long enough for a tumble in his water bed, and made sure I knew she had. Now she wanted Appermoy's child. At first I thought all she wanted was a child. She could have had one easily enough, with all those young studs sniffing after her; I thought what stopped her was, a little, the bother of marrying one of them or, most of all, the unpleasantness and pain of actually giving birth. In that I was wrong. What she wanted was James Reginald Appermoy, with all his tantrums and colics, and only because he was May's.

So for half a year May was the perfect young mother bereft, with the imperfect wretch of a babe. Then the brat was weaned, and she seemed to come back to the world. Perhaps she realized at last that she was lonely. She had no friend but me on the oaty-boat. If anyone in the huge seven-thousand-man crew showed signs of becoming a friend, Betsy told Ben, and Ben transferred him away. Even the four other Mays could come on board only for a day or two at a time, with all the long flight to get there and the other to leave again, for we were mostly far from any land. So it was no wonder that my sweet girl began to look elsewhere for pleasure. It was a house party here, and a fox hunt there, and Switzerland for the skiing, and Tokyo to see the shows. If she was to be away for just a few days, she would leave Jimmy Rex with me, nasty

child whom I tried with all my heart to love. If it was a matter of weeks they would both be gone, and I had nothing to do and no one to do it with, for my friends were suddenly needed badly on another boat as well. I wished for another Elsie Van Dorn, but Elsie herself was now a second engineer on the old boat, and I did not want to involve her in Ben's anger. So I had a succession of cooks' assistants and young things from the typing pool. None lasted more than a few weeks. The ones who were not kind enough and strong enough to put up with the brat I had to send back to their regular work, and the others Ben transferred away.

And the unsigned messages came in. One a month. Some came from Australia and some from Seoul, and one from Capetown, but they all said much the same thing:

"If you value your life, help her now."

But how was I to do that?

I did not need the unknown assassin's reminder to want to help my May. I made an excuse to slip away again and this time found a better lawyer, or at least a more high-priced one. He did not simply tell me the Commodore's will could not be broken. He gave me two days of his time, quoting the Law of the Sea and citing precedents. He charged accordingly, and it all came out to much the same. Ben had the law on his side until May was thirty.

It was the only time I was on land that year. I thought of following May to her parties, to see if she would talk freely off the boat, or more truthfully just for the pleasure of being near her. I could have done it. I would have, I surely would have, if she had said a word or given a look to say she wanted me. The word never came. The look, maybe.

She was off to New York City this time, May and the child. I carried Jimmy Rex to the airplane and handed him over to her at the door. "New York for the opera season? I didn't know you loved opera that well," I said, and May smiled at me.

"A little culture would do neither of us any harm, Ja-

son, dear," she said, and paused, and thought for a moment, looking out over the wide, warm sea. I knew that look. I almost expected to see her with her thumb in her mouth and her hip-huggers sagging to the ground, for it was a lost and thoughtful look. The pilot was flipping his control surfaces back and forth and glancing back over his shoulder at us, for he had a schedule to keep, but May stared at the sea for some time. Then she turned back to me as though she were about to speak.

She did not. She looked past me, over my shoulder, and changed her mind. "Good-by, then, dear Jason," she said, and kissed me. She took the baby from my arms and was gone.

As I stepped back to get out of the way of the VTO jets, I bumped into what had changed her. It was brother Ben. He was looking worn and fretful, for all he was only a dozen years older than May, and sullen Betsy was scowling at his side.

The hydrogen flame screamed and licked against the baffles, and the plane lifted in a blue-white burn too bright to look at. Betsy turned to me. "We came to say good-by," she said nastily, "but I guess May doesn't want to waste good manners on the family."

The plane was a kilometer up now, and moving away. Ben shaded his eyes to squint after it. "Jason," he said without looking at me, "let's talk business. I'll buy your stock."

"You will not," I said, "for I don't want to sell to you."

He gave me a hooded look. It was the look of a man who has some pieces to a puzzle, but not enough to make the pattern clear. "Have you been enjoying your trips to Iceland?" he asked.

I had never doubted that he was spying on me. I didn't bother to answer. He said, "I'll pay you more than your shares are worth."

"They're worth more to me than they are to you, Ben," I said, and turned my back on him. As I walked to the lift I could hear him coughing behind me. He was a sick man.

I went to my desk and began to study my reports, but I did not have my mind on them. Part was on May, as part of my mind was always. But part was on Ben. I wished the bastard no good at all, but I did not wish him dead. I knew who would inherit his stock when he died. And the Reykjavik lawyer had told me that Ben could name his successor as May's guardian and, for all that she was years younger and the guardianship a mockery, I knew who he would name.

I could not get out of my head that May had been about to say something to me before she left, and so I decided to hear what it was. Three days after she was gone, I called in my assistant and told him he was on his own for a week, and took the same plane.

We were cruising in the Philippine sea at the time, so it was VTO jet to Manila, then orbital craft to the great floating terminal off Sandy Hook, and a helicopter to the roof of my hotel.

I do not like the land. I do not like the crowds and the roar and the stink of the land, and especially I do not like a city. I had taken rooms in the same hotel where May was staying, and I did not intend to leave it except to see her. So as soon as I was settled in my suite I walked out into the hall and took the elevator a dozen flights and knocked on the door. Tse-ling Mei opened it. "Uncle Jason!" she cried, with pleasure and surprise in her voice, and maybe a little worry, too. "Oh, come in, please!"

All four of the other Mays were there. So was little Jimmy Rex, bawling at the walls of his room because he was being made to take a nap, but my May was not.

The young beauties sat me down and clustered around me like meadow flowers in the spring. "Some tea?" asked Mei, and, "Have you eaten?" from Maisie, and "What Jason probably needs most is a drink," from May Bancroft, and from May Holliston-Peirce, "Oh, tell us what's new on the boats!"

So we chattered for a while and I felt almost at ease,

though concerned that they seemed to have no idea when
May would be back. Then May Bancroft sighed and said,
"Oh, hell." We all turned and looked. Jimmy Rex was
standing in the doorway, glowering at us, escaped from
his crib and come to make us unhappy. In one hand he
waved the perfectly dry diaper he had managed to squeeze
out of. With the other he guided himself as he pissed
deliberately on the Aubusson rug. Do you see what a
foolish lottery we gamble in when we make a child? He
could have taken after his mother, May. Even after his
father, and been nothing worse than a fool. But in the
random lottery of the DNA exchanges he had caught the
very soul of May's bitch mother-in-law, and how heavily
that has cost me since.

It cost me then, too, because it broke the mood of the
party. I got up to go. Tse-ling Mei was holding the brat
down while Maisie tried to pin the diaper back on him,
and May Holliston-Peirce was bringing towels from a
bathroom to mop up the rug. May Bancroft said, "I'll
walk you to your taxi, Uncle Jason." I had no intention
of a taxi, but the look on her face stopped me from saying
so.

So we walked through the hall with her hand in mine,
and dropped like stones in the elevator—my heart in my
mouth, for there are no such high-speed lifts on the oaty-
boats—and she walked me through the lobby to a back
entrance, and around a corner and another until she found
a taxi that suited her. I was dressed for the Philippine
sea, not New York in November, and May not much more
warmly, not to mention the crush, and the stink, and the
noise. But I let her keep up her chatter all the way without
interrupting. Tse-ling Mei had been given a marvelous
new part, and one May was to be married and another to
run a hospital somewhere in New Jersey or Indiana, and
May Bancroft herself was back in school for a law degree.
And then she peered inside a parked cab and nodded her
head and leaned forward to kiss my ear. She did not give
me just a kiss. She gave me an address and a room num-

ber, and then turned and hurried off without looking back.

I had wit enough to change cabs and walk a bit before I hailed the second one, although I nearly froze while I was doing it, but in five minutes I was there.

The address was the seediest of old hotels. The room number was on the seediest floor. The air in the hall was choked with marijuana fumes and the smell of human sweat, and the door was opened by a man of forty or more. He was wearing pants that he had zipped but not belted, no shoes, and a shirt that he had left unbuttoned. He was a sober-looking, serious sort of a man, not what you would expect to find in a whore's hangout like this, far from good-looking but solid.

And behind him, lying on an unmade bed, wearing a thin muumuu, was my May. Her expression was filled with fear.

"It's not what you think, Uncle Jason," she said to me at once, and to the man, "Hurry! Let him in!"

The man moved quickly to do it. He pulled me in by the elbow, showing surprising strength for a pudgy little man not much younger than myself. He stuck his head out into the hall, and looked both ways before he closed the door. Then he turned to me.

"I'm Jefferson Ormondo," he said, "and I'm an investment banker. I apologize for this place and the way we look, but the windows don't open and the heat won't turn off. And Ben Zoll has willing ears in too many places." He was buttoning his shirt while he spoke. He sat to put on his shoes and said, "I'll take a look around the lobby to make sure it's all right. May will tell you what's going on." And he was gone, and there I was in a sweaty half-hour room with my sweet May gazing up at me out of a rumpled bed.

"We're going to get Ben's guardianship set aside," she said.

"That's impossible," I said—with my voice, but I know that what my face was saying was, *That's unfair, May,*

to try such a thing without me! And she answered my
face.

"Jason, dear, it's no secret from you. I can't do it
without you."

"The best lawyers in Reykjavik say you can't do it at
all," I told her, "for the will is in proper form."

"But what if it is forged, Jason?"

I goggled at her.

"Forged," she said, nodding. "Not all of it. Just the
matter of dates. The guardianship was supposed to stop
when I was twenty, and Ben had someone get into the
datastores and add ten years to the time."

Now, that was getting close to a line of conversation
I did not want to pursue. I didn't know—I have never
known—if the Commodore ever told his daughter about
the favor I had done him. She did not say anything then,
or ever, to give me an answer one way or another, but
hurried on: "And that is fraud, Jason, and somebody may
well go to jail. But proving it! It's so hard. And Ben has
everything on the boats bugged, of course. I couldn't
speak to you there—and besides," she said, sitting beside
me and touching my arm, "he knows you're smarter than
I am, so he watches you twice as hard."

I said, "You don't have to explain anything to me,
May." But I wanted explanations all the same. I got them.
The plump little bald-headed man, Ormondo, worked for
the bank that held Ben's stocks, and it had seemed to him
that there was something funny about the records. For
one thing, the will should have existed in several datastores, not just the bank's. But the Commodore's own
bank had been swallowed up by another and its records
were unavailable, and in the hall of records where the
will had been filed the system had crashed, all the data
lost.

Ormondo came to believe that there was a forgery. He
could not prove it, but it made him curious to look further.
There was plenty to find.

Ben had been milking the Fleet. He had set up cor-

porations of his own to buy the hydrogen from the oaty-
boats and to sell the ammonia on land, and to lease to us
the pilot cutters that prospected for cold, deep water, and
even the aircraft that carried us to shore. Everything the
Fleet bought cost a little more than it should, and everything we sold went for a little less, and the difference went
to Ben.

And then Ormondo had met May at a party, not by
chance, and whispered in her ear.

And ever since then, for the best part of a year, the
two of them had been searching out records and inter-
viewing people who might know things. Whispers had got
back to Ben, surely. But Ormondo was a careful man.

And they had the pattern almost complete.

"The next step, Jason," she said, "was going to be to
talk to you. I almost asked you to come with me this time.
I'm glad you didn't wait to be asked."

"Of course I'll do everything you want," I assured her.

She smiled sweetly and touched my arm. "Of course
you will, dear Jason. There's one other thing."

She looked embarrassed. She pursed the pretty lips,
hesitating, her eyes gazing at the chipped paint on the
ugly wall as though she were staring over the wide sea.
Then she said, "I need a husband, Jason."

She had caught me unaware. "A husband?"

"I need a husband for me, and for help in this fight,
because it will be a terrible one. And most of all I need
one because of Jimmy Rex. He must have a father, Jason.
Not a silly boy. A grown man, wise and kind and sensible.
It doesn't matter if he's older than I am. It only matters
that he be someone I can trust and love with all my heart."

These were the words I had been dreaming of hearing
for all the long years. I could hardly speak. "Of course,
my dearest," I said, and reached out for her, and was
puzzled by the astonishment that sprang into her eyes.

It was a terrible fight, indeed. For months we were
more on Iceland than in our proper homes, all of us. That
was a high enough price to pay in itself, for me. Iceland

is where the Law of the Sea is administered, and indeed
it is land that has come from the sea, bubbling up in roaring
steam, some of it within the memory of living men. But
it is still the land, and all the geothermal steam and hot
swimming pools do not make up for losing the warm
breezes of the southern seas.

But we won. Or mostly we won. Bastard Ben might
well have gone to jail indeed, if he had not gone to the
hospital instead and did not come out alive.

So it was Betsy who lost the suit, not Ben, and she
did not lose it all. We could not prove the falsification of
the will. The litigation was long-drawn and savage, and
three of our witnesses disappeared, but the records of the
dummy corporations did not. So May settled at last for
a division. The guardianship was annulled. All Ben's contracts to buy and sell were voided. The Fleet was divided
in two. Half the oaty-boats went to Betsy, the rest, with
half the money from Ben's loot, to May. And Betsy began
at once to build more . . . but we were at ease at last, back
at home on that first old boat, steaming slowly through
the Strait of Malacca, and the Commodore's daughter was
at last the undisputed queen of the grazing isles. She ruled
us happily, along with her child. . . .

And with her husband. Who was not me.

She was the kindest of women, my May, but she could
not be kind enough to allow me to forget how foolishly I
had missed her meaning when she was trying to tell me
that she meant to marry Jefferson Ormondo.

III

For the sake of her son and to claim her due,
At four and twenty she wed number two.
They battled and won in the struggle to keep
Her fair-owned gifts from the generous deep.
Blest was the respite from worries and trials
In this short happy time for the queen of the isles.

Although I had lost her again, it was a good time. May was happy. Jefferson Ormondo had the good sense to be happy—well, what else could he be? Even little Jimmy Rex became more tractable, since he was away from Betsy's constant need to spur on his own born-in meanness.

We even made a sort of peace with Betsy herself. It was not easy or comfortable. Yet she came to pay a visit to our quaint old thermal grazer, and then there was nothing to do but for us to visit her great new flagship. Though I took no joy in seeing Betsy, I was glad enough of the trip. Her Works Captain was a decent enough man—we'd sailed together under the Commodore—and besides, I wanted to see some of their engineering.

What we want for the heat exchangers is the hottest surface water we can get, the top meter if we can get it, for that's where the sun's heat is strongest. But when you pump a hundred tons a second, the suction tubes are not fastidious about what they take. So when Captain Havrila took me up on his bridge, beaming with pride, I knew what he was going to show me. I'd seen it from the air. The boat was surrounded with a screen that lay thirty meters away from the hull in all directions; I'd seen it, and realized at once that there was a shallow lip all around. "You pump direct from the hull," I guessed, "and you've trapped surface water in a moat. The screen's to keep out fish?"

He grinned ruefully. "I knew once you laid eyes on it, Jason, I wouldn't have to say a word. We pump from a reservoir ten meters deep, but all that comes in to replenish it is the very top of the sea."

"It's a nice solution." I complimented him. "But doesn't it cut down your maneuvering, with all that drag?"

"It *destroys* it," he said happily, "but we're not going anywhere very fast anyway. And we've been getting delta-Ts of twenty and up—well, most days," he corrected himself. "Tell me, Jason, what are you doing about organic fouling?"

"Same as you, I guess. Reverse flush every ten days

with little plastic marbles. We lose nearly half of them every time, though." The sea is full of little living things that want something to cling to—unfortunately, they don't care what. The lining of our intake tubes is as good a place as any. There's not too much trouble with the deep-water intakes, because the water down there is too cold for them to be very active. But the surface intakes are another story.

"We're recovering nearly a hundred percent on the surface," he boasted. "It's all trapped in the moat, you see, so we just scoop them up again."

"Good job. But what do you do when the perimeter screens begin to foul?" And he laughed and offered to buy me a drink, for that was the weakness in the system.

I took his drink, and a lot more than one over the three days we were there. I had no quarrel with Betsy's captains or Betsy's crews, but I did not like Betsy's friends. I didn't like May's liking them, either. The women called themselves actresses or models—polite lies. The men lied less politely. They called themselves men. There was Simon Kellaway, Las Vegas–born, slim and quick and temporarily living at sea on Betsy's charity because there was a murder charge in Nevada that he couldn't hush up. There was Dougie d'Agasto from Miami Beach, tall and fair and a pimp's recruiter if I ever saw one. They came from Chicago and Los Angeles and New Orleans, and they all had money, or acted as though they did, and I did not believe that even one of them had got it inside the law.

The one I liked least was d'Agasto, the handsomest and emptiest of men. What I liked least of all was that May did not reject his company. They sat together at dinner the first night. I assumed he was Betsy's bedmate. I assumed that of every man I saw her with, for she was always, and after Ben died openly, available, accessible and even aggressive about it. Even, to my surprise, with me, for at two in the morning she knocked on my door to announce that she wasn't in the mood for sleep. When I told her that I was, she shrugged and said, "Well, you'd

probably be no good to me anyway, old man, especially
after you've starched your sheets already over May." She
left without protest, and I—I wished we had never come
there.

So I spent my time as far away from Betsy and Betsy's
friends as I could. Captain Havrila fed me in the ship's
officers' mess. We talked shop—openly—pretty openly,
because there were things I did not mention to them, and
I know there were a good many they didn't tell me. A lot
of what we talked about, though, was no secret. I knew
that Betsy was diversifying, because what she sold to the
land became public knowledge the minute she sold it. I
didn't know, but I would have found out shortly anyway,
that she was planning to try total manufacture—refining
steel, even. Electric refining, mostly. "The ships that come
in are in ballast anyway," said their marketing chief, Jim
Mordecai, "so they might as well carry ore—and we've
got the electricity—and we've got a lot of extra oxygen,
because if we keep on expanding L-H-2 production the
way we're going, the extra oxygen's sure to depress the
world market. And then there's pollution."

"Pollution? Out here?" I asked.

"Here's the place for it, Jason, at sea, where it won't
make the land worse than it is—although—" he grinned—
"I don't know if the folks in Tahiti are going to agree with
me." He glanced at the captain before he went on, "We
do have a kind of pollution problem, though." The captain
must have signaled it was all right, because he completed
his thought. "We're pumping so much deep water here
that the dissolved CO_2 doesn't dissipate right away. We're
up to pretty nearly five hundred parts per million."

"Oh? I didn't notice anything."

"Well, you won't," boomed Captain Havrila. "As far
as we can tell there's no health risk—and actually, Miss
Betsy says she kind of likes it. It does make the plants
grow in her garden! Care for a brandy now, Jason?"

I did. I had one. I even had two with them, but they
all had work to do, and I couldn't keep them from it. So
I volunteered to take Jimmy Rex for a walk, and we headed

for the gardens so I could see for myself, and indeed it was true. Bougainvillea and orchids and flowering ginger—everything was lush and beautiful.

Jimmy Rex was being not particularly awful, for he liked picking flowers. He crushed them as soon as he picked them, threw them away and picked more, but there were plenty of flowers. I let him do pretty much as he pleased, following slowly after him and thinking the unpromising thoughts of an aging bachelor, till I heard voices and saw him dart into a cluster of dirty-boy shrubbery. "Come back, James Reginald," I shouted. For a wonder, he did, looking abashed. I heard someone moving away out of sight, and in a moment some other someone came around the shrubs to see who I was.

It was Dougie d'Agasto. He was partly dressed in shorts and unlaced tennis shoes, carrying a sports shirt slung over one bare shoulder. "Oh, it's you, Jason," he said, smiling—at least I give him the credit of saying that he probably meant it for a smile, though it had a lot of smirk in it. "I figured if Jimmy Rex was here you couldn't be far behind. I'm glad you two didn't get here ten minutes sooner!"

Well, I had no interest in his tacky whoring in the bushes. I put my hand on Jimmy Rex's shoulder—he was behaving well enough to let me—and said, "We were just going."

He nodded absently, stretching, yawning, pulling the shirt on over his head, but he kept his eyes on us. "You're smart to keep close to the kid," he said.

I said stiffly, "I don't let him near the rail." D'Agasto looked at me as though I were talking a foreign language.

"I'm not talking about accident, for God's sake. I'm talking about snatch. Kidnap," he amplified, and this time it definitely was a smirk. "Do you know what that kid's worth for ransom?"

Now, if you'd met d'Agasto on a tennis court, say, you might easily think he was just another bright and handsome young sportsman, because he had the wide-eyed good humor and the trim, strong body of healthy

youth. I had never thought that. Not for a single second, because before I ever met him I knew he was some sort of second-rate kin to one of the lesser Mob families in Florida. Even if I had ever thought it, listening to him talk would have straightened me out in two sentences. The way his mind worked!

And went on working. "What is it you've got now, Jason?" he ruminated. "Eighteen boats in May's fleet? There's probably construction loans against every one of them, but, say, ten million dollars apiece average net worth? And that's only pocket change, because when old lady Appermoy kicks off, there's no heir left but the kid. Why, you've got your hand on a billion dollars, pal! What say you just quietly sneak him on the plane when I leave and don't say anything until I'm in San Francisco—we'll split the ransom fifty-fifty!"

He was watching my face, so he winked and turned away and left without waiting for an answer. Jimmy Rex stared after him with scared delight. "Was he just making a joke, Uncle Jay?" he asked.

"What a stupid question! Of course it was just a joke!"

But it wasn't.

I was glad to be back on our own ship, and the first thing I did was have a talk with the security chief. From that moment on there was somebody near Jimmy Rex every minute he wasn't with me or his parents.

I didn't stop worrying, but after a while I didn't worry as much. For May and Jefferson Ormondo it was the best time of their lives. When they walked about the boat, they were hand in hand. He was a good husband to her, for all he was no beauty, and would have been a good father to Jimmy Rex if the boy had been capable of being a son.

The money grew and grew. The more fuel we made, the more hungrily the land people clamored to burn it. We could not fix nitrogen fast enough to meet the demand for fertilizer, and so the price went up and up. We weren't the only boats on the sea anymore—now and then we'd catch sight of Japanese ones, or Australian. We built more

of our own, and bigger ones, and yet there was plenty for all.

When Jimmy Rex was three years old, we moved us all to the newest and hugest oaty-boat on the sea. Two million eight hundred thousand tons. We could have run a nation off the power we produced. It was well along in the shipyards before Jefferson Ormondo ever saw it, but he cherished it as his own, for the last of the fitting, and most of the owner's country, was his own design. May encouraged him to plan on a grand scale. And grand it surely was—but I had been happy enough on the old one. "You're a sentimental man, Jason," said May when I told her as much, "and a very dear one to me. But it's such an *old* boat. And little—why, it doesn't even have a decent bridle path!"

She was trying to tease me cheerful—she knew I'd never ridden a horse. "So we're going to sell it for scrap metal, then?"

"No!" Then less emphatically, "I don't think so. What can we do with it, Jason? The Gulf of Mexico?"

I'd thought of that myself, but it wasn't good sense. There was good grazing in the gulf for smaller boats, but it didn't seem to me there was enough sea room for an aging oaty-boat to get out of the way of bad weather. "Maybe the Brazil Triangle," I said—that was good, too, from the eastern coast of South America to the African Gold Coast—but how did you get it there? It would never go through the Canal, of course, or even the Straits of Magellan, and the seas south of Cape Horn would probably sink it. "I'll think of something," I said, and after a while I did. I sold it to May's old in-laws. They moored it for a fixed OTEC station in the straits off Lahaina, for the gray whales to stare at. It was no joy dealing with the old witch, but she made us a fair price, and even sent May a wedding present into the bargain—a year late and a lot too little, but May took it kindly and even offered to let Jimmy Rex visit his grandmother now and then out of gratitude.

But I missed the old boat. The big one wasn't just

bigger. It was better designed. We put in a new cold-water intake system, with a single pipe five kilometers long and six meters wide. The thicker the pipe was, the better the surface-to-volume ratio, so the water didn't warm up as much on the way up. It does warm a little, of course. But the dissolved gases expand a little, which tends to cool it—in fact, we had to install relief valves along the pipe to bleed out the excess pressure; otherwise it would have ruptured. We were reliably getting a delta-T of 26 or 27—once even 29 for five days in a row. But the damn pipe was so long it wanted to curl up like spaghetti, and so we had to divert scout subs from prospecting for cold-water lenses to pushing it back into shape almost every day. And because we were bringing up so much in the way of nutrients, the fishing fleets from Korea and Peru followed us around. I didn't begrudge them the fish, but I liked it better when we couldn't see other ships on the horizon.

May just laughed at me when I said as much. "You just don't like to change anything," she told me, halfway between teasing and tenderness. We were on a lower deck, Jimmy Rex pretending to shoot the dolphins that were larking around our moat. Naturally, I'd installed the same sort of warm-water trap as Betsy's flagship, and naturally, the dolphins weren't going to let a little two-meter-high screen keep them from jumping over into a new playpen.

I said, "I like things to get better, not just different."

She sighed and pulled Jimmy Rex back from the rail. "And isn't this better?"

"It is in some ways."

"Name one it isn't!"

I pointed over the screen, at the open ocean waters. "We didn't see dead squid floating around the old boat."

"Jason, be fair! That's not the boat's fault. There are fish kills all over this part of the Pacific—" And then, out of the corner of her eye, she saw that the boy had climbed up on the rail to get a better make-believe shot. "James

Reginald Appermoy!" she yelled, and dragged him back just as he was about to go over.

Well, it wouldn't have hurt him much, a twelve-meter fall into a warm bathtub, but he wouldn't have liked it, either. He was good for almost a minute, and even let me put my arm around him for almost that long. But I was still worrying about the squid. A dead fish at sea is a curiosity; as soon as anything slows down enough to be dying, something else is sure to eat it. "I hear they're worse off on Hawaii," I said, and May said:

"Oh, that reminds me. Jimmy Rex is going to see his grandmother next week."

I said nothing, but I didn't have to. "It's all right," she reassured me.

"It's all right if he can take Pan and Jeremy along," I bargained—they were the two security men Jimmy Rex hated least.

"Well, if you don't think Grandma's feelings will be hurt—" She saw my eyes and dropped it. "They'll go," she promised. "But after all, the Appermoys are family. And so's Betsy, and when Jimmy Rex comes back from Hawaii, I'm thinking of inviting some of her friends over."

"Betsy's family," I admitted, "but the trash she keeps around her are not."

"But they're amusing, Jason. With all the space we've got now, it's no trouble to have a few guests."

"That," I said, "is another way the old boat was better."

But I could not really argue against family. And if we entertained Betsy and her friends, then Betsy must entertain us and ours, so May and Jeff and the boy and the four Mays and I flew over to visit good queen Betsy. Our flagships were not usually very far apart—I speak geographically. With the scouts for both our fleets getting better at finding the best delta-Ts and the hydrologists improving their predictions about how stable they were and the navigators getting more skilled at plotting courses that would graze where the deltas were greenest—well,

there are only so many optimal solutions to a problem, especially as we each copied the other's technology as soon as it was proved. It was no wonder that we often came to the same solutions. And the same problems, for looking over the side of Betsy's flagship with Havrila by my side, I said, "I see you've got dead squid, too."

"The fishing fleet's complaining, too." He nodded gravely and then laughed. "Best thing we ever didn't do," he said, "was diversify into fishing."

"We thought about it for a while, too," I said, "and decided to stay out of perishables. There are plenty of other fields!"

And there were. We were getting into dozens of them. Mining the hot heavy-metal brine from the springs of the East Pacific Rise. Scooping up manganese pellets from the ocean bottom. The only "perishable" we got into was fresh water—we built two experimental sailing tugs, huge devils with revolving masts to catch the winds, and used them to tow icebergs from Antarctica to the Persian Gulf.

All the ventures prospered—though nothing more than the ocean-thermal that was our core money spinner—even the icebergs. They were Jefferson's own pet. He was land-born and land-oriented, and he could not resist something that would make things better for people on land. He went off to supervise the project now and then, a week at a time. I didn't like his leaving May alone. I liked it least when it began to be so that, as Jeff was leaving, some of Betsy's giddy friends would arrive. The one who came most often was Dougie d'Agasto.

There was bound to be trouble, and it came. Dougie stayed a day too long. Jeff came home, and he must have been looking for his family with field glasses as the plane came in, for he didn't bother to go to their rooms. He dropped his bags with a deckhand and headed straight for the pool. May, looking ethereally ravishing in her skimpy suit, was watching to keep Jimmy Rex from drowning himself—heaven knows why. Dougie d'Agasto was standing beside her, whispering in her ear. His arm was around her waist, and his fingers were toying delicately

with the elastic of her trunks. Jeff did not look like a
fighter. His bald head gleamed sweatily in the Pacific sun,
and he was shorter and fatter. But he spun d'Agasto around
and decked him with one punch. Into the pool went Dougie
d'Agasto, and came up screaming and fingering his bloody,
but not broken, perfect nose. He was off the boat in an
hour, and what May and Jefferson said to each other about
it I do not know.

I know what I said to May. First chance I got her alone
I said, "You're a fool to risk Jeff for that little pimp."

Was it any of my business? At least she didn't tell me
it was not. She said seriously, "I am not risking Jeff, Uncle
Jason. Dougie's flattering, though. He's such a beautiful
boy."

"He's a louse."

"He's almost family."

"He's some kind of poor relation to your former mother-
in-law, yes, and that's Mob family. Those people are criminals. Drug pushers. Arm breakers. Murderers."

She laughed good-humoredly and pecked my cheek.
"Dougie never murdered anybody, Jay, except maybe a
few women he loved to death. But you're right. I shouldn't
let him think he's being encouraged. And I won't."

So for six months I saw nothing of Dougie d'Agasto,
but long before that he'd written both May and Jefferson
most abject letters of apology. Jeff relented—he didn't
ask my advice. Then Betsy came over for a party, and
she brought d'Agasto with her.

We were competing in earnest then, and actually the
visit was partly so that we could talk over some business.
There's a lot of ocean, but only narrow bands of it, and
short, where the temperature difference between surface
and chilly deep is enough to run the turbines at full speed.
We both were sticking pretty close to the equator, too.
It wasn't so much for the solar heat, although there was
plenty there. It was for protection from the storms. Our
boats were getting a lot too big and clumsy to risk in a
hurricane. You don't get hurricanes on the equator, or

anyway very rarely. The equator isn't north and it isn't south, so there's no Coriolis force to speak of. The funnel doesn't know which way to turn, so the big funnel storms don't develop there.

So more often than not the ocean wasn't empty any-more. There were other oaty-boats in sight, often ours, more often hers—or Russians or Japanese or Norwe-gians. The time was coming just beyond the horizon when there might be more grazers than forage for OTECs. So there was some high-powered arguing between Betsy's nav chiefs and ours before the party started, and I can't honestly say the question ever really got resolved. Still, the guests had a good time at the party. It was New Year's Eve, and we'd given everybody any time off that could be spared at all. The guests were all over the boat, the crews were welcomed in owners' country; I saw Betsy and May singing "Auld Lang Syne" with the kitchen staff and Dougie d'Agasto slapping the back of an assistant pipe fitter, and if we were out to cut each others' throats in the marketplace as soon as the party was over, the swords were sheathed while it lasted. And the next morn-ing, while most of the ship was nursing hangovers, Jef-ferson Ormondo was inspecting intake gauges on a hydrogen freezer-ship line.

There was a leak. Any leak was dangerous, but it shouldn't have been a disaster for two reasons. The first reason was that hydrogen in the open floats quickly up and away. Anyway, as soon as they heard the shriek of escaping gas, Jefferson and everybody else broke for the rail—it was only a twenty-meter drop, and the water in the moat was calm and warm. The second reason was that there was no reason for a spark to ignite it. Nothing that could make a spark was ever on a hydrogen ship's intake stage.

Except this time. I had guarded the wrong member of the family.

Even if there had been an explosion within a few meters of Jeff, he should have survived. But he was within the

explosion. He was inside a mass of mixed hydrogen and air, and the same mixture was inside his lungs. When the explosion came, it exploded outside him and in. He lived an hour. The whole time he kept trying to scream in agony, but he hadn't lung enough left to scream with anymore.

The only damage to the oaty-boat was some scorched paint and a few fittings. That didn't matter to May. She didn't want to live on it anymore. Jimmy Rex needed a good school, she said, and so she was taking him and herself off to live in Florida. What it was that May needed I only guessed. Did not want to guess. Could not helping guessing when, a few months later, she phoned me and said, "I have news for you, Uncle Jay."

That sweet, sad face on the phone, it melted my heart. All I said was, "Who's the lucky man?"

Pause. "Please don't say anything against him when I tell you, promise?"

My mouth was dry and my heart was pounding, but I managed to smile. "It's Dougie d'Agasto, right? And you've made up your mind?"

"I have, dear Jay. He's a nicer man than you think he is."

"I hope so."

"Oh, Jay, please! Try to see it my way. I married one husband because Ben insisted, and another because I needed his help. This one's for me, Jay. Please say it's all right!"

"May," I said to my lifelong love, "whatever you do is all right with me, always." Twice a widow at her age—could I blame her?

No. It was easier to blame myself. And bastard Ben had been right. He said she would marry a rich boy and a sensible boy and a handsome boy. He never said they would all be the same man.

IV

Consort the first was slow to learn.
Consort the second was quick to burn.
The higher her worth, the meaner her fall,
And consort the third was the worst of them all.
Sweet Truth despises and high Honor reviles
The last man to king the queen of the isles.

They made their home in Miami. Miami! I could not
imagine how my May could be happy among land people,
especially those land people, but her letters were cheerful
enough. They were short, yes, and infrequent. But the
only news they ever contained was good. Dougie, she
wanted me to know, had buckled down and was studying
ocean-thermal engineering! It was too bad that it kept him
away from home so much, but he was very clever at
learning it. May herself was swimming, golfing, riding—
always busy. And Jimmy Rex was happy to be back in
his school. There was no word of whether the school was
happy to have him. So there was some kind of a bright
side for me. If I didn't have May, at least I didn't have
Jimmy Rex, either.

So owner's country was all mine, and I rattled around
in it lonesomely. I was in no mood for parties, and if
Betsy wanted to be invited, she had the good sense not
to tell me so. I kept busy. We were in a dozen big in-
dustries by then. We were selling liquid gases—oxygen,
nitrogen, hydrogen; solid CO_2; ammonia, methanol,
chlorine, caustic soda; small quantities of argon and he-
lium, too, when we could find anyone to buy them. I was
toying with the idea of microwaving energy to a low satellite and beaming it back to, say, Australia or Japan.
Betsy's steel industry wasn't going anywhere, but I'd taken
a tip from what Captain Havrila had said about the ships
coming in in ballast: I had ours siphon sand up from port

bottoms for ballast, and then we used the sand to make a slurry to scour out the fouling organisms in our deep intake pipes—no need to try to recover it! Of course, I wasn't the owner of the Fleet, and everything I did I had to ask permission of May for. But she gave it, every time. Because I had plenty to do, I should have been happy— or as happy as I could be expected to be, with my May married to a rodent that walked like a man. If I wasn't happy, part of the reason was that I got the letter I had been expecting for weeks. No return address. No name. Just the message:

> The Commodore's orders are still in effect. I didn't
> know whether it was time for me to carry them out
> or not, so I flipped a coin. You won this time.

I almost wished the coin had come up the other way— better, I wished that my unknown pen pal would come and talk to me about it. If he decided to kill me afterward, well—I didn't want him to, but there were some bad nights when it seemed like a way out of a place where I didn't want to be. But God knew I needed advice—even from my assassin.

And then May's weekly letter said, "Please come and visit us," and enclosed with it was one from Dougie d'Agasto:

> We have some important business to talk over,
> Jason. You'll come out of it rich. Besides, it's what
> May wants.

Even when the man was trying to be ingratiating he raised the hackles on the back of my neck. I had not forgotten the last deal he had offered me! I did not for one second think that he wouldn't have made the same offer again—except that he'd found a better one for himself. You don't have to steal the child when you can capture the mother.

I certainly did not want to talk over anything with

Dougie d'Agasto, no matter how rich he proposed to make me. But it was May who'd asked me to come.

It is not a long flight from Papeete to Miami, but it uses up a whole night—you cross over five time zones. And so I arrived at ten in the morning with no more than an hour's sleep and my disposition cranky. I took a taxi from the airport to the address Dougie had given me. What I wound up in looked like a warehouse district and smelled like the city dump. A couple of gasoline-burner cars, half dismantled, rusted along the curb. We were only a block or two from Biscayne Bay—that accounted for part of the smell. At least two of the low-rise buildings on the block had been burned out and boarded up. An elderly black woman was throwing a bucket of hot, soapy water on the sidewalk in front of a little grocery store and attacking it with a broom. I walked up to her, carrying my overnight case. "Excuse me, I'm looking for Douglas d'Agasto," I said.

She straightened up. "Round back," she said. I thought there was some hostility in the way she looked at me, but she added, "You want me to help you with that bag?"

"Thank you, no. But it's kind of you to offer." I gestured at the soapy sidewalk. "I didn't really expect to see anybody doing that around here."

"I ain't from around here," she said, dismissing me. At least there seemed to be one decent person in the neighborhood to keep May company, I thought—but could d'Agasto really have May living in this wretched slum? Well, of course he could, if it suited his purpose—but not himself!

Of course, I had made a wrong assumption. Neither of them lived there. It was an office, not a home, and once you got to the inner courtyard, obviously a luxurious one. A slim black man appeared from a vined trellis and circled a marble fountain to ask what my business was. When I gave my name, he passed me on through a door— there was a very thick frame around it; weapons detectors, I realized—and into a handsome, huge waiting room.

There a handsome small woman with rose-red hair conducted me to the very office of Douglas d'Agasto himself.

I've seen pictures of a bigger office. It belonged to that old dictator, Mussolini. "Uncle Jason," d'Agasto cried welcomingly, rising to wait for me to cover the fifteen meters to his desk before he stretched out his hand. "Glad you could come! Sorry to make you come to my office first, but I figured we might as well get the business out of the way so you could relax when we get to the house."

I let him shake my hand. "What's the business we're talking about?"

He nodded approval of my directness. He was just as direct. "May wants to own the Fleet free and clear. No more trustee. No other owners. So we want you to turn the trust over to her and sell her your stock. We'll pay you fifty million dollars for it, Uncle Jason."

He had not invited me to sit down, but I sat down anyway. "I'm not your uncle," I said, "and my stock's not worth that much. Fifteen or twenty at most. It doesn't matter, though, because I don't want to sell."

"May really wants you to—"

"What May wants me to do, May will tell me to do herself."

The look he threw me was instant anger on top. That didn't bother me a bit. Underneath was a cocky confidence, though, and that did. "In that case," he said, spreading the dimples on the sun-tanned face with a wide smile, "we better just get our asses out to the house so she can do that little thing. I think you're going to like our place."

If what Dougie meant was that I would think it very luxurious, I knew that sight unseen. I had been signing the fund transfers into May's account to pay for it. The luxury started long before we got there. We were only a block or two from Dougie's boat dock on the bay, but there was a chauffeured car waiting in the courtyard to take us there. As we pulled out into the street, I saw the old black woman pause in shining her cracked store window to glare at us over her shoulder. I appreciated that;

at least now I knew who the hostility belonged to. We got in a hydrofoil with a three-man crew and screamed down the waterway, under causeway bridges, past small islands, until we came to a large one. We coasted along it for a while. There were lavish estates along the shore; then there were none, just mangroves and cypress, until we came to a dock that could have handled an oaty-boat. Well, not really. I exaggerate. But the dock was an exaggeration, too. There was no vessel he might want to own that would need that much space.

The house was as grand as I could have expected, but the grandest part was May running down the green, green lawn to meet me. She hugged me twice as tightly as I had expected, then leaned back to look at me. And I at her. It was my veritable sweet May, as ever was, the clean, clear face, the thoughtful, wide-set eyes, the silky hair— "You look tired," I said. I hadn't meant to, but it was true. It was not polite, so I added, "Too much golf, I suppose."

The smile flickered, but it came back fast. "It's more like too much not seeing you, Jay. Come on in! Oh, Jason—I've missed you so much!"

If consulted by the tribunal when it is time to decide how long Dougie d'Agasto should roast in hell, I will say on his behalf that at least he let us alone to talk. He excused himself at once. He went up to his "study" for an hour, came down for lunch, and immediately took off in the stiltboat for most of the afternoon—it was for his tutoring in thermal engineering, he said. So I had May to myself. I saw the house. I heard how Jimmy Rex was doing. May told me that the secessionist mobs were pretty worrying when they rioted, but maybe they were right and this part of Florida should anschluss with Cuba. She wanted to know if I'd seen much of the big new Chinese boats that were being launched, or any more dead fish. I even had time for a nap before dinner; and not once did she bring up the trust, or I.

Dinner wasn't grand—just very good, with all the things in it that May had known I liked all her life. When the

coffee was on the table, Dougie chased the servants out
of the dining hall and leaned back.

"So tell him, honey," he said with that smile that was
on the very verge of curdling into a smirk.

May looked reluctant, but she didn't put it off. She put
her elbows on the table and her chin in her hands, and
she gazed at me. "You've been as good a father to me as
my father ever was, Jason."

Those were not the words I most wanted to hear from
her, but under the circumstances they were about the best
I could expect. I reached across and patted her hand.

"So don't think I'm not grateful to you, dear, because
I am. I always will be. But I'm not a child anymore. I'm
a grown woman, married—" Three times married, I
thought, and she was thinking the same because she hesitated—"married, with a child. As much of an adult as
I'm ever going to be, Jason. So I'm asking you to dissolve
the trust." Dougie pursed his lips and nodded judiciously,
as though he had just heard the idea for the first time and
thought that by and large it might be sound. He didn't
say anything. That was just as well, for I might have said
something in return that could never be unsaid. "You
don't have to sell your own stock if you don't want to,
Jay," she went on. "Dougie thought that might be a good
idea for you, but it's up to you. But, please, will you do
the other?"

I didn't look at Dougie again. I didn't have to, for I
could feel the temperature of his smile . . . and I could feel
it drop to zero as I said, "If I do that, May, I will be
killed. It's your father's orders." And I spread before
them the nineteen letters I had received from my unknown
assassin. And I told them what the Commodore had said
to me.

Dougie slammed his fist down on the table. It was thick
teak, but it shook. I didn't look at him, and he didn't say
a word. May, with tears in her voice, said, "You mean
my father paid someone to have you *killed*? But that's
horrible!"

I touched her hand again. "No, love, it's not. He was

right to make sure of me. If I'd failed you, it would be fair punishment." And wished I were more sure that I hadn't failed her already.

May was crying openly now. It was her husband's place to comfort her, but her husband was studying the nineteen letters, their envelopes, their postmarks. I got up and went around the table, knelt beside her, and put my arms around her. No one said anything for a while. I would not have minded if that while had gone on indefinitely, with May warm and unresisting in my arms, but at last Dougie had finished his chain of thought. He swept the letters in a fan across the table and sat back. "I guess you're not lying," he stated.

In my arms May stirred and detached herself. "Jason doesn't lie to me," she told him, "ever!"

"I don't think he could have cooked up all these letters," he said, "so let's say you're right. What about it, Jay? Don't you have any idea who this person is?"

I hesitated, but it was too late to do the person any harm. "I thought for a while it might be Captain Havrila," I admitted, "but he died six months ago, and I've had letters since."

"Never tried to find out? See where they were mailed from? Find the people who mailed them?"

"How could I?" For that matter, why would I want to? I had accepted the situation as just when the Commodore had laid it on me.

He nodded. He wasn't agreeing, he was only recognizing the fact that I didn't have the guts or the determination to do anything about the situation. "What we can do," he proposed, "is get you the best damn guards you ever saw in your life. Twenty-four hours, round the clock. As long as you live. And forget about fifty million, I'll go to—"

"Dougie, stop it!" cried May. He blinked at her, but she stared him down. Then she turned to me. "What you've said changes everything, of course. So that's out. We'll go on the way we are for the present."

And I expected an explosion from Dougie. I didn't get

one. I was slow to learn that the only safe expectation about Dougie d'Agasto was that he would never do what I expected him to do, but always something worse. He nodded, and picked up the letters and stuffed them in a pocket and gave us both a sunny smile.

"In that case," he said, "anyone for a game of billiards?"

If Dougie d'Agasto did not get what he wanted out of our meeting, he got quite a lot in other ways. He got the right to tell me what to do. Every one of his letters of instruction was countersigned by May herself, but there was no doubt who had written them.

His instructions were not all that wicked or dumb, to be honest—perhaps there had been worse ones that May refused to sign. Cancel the plans for another ore pumper—well, the manganese nodules were a drug on the market these days, with so many boats fishing for them. Kill the iceberg project and sell off the tugs—it had become a running sore in our cash-flow accounts anyway. He never attempted to keep me from spending any sum on keeping the Fleet seaworthy and comfortable for its crews, but he did veto almost every plan for expansion. He was hoarding capital, it seemed. No doubt there was a plan, and no doubt I would find out about it sooner or later.

Meanwhile I followed his orders, and life was not all that bad. The officers and crews liked me, I think. Not just on the flagship. When I flew to Dubai to sign the sale papers on the sailing tugs and pay off the crews, they took me out for a night on the town. I could not have expected that from forty men and women I had just fired, and they weren't angling for other places in the Fleet—they were all fine sailors, and there were plenty of jobs. They were simply saying good-by to a friend, and I was touched. I was also very, very drunk, and when at last I got back to the flagship I was still parched and headachy, but not unhappy—at least not until I saw that Betsy's private VTO was parked on the landing deck.

"I thought," she said, "it was time I paid you a visit, since you don't ever come to see me."

She was not a person I wanted for a friend, but I didn't particularly want to offend her. "You are always welcome on May's fleet," I told her, with a great deal of politeness and not nearly as much truth, and I called the house-keepers' section chief to tell them that they were to prepare suitable accommodations. Of course, they were way ahead of me. They had put fresh flowers in the vases and ice in the bowls in the suite that sheikhs and sovereigns occupied when they were our guests. For a wonder, Betsy didn't pout when I told her I had to work for a bit— "I've been away quite a while," I said, "and I really need to—" And she put her finger against my lips, with a smile that under any other circumstances I would have called flirtatious.

"May I try your pool out, Jay?" she asked, quite politely, and she occupied herself with swimming and lazing around the big waterfall that sheeted down the glass of the owners' suite and into the pool, while I did what I had to do. Which was only partly business. Mostly it was sucking oxygen out of a bottle and swallowing aspirin, because if I had Betsy for a guest I wanted a clear head.

She had asked that dinner be served out in the garden, and when I came out to see her, she was wearing something long and filmy and white, with white hibiscus tucked into a diamond tiara on her hair. "How very nice you look," I said, as required. She smiled dreamily, watching the butler pour the wine.

"To us," she said, and then, when we had each taken a sip, "How fresh and clean the air is here, Jay."

"I hope it stays that way," I said, because there had been rumors of Betsy's next plan for expansion and diversification. She gave me a thoughtful look, but she was too busy being sweet to follow it up. All through the meal she was all sweet prattle and gossip about rich friends and reckless doings. It was quite a meal. The chef had had time to do his best, and so it was mahimahi and rack

of lamb from our own flock, and a compote of mostly
ugly-fruit for dessert with enough kirsch in it so that I
didn't require an after-dinner brandy. Or, after the previous few days in Dubai, at all want one. Betsy had no
such restraint. She ate every scrap and drank all that was
poured, and when it was done she sighed, "I wish I had
your cook, Jay! I guess I can tell you that I've tried to
hire him away."

"I know," I said. I also knew the reason he had told
me for turning her down—young Betsy was a terror to
her servants.

"You know a lot about my business, don't you?" she
purred, watching me. "I think you meant something by
that remark about the air pollution."

I shrugged. "I have heard," I said carefully, "that you
are contracting for large amounts of Australian coal. The
only thing I can think of you wanting to do with it is
pyrolize it into gasoline, so we'll have a floating Galveston
out here."

"You have very good sources of information, Jay. I
do too. You were a fool to turn Dougie down, you know."

She was sitting between me and the setting sun. I moved
to get the sun out of my eyes so that I could see her
better, and she laughed and hitched her chair closer to
me. "You're always a surprise to me, Jason," she said.
"Those nineteen letters coming in all these years, and
nobody knew but you."

I had finally puzzled it out. "You've got a spy in May's
house," I said.

"My dear Jason! Of course I'm always interested in
what's happening with my sister."

"She's not your sister."

"I think of her as my sister." She hitched her chair a
bit closer, and our knees touched. "Would you like to
know how I think of you?"

Now, the advancing years had not made me any more
handsome. I was older than Betsy's father. I could not
think of any reason why she would be after my body, but

her eyes were half closed, and her lips were half smiling, and her voice was husky.

I got up to replenish her drink, and when I was seated again, we were no longer touching. "Why was I stupid, Betsy?"

"Accidents happen," she whispered over the rim of her glass. "You've got a few good years left if you're careful, Jay." I moved restlessly, rejecting the implication. "May has more than that," she went on, "unless there was an accident. Why, do you know, Jason, under the terms of the Commodore's will, if May died your trusteeship would terminate? And then you'd have nothing to say about what happened to her stock."

"It would just go to Jimmy Rex."

"And if something happened to Jimmy Rex?"

I was getting angry—it was not because she was putting new thoughts in my head, for what angered me was that these same thoughts had occurred to me long since. Fortunately for my peace of mind I had reasoned out an answer to that. "May's money," I said, "is a lot, but it's nothing compared to what Jimmy Rex is going to inherit from his grandmother. The Appermoys have *billions*, and Jimmy's the only heir."

And Betsy laughed out loud. "To think," she marveled, "that you were the one who got us interested in the dead fish!"

I nodded as though I understood. I doubt that I fooled her. I did not understand at all, and to make time to help puzzle it out I poured myself a brandy after all. I dawdled, savoring the Courvoisier. Either she was being deliberately mystifying, or I was more tired and hung over and, yes, already slightly drunk all over again than I thought. Perhaps I had not made myself clear? The logic was very simple. Nothing would happen to Jimmy Rex—at least nothing that Dougie might arrange—as long as his grandmother was alive, because Dougie would not endanger his chances of somehow getting his hands on the Appermoy fortune. What dead fish had to do with all this I did

not know, and Betsy was not helping me think. She leaned forward, with her eyes as close to sparkling as she knew how to make them, and licked the lobe of my ear. "You're an exciting man, Jason," she whispered.

"For God's sake, Betsy!" I protested, not quite sure whether it was the sense of what she was saying that I objected to, or her warm, moist tongue in my ear. I was getting to be an elderly man, but I wasn't dead. I didn't like Betsy at all. She was not beautiful. But she was young, and she was healthy, and she was wearing at least a hundred dollars' worth of French perfume in the folds of the clinging gossamer gown. I tried to redirect the conversation. "Will you please tell me what you're trying to say?"

She smiled mistily and leaned back—it was not a way of putting space between us, it was only so that she could throw her breasts out. I did not fail to notice them. "Jason," she murmured, "I think better when I'm lying down. In bed. With a nice warm body next to me."

There was no possible doubt in my mind that it was Betsy's intention to add me to her already outstanding collection of lovers. I am embarrassed to say that at that moment I could almost believe that it was for my own aging body's sake—almost. I croaked, "Why are you doing this, Betsy?"

"Aw . . ." She pouted. Then she shrugged. "Because I want everything that belongs to May. But I promise you it'll be worth it. I'm really good, Jason. And I also promise you," she added, getting slowly up and tugging me to my feet, "that in that nice big bed that you sleep in, that used to be May's, after the important stuff has been taken care of, I will tell you everything you want to know, and it will truly fascinate you."

On that promise she cheated me, though not on anything else. I did not sleep much that night. When I woke at daylight and remembered who I had for a bedmate, she was gone. I pulled myself raggedly out of bed and threw

a robe on, and while I was puzzling over what had happened, I heard a jet scream. I went to the lanai and there was Betsy's plane, a bright blue-white trail streaking across the pink morning sky. She had gotten what she wanted, and gone.

She spoiled my sleep for more than one night. I could not get out of my mind what she had said and hinted. The worst was the implication that Jeff's death had not been an accident. Dougie was filth, of course. I had not thought he was a murderer, at least in my conscious mind; but now that Betsy had made me think about it, I could not doubt it anymore.

I called in the security chief again, and from then on I was never without a couple of huskies within call.

But that protected only me. What could protect my May? Logic told me that it would not make sense for Dougie to harm May as long as the boy would simply inherit—nor would it be reasonable for him to want the boy out of the way as long as Jimmy Rex stood to inherit the vast Appermoy billions. It would surely pay Dougie to bide his time, at least until the old lady died.

But the stink of dead fish showed me there was something wrong with that chain of reasoning. Betsy knew what it was but, typically, had not told me. So I started other inquiries into motion.

They weren't necessary. Before my agents had a chance to report, a morning came when I was awakened by the Fleet bursar pounding at the door, bursting with news.

The dead fish had done the Appermoys in.

For old man Appermoy had not been able to resist one more villainy before he died. The glassy pellets he dissolved the radionuclides in for disposal were not expensive. It was not usually worth his while to steal in so trivial an area. But there was a strike in a settling farm that he had not been able to buy off, and an accident to one of the vitrifying plants that put him behind schedule, and so he had eight hundred ton lots of high-level radioactive waste with no legitimate place to put them. He had

dumped them, raw, into his seamount. Of course, they had begun to dissolve into the sea almost at once.

Appermoy had not killed the Pacific Ocean, for it was too big for even him. But he had so polluted three million square kilometers that fish were dying. The family had been able to keep the lid on—it is cheaper to bribe than to comply—until the weather betrayed them. For a solid month the Hawaiian winds blew the wrong way. They swept the waters out of the west, and washed radioactively hot waves onto Oahu and Maui and the Kona coast.

The damage was too immense for bribes to work anymore, and they were a land-based conglomerate. So the land law could reach them, and that meant something like twenty billion dollars in damage suits already, with more in the offing, and the lax government agencies forced at last to stir themselves. "I'm sure," said the bursar gleefully, "that the old lady's tucked a few million away in pocket change here and there. But the company's bust!"

So Jimmy Rex had lost most of his legacy . . . and May had lost her insurance.

Since I no longer believed that Jeff's accident had been an accident, I had to believe that an accident could easily happen to May and her son. What could I do to prevent it? I ruminated a thousand plans. I could confront Dougie with my suspicions and warn him that he was being watched—foolish idea! The one thing you could not do to Dougie d'Agasto was frighten him off. I could warn May. I could tell her what I believed and beg her to leave him. But that was almost as foolish. If she had been willing to listen, she would never have married the creature in the first place. The best plan was the one that I rejected most positively and at once. I could, I thought out of my anger and despair, do to Dougie himself what I feared he would do to May.

But I could not stoop so low, though for many years I have wished I had.

And while I was stewing over whether to call May, and what to say to her if I did, I got a call from her. She looked troubled and very weary, but she was trying to sound happy. "Good news, Jason," she cried, though her eyes made liars of her words. "Dougie says we won't have to worry about that—that *letter* problem, anymore. He says he is certain of it. He has gone to get documentary proof, and he'll bring it to you." But she added, although I could see that it cost her, "But you're the one who has to decide if the proof is enough, Jay. I'll abide by whatever you decide."

And two days later, before dawn, Dougie's plane screamed in. It woke me from my sleep. By the time I got to the landing strip he was gone, the pilot waiting by the ship to pass on his instructions for me. Mr. d'Agasto had had the deck crew take his materials down to the scavenging deck. Mr. d'Agasto would wait for me there. Mr. d'Agasto asked that I join him at once.

Mr. d'Agasto was getting on my nerves. Why the scavenging deck? It was not much more than a sewer head—when we built lips around the oaty-boats, we could no longer throw our garbage over the side, so there was a well that opened out under the hull. It was a tiny, dirty chamber down near the waterline, not a place where anyone went for choice. I didn't like Dougie's choice of a place, I didn't like getting orders from him—most of all, of course, I didn't like Dougie himself. But I went. And all the way down on the hoist, and all across the wide, hissing, rumbling of the boat's workings as the tram carried me through the low-pressure turbine decks, I was wondering if this was a scheme of Dougie's to kill me and dump me down the scavenging well. I had not forgotten what he was.

I also had not forgotten some of the other things Betsy had told me. They were not useful things. They were what she thought were sexually stimulating things. They had to do with Dougie's tastes: How he liked to do that, she said, showing me *that*, and also this, demonstrating *this*,

and most of all he likes to do these others... But some of those others I would not allow at all, and my stomach turned as the images formed in my mind of what went on between Dougie and my May in their private hours. So I did not want to see the man at all. And if it was his plan to kill me—well, then at least I would never again be troubled with these poisonous thoughts.

He did not have any such plans, it turned out.

He was alone in the scavenging chamber. It reeked, for he had opened the main access hatch and the oily, warm water was only a few meters below, with all its leftover stinks. Dougie had a great packing case at his feet, and he was smoking a joint to combat the stench. "Close the door," he ordered.

I did as I was told. Dougie could see that I was ill at ease. It amused him. "This won't take long," he promised. "Help me open the box."

I did that, too, very obedient to his instructions. The box was very heavy, and there was waterproof sacking around it, a metal container nearly two meters long. It was sealed and locked. "You take good care of your documents," I panted as I lifted one corner so that Dougie could unlock the strapping.

He laughed—I did not then know why. It took him some time to get the lid open—

The lid of the coffin.

A terrible miasma of decay poured out. The body inside was days dead, but I could recognize the tired old face. In life it had belonged to Elsie Van Dorn. "I never thought of her," I gasped.

"You don't have to think of her anymore," chuckled Dougie. "You're really pretty dumb, old man. It stood to reason that the Commodore would have arranged for your guard dog to get some money. All I had to do was get a look at his private bequests—you know how that's done, don't you?" I flinched, but didn't meet his eyes. "Once I found her, it wasn't hard. She even had copies of the letters in her safe-deposit box."

I could not speak. I could only stare at poor Elsie, who had loved the child she had cared for and at the last paid the tariff on that love.

"You've seen enough? You're convinced?" And Dougie shoved the box into the scavenging chute. It was a two-meter drop, splash, gone forever into the secret deeps of the ocean. "So you don't have any excuse anymore, old man," said Dougie, "and I've had the papers drawn up for you. Here they are. Sign."

And of course, as soon as he could get back to Miami with the signed papers, May turned over all her stock to him. I had begged her not to. She wouldn't meet my eyes on the phone as she said, "I feel—anyway, I hope—that once he has what he needs, he won't have to—"

She stopped there and shook her head, not wanting to name what he "had" to do otherwise. And Dougie d'Agasto was crowned king of the grazing isles.

Toll the bell, sound the knell,
My lady she married the lord of hell.
Her life she gave as wife and slave
To a treacherous, lecherous, blood-soaked knave,
An impudent villain whose touch defiles
The sweetness and woe of the queen of the isles.

The oaty-boats had a long run for their money, but there were clouds on the horizon. There was a new land-based energy source, deep methane from far under the crust; there was a new sky-based one, with MHD generators in orbit beaming down floods of microwave power. And every month a new huge oaty-boat appeared, or more than one, to add to our fleet or Betsy's or some foreigner's. They all had five-kilometer intakes now, and we were all huddling in the same patches of ocean, sucking out the delta-Ts. It was not just that the sea was never empty now, it was worse than that. The sweet Pacific reeked of oil. My suspicions about Betsy's plans were correct,

though it wasn't just gasoline she was making. She bought cheap coal from Australia, pyrolized it to make liquid hydrocarbons, and reacted them with her electrolysis gases to turn the waste char into fuel alcohol. It was cheap fuel to ship and cheap fuel to store, for it needed no liquefying, and she sold every drop of it back to the Australians, or to the Americans or the Europeans or the Japanese. And left the stink of her oil and the smudge of her filth far beyond the horizon.

Half the other fleets were beginning to do the same, and Dougie called me on the carpet to find out why I had not proposed it for ourselves. They were back in the owner's country now, he and May and the boy, for he simply had overruled her objections to living in the place where Jeff had died. He kept me standing before his huge teak desk for ten minutes while he punched out data sets to study, face impassive, head twisted back to avoid the drifting smoke from the joint he never took out from between his lips, and then he confronted me: "Well? Can you explain why we missed the boat on this?"

Dougie d'Agasto's opinion of me didn't matter at all, but I didn't want him convincing May I was an old fool. "The market has peaked already," I said. "There's too many boats doing it."

"Because we're getting to it too late!"

I shook my head. "Because hydrogen's a cleaner fuel—" I saw that wasn't registering with him—"and will always get a higher price—" that did—"and this little boom won't last long enough to amortize the cost of the pyrolytic converters. All it will do is turn the Pacific into Los Angeles." And indeed, there were days when my eyes stung out in the open sea wind.

"Well," he said, as though he were giving me one more chance and begrudging it, "we'll say no more about it. Anyway, I've got plans of my own."

But he didn't tell me what they were. I didn't ask. I confess to curiosity, though, because to give the reptile his due, Dougie had not entirely wasted his time in "study-

ing" oceanthermal industrial processes in Miami. He hadn't wasted much time doing any actual studying, either; I do not believe more than one hour a week went to his tutoring, and where the rest of it went I could guess—and so could May, for the lines on her face were not all due to too much golf and sunshine. He found that there was a simpler way, though. He simply bought the school. He hired away twenty of the expert instructors and flew them to the Fleet. He knew enough to make good choices, anyway. All of them were skilled, and one or two I knew myself—Desmond MacLean had worked as a junior engineer on the Commodore's first boat, before going back to school and winding up a teacher. But even Desmond did not volunteer what Dougie's plans were.

I must give the devil one more measure of due. He was a worker. He worked as hard as Jeff Ormondo even, though how he found time for it all I could not guess. When they were aboard the boat, he was everywhere, looking into every hold and engine room and control point; but he and May lived jet-set lives, parties everywhere, on all the seas and on the land. He took May away from me for three weeks out of four. It was not only May he took. Dougie was grossly and tastelessly—and after a while almost openly—an addicted womanizer. I could not forgive him his infidelity, for was there any other man alive in the world who would have wanted more woman than May?

I understood at last what Dougie wanted: Everything. He wanted it all. He had grown up as a very junior poor relation in his mob family. Now he was almost the richest of them—but that "almost" was the iron in his soul. He wanted Betsy's half of the Fleet back to add to May's. If he had twenty thermal engineers on the payroll, he had ten times as many lawyers—but so did Betsy. When they met, which at one ball or race meet or another was often, they joked with each other about their lawsuits, and both would have pointed the jests with steel if they had dared.

* * *

"Mr. d'Agasto," said Desmond MacLean, "says I can tell you now. Come up on the weather bridge." And he only grinned at me without a word as we rode the hoist up to the snug cabin on top of everything. He punched in his present location to the ship's circuits and waved an arm in a half circle. "What do you see, Jason?" he asked.

What I saw was what I had seen every day. The great mass of the vessel stretched out for hundreds of meters in every direction, and beyond our decks was the sea with its dozen vessels steaming slowly through the sooty air.

"I see stink," I said.

"So you'll be glad to see us making more hydrogen and cheaper, won't you?" he asked cheerfully.

I shrugged. "Where are you going to get the delta-Ts?"

"That's the problem, right." He punched in the commands and displayed on his intercom console a map of the Pacific Ocean. "Here's where we are—" pointing— "in the middle of this shaded green oval here, stretching from New Guinea to Hawaii. There are now four hundred oaty-boats grazing it, and each one pumps nearly a hundred tons a second average. That's—" he punched out the calculations— "eighty billion liters a day, thirty trillion a year. Every year we move thirty cubic kilometers of water from the deeps to the surface!"

"There are plenty of cubic kilometers in the Pacific," I said, unwilling to believe that our puny pipes could change anything in the majestic mass of the ocean.

"But not plenty that we need at the five-kilometer depth," he said.

"Well, of course. That's why we stay out of each other's wakes—or try to."

"We do," he agreed, "as long as we can. But either we settle for coming close to another boat or we work lenses that aren't quite as cold as we'd like. Look at the arithmetic. When we have deep water at six degrees and surface water at thirty-two, which is what our turbines are designed for, we've got a delta-T of twenty-six. The efficiency of the boilers goes up with the cube of the tem-

perature difference. So the figure of merit for those temperatures is twenty-six cubed—17,576."

"We've not had a twenty-six degree delta-T for some time," I admitted.

"And we won't for a while longer, because we're competing with the heart of the oaty-boat fleet. We're cooling the surface water and sucking up the best lenses of cold. So most of the time we're dealing with top water that's as much as three degrees cooler than it should be, and bottom water sometimes three degrees warmer. Delta-T, twenty. Cubed figure of merit, eight thousand. Which means just about half the energy we should be getting."

"As bad as that!"

"And going to get worse," he said, but cheerfully, so that I asked irritably:

"All right, come on! Tell me what you've got up your sleeve."

"We go deeper!" he said triumphantly. He shook his head when I started to object, and keyed the map back. This time it was featureless. "Here are unexploited areas with a surface temperature of thirty or more—" He displayed areas hatched in red lines, and as I peered at them I began to object again— "Wait a minute, Jason! And here are huge lenses of three-degree deep water. Three degrees, you understand me? And look—there's a patch five hundred kilometers across where we've got both. Thirty-three degrees on the surface, three degrees at depth—delta-T, thirty—cube that for a figure of merit, Jason!"

I didn't have to. It was an oaty-boater's dream. "Shit, Des," I said contemptuously, "you're talking about *bottom* water."

"Damn near. Ten kilometers down, most of it."

"And I know those charts. What you don't show there is that there are mid-depth warm currents. You try to drop a suction intake down through them, and they'll curve into spaghetti!"

He grinned smugly. "Right," he said, "and wrong. I'm not talking about a rubber hose. I'm talking about steel tubing, buoyed along its length to keep it neutral, dynam-

ically positioned by its own engines. Of course, those figures of merit aren't all profit. A hell of a lot goes into energy to keep the currents from tying the tubes in knots, and a hell of a lot of capital into building them in the first place. But I did the feasibility studies myself! With a figure of merit of twenty-seven thousand you can afford a lot."

I only had one question left. "When?" I begged.

"It's already started, Jason! The contracts have been let out for the new gear, deliveries will start in sixty days. Mr. d'Agasto has started hiring construction crews and they'll be coming aboard next month—"

"Aboard? Here?"

There was a shadow on Desmond's happy face as he said, "Well, yes. The conversion's going to be done at sea. That's Mr. d'Agasto's plan. I really think," he said wistfully, "that we'd do better taking the boats in one at a time to some nice deep harbor, maybe in the Sunda straits, and refit there. I showed him the figures. It'd be cheaper and faster...but he's the boss, Jason."

I nodded. He was. He was showing it. He hadn't said a word to me—hadn't even allowed Desmond MacLean to whisper it to me until now, when the work was already begun and the secret would be no secret anymore. He was the boss. And I—was superfluous.

Prophecies fulfill themselves; a man who thinks himself useless becomes so. The best estimate I could make of myself was that I was an old fool who was in the way.

So I got out of the way. I took myself off to New Zealand.

It could just as easily have been Okinawa or Iceland. There was no place on the Earth where I was particularly needed, or had any particular reason to be. I thought I might like to see geysers before I died, so New Zealand won the toss. There were one or two people there I had some sort of friendly relations with—shipping agents and freight forwarders, and a banker named Sam Abramowitz whom I had known for forty years. I was shy of meeting

Sam, for I had known him first while I was a scared kid in the accounting department of the bank, and he was one of the few people in the world who knew I had juggled the books to give the Commodore his start. But he made me at ease when I hinted at the subject. "Ah, Jason," he said, "that was a hundred years ago in another world. That was back in America, and we've both gone a long way away from what we were then." For he'd been personal banker for a lot of Mob money, until his stomach wouldn't take it anymore and he emigrated. "Forget it. Have a drink. And in the morning I'll take you to see all the damn geysers you want."

So I dawdled away a month, and then half of another. The geysers didn't keep me interested that long. Neither did New Zealand, for when all was said and done it was still land, though only a fairly small piece of it and remote. I longed to be back on the sea, but more than I wanted that I wanted to be wanted there. And so when at last May phoned me, it was all I could do to keep my voice calm and my face bland. "A party?" I said. "Well, I'm not much of a one for parties, my dear."

"Oh, please, Jason! The Mays are going to be here, and a lot of our other friends—it'll be the biggest party we ever gave."

"I would like to see the Mays," I admitted.

"Not as much as they want to see you! I don't know if they'll even come if I can't tell them you'll be here. And, Jason—" there was real sweetness in her voice and in her half-fearful smile—"I've missed you *so*."

Well, of course I went! I was getting pretty sick of sheep, anyway—and even sicker of being on the land.

May had kept my rooms for me, but there was going to be a crush of guests. I gladly vacated them for May Bancroft and Tse-ling Mei to share, and I moved in with the crew. There was not much more room there. The work crews were coming aboard for the refit. When I looked them over, they were the sorriest, meanest bunch of roughnecks I have ever seen. If I had not been told they were deep-water construction workers, I would have

guessed them to be knee breakers for the Mob. Every one of them was allowed a hundred and fifty kilos of personal luggage, and I did not believe that any of it was musical instruments or books.

They did not help morale on the boat. Dougie cleared six hundred of our own people out of their quarters and put the new ones in one whole section together. They ate together, they talked together, they kept together. The rest of us were doubled up and excluded. In the first day the boat's security staff arrested a couple for hard drugs, but Dougie was having none of that. He ordered the charges dropped, and then ordered the security forces to stay out of the construction workers' area entirely. Not just the security forces. All of us were told to stay away, and hard-nosed types that had come aboard with the new work crews stood guard at the passages to keep the rest of us out. The new ones all wore a new kind of uniform—scarlet sea jackets and crash helmets—and they looked as much like an invading army as anything else.

They felt that way, too. There was a meanness in the air on our boat that I had never felt before, not even when bastard Ben was king triumphant. I tried to talk myself out of it. Old man Jason, I said to me, although I was still not yet sixty and not really old at all, old man, you are seeing ghosts and worrying without cause, for how can things get worse than they are already? They can't, I said, to reassure myself. But at sixty I had a lot still to learn.

I went to May and told her I didn't like the new people. She was trying on her new party dresses, with two of her maids fluttering around and admiring her and them, and indeed she was as beautiful as she had ever been—a little thinner, a little sadder, but the most beautiful woman in the world—and the dresses nearly did her justice. "These people are only for a little while, Jason, dear," she said. "As soon as the new intakes are installed, they'll be gone."

"I'd hate to be the one that had to throw them off the ship," I grumbled. She didn't look at me for a moment. She stood there, staring out over the gardens toward the sea, as she used to stare when she was two years old.

Then she said, "Perhaps you ought to talk to Dougie about
them instead of me." She had made up her mind not to
interfere with her chosen love's way of running the empire
she had given him. I had to respect her wishes.

So I did talk to Dougie. He laughed at me and told me
to get lost. He was busy, he said.

That was what he said, and that, in fact, he was, for
the refit was a huge task, and there was the party coming
up. The party was to celebrate the public announcement
of what everyone in the trade had known for weeks, that
we were going deeper and finding more. He had invited
people from the Russian and Japanese fleets. He had invited a few of our principal customers from even the land.
And of course he had invited Betsy. Because May asked
me to be, I was polite to her—as polite as to Captain
Tsunehshov or to old Baron Akagana when they came
aboard. I greeted her politely and offered her a drink and
helped her get settled in her rooms; and I did the same
for the Japanese and the Russians, and then went off to
see the Mays. If they were a little older than the last time
I saw them, they were at least that much more charming
and beautiful, too. Tse-ling Mei was one of the world's
most loved movie stars. Maisie Gerstyn, who had once
been Maisie Richardson, had brought her handsome husband and her two fair, bright twin boys. We all sat around
the lanai that was part of my suite—theirs now—gossip-
ing and enjoying one another's company until the sun was
low and it was time for them to dress for the party.

I was in no hurry to dress, or to go to the party at all,
for that matter. I was ambling slowly toward my room
when the pager called my name. Desmond MacLean
wanted me to join him in the high bridge, and his voice
sounded strange.

The principal reason his voice sounded that way was
that he was half drunk. He wasn't alone, either. He was
sitting there with his face flushed and his tongue tripping
over the hard words, and there with him, matching him

drink for drink, was Betsy Zoll. "You idiot," I snarled at him, "you're out of your class! Can't you see she's pumping you for information?"

He shook his head stubbornly. "Other way," he mumbled. "Y'unnerstan' me? It's the other way. She's doing the talking."

I had no patience with the man—or with Betsy, either, who sat there serene and smiling. I called for a medic with a tank of oxygen and some black coffee. "You'd better stay away from the party," I said bitterly, "for you'll disgrace the boat." He shrugged hopelessly. "Damn it," I cried, "what's the matter with you? Don't you see what a fool you are? And what did you call me for, anyway?"

He pointed to Betsy. "Tell'm," he mumbled, and submitted himself to the attentions of the medic, who had just arrived.

While MacLean was choking down coffee and inhaling as much of the O_2 as the medic could force into him, Betsy stood up. I'm sure she'd had as much to drink as Desmond, but the only sign was that she moved very carefully, as though the floor were rocking. There was nothing wrong with her speech. "What I told him, old man," she said, "was nothing you couldn't have seen for yourself. Just look around you."

"At what?" I demanded. She pointed out the window.

But there was nothing to be seen that I didn't already know was there. True, Betsy's own flagship was hull down on the horizon, and two others of our own fleet and one of hers in sight—but I'd known that, for some reason or other, we'd been steaming closer and closer to other boats for the past few days. The only other thing that was in any way unusual was the flotilla of stiltboats and fast hovers in the water just outside the lip. And that was easily understood. It was to ferry our guests back and forth, of course—though it was, I thought as I looked closer, a touch strange that the crews manning them all wore the scarlet sea jackets of the new construction crews.

"I don't know what I'm looking at," I admitted stiffly.

Betsy laughed and turned to the medic. "Out," she ordered. The woman glanced at me, then left, her expression resentful. "Have you looked at the landing strip?" Betsy demanded.

"Why should I?" But I did, and then I looked again. There were a dozen aircraft parked at the side of the strip, and instead of bringing them down to the hangar deck, more were coming up on the elevator.

"Old man," she said contemptuously, "what you won't see, you can't see. I knew this was happening weeks ago. I only came to make sure."

"Sure of what?"

"Ah, Jason, what a fool you are! Can't you recognize an invasion force when you see one?"

"There's no need," I said, misunderstanding her, "for Dougie to invade the boat, since May has given him the whole fleet."

"Not her fleet, you old fool! Mine! He wants to steal my ships!"

"You stole them yourself in the first place," I said stubbornly, not quite taking it in, "or your bastard father did."

She stared at me with scorn. "Everybody steals everything; how else can anybody ever get rich? How did the Commodore get them in the first place, but with you to help him in the stealing? God help you, old man, you've blinded yourself. If you won't believe me, ask your drunken friend," she cried, grinning, and left the bridge.

By then Des was nearly coherent. Still, it took him a long time to get the story out. Betsy had plied him with drink and got him babbling, and what he had babbled was what I should have known for myself. He had poked among the incoming stores for the new "work crews" and found that there were pumps and engines and tubing, all right, but there were also rifles and grenades and bigger, worser weapons than that. It was true. The reconstruction was a ruse to import his storm troops; the party was a ruse, too, to get Betsy aboard as hostage.

God knows how long Dougie had planned this madness. God knows how many of Betsy's people he had offered bribes or how many fortunes he had squandered to buy arms and hire his battalions. God knew—but I should have known, too! If I hadn't let myself fling off to New Zealand in a fit of pique, I might have seen it happening in time to prevent it. But even so, I should have known. I should have realized months earlier that Dougie would never settle for half of anything. He wanted all of the Fleet, not just May's boats.

And he wound up with nothing. For God knew, and I should have known—but Betsy did know. People who take a bribe will take a bigger one. As I was scrambling down the ladder to Dougie's command bridge I heard the distant scream of a stiltboat and saw Betsy's boat rising on its skis. She was on her way back to her own ship, and Dougie was caught with egg on his face. For by the time I got past his uglies to confront him, she was home free and talking to him on the intercom. "Give it up, sonny!" she taunted. "You missed your chance!"

He roared obscenities into the microphone, and finished with threats, but she cut him off. "It's too late," she said. "Look to your starboard!" He did. I did, too—we all did.

And wished we had not.

I had never seen a mininuke at work before. The oatyboat next to us in the grazing comb was a sister ship to our own. Two million tons, and most of ten thousand people aboard. You would not think to look at that vast, slow juggernaut that anything could halt it, or even slow it down, much less do it harm—you might as well try to sink Gibraltar! But a hundred-K nuke into its engine room was too much weapon for even an oaty-boat.

It was God's grace for us that the explosion was inside the hull, for we were spared our eyes. Even the second-hand radiation that bounced off the water and made a bright haze of the smoggy air blinded me, and the concussion shook our boat. When the wave came, it swamped Dougie's attack flotilla and drowned hundreds of his thugs,

but then it was over. The only real change was that our sister boat was not there anymore. All that remained of it was a glowing, rising cloud of steam.

Dougie did not know when to give up. He actually thought, I believe, that his hired killers would be loyal to their pay. When he tried to get them to attack Betsy's boat as planned, no matter that the same torpedo tubes that had just disintegrated one oaty-boat were now trained on ours, the mercenaries did what mercenaries do best—changed sides—and told him they were arresting him. He would not submit. That didn't help; they only killed him instead.

The Russians and the Japanese ranted and raved, but what could they do? There was no law left on the sea. And no peace, either. When Betsy came aboard again, it was as a conqueror, with twenty armed hoodlums at her back, and she demanded that May sign over every vessel in the Fleet to her.

My May was poised and lovely, but very pale. She looked at me for strength but, chained and gagged in a chair, I had none to give her. "The world will not condone piracy!" she cried, but Betsy only grinned.

"The world," she said, "has troubles of its own, and besides, who would lift a finger to help a murderess?"

I groaned and struggled, for I could guess what was coming. May could not. It was her greatest weakness, that she could never gauge what evil really was. "You murdered your husband," Betsy announced. "The second one, anyhow—I don't know about the others!" May didn't bother to tell her she was lying; she only waited to hear what form the lie would take. But it wasn't all lie. For Betsy said, "I have a confession from the oiler who helped Dougie d'Agasto murder Jeff, and proof that it's true. And the confession says that you were as guilty as Dougie. Planned it together"—she grinned—"for everyone knows that you and Dougie were lovers long before you killed Jeff to get him out of the way!"

And all I could do was groan.

Later, when the papers were signed and May was taken away, Betsy got around to me. "Well," she said when the gag was out of my mouth, "what shall we do with you, old man?"

"Whatever you want to," I said. "But you know May was no part of that murder! You have no evidence that will stand one second in court!"

"But the only court there is, old Jay, is me. No land court will try her. She'll never be on land again, you see, because I'm going to keep her near me as long as she lives."

"Treat her kindly at least," I begged, abject at last.

"Why not? In fact," she said, in high good humor, "I'll let you be her jailer, old man—providing we can make an agreement on what your other duties are! And then you can treat her as kindly as you like."

And so all the years of peace were over, forever.

V

Thrice widowed was wasted her beauty fair.
Her son, no son, was her only heir.
Her sister, no sister, pent her there,
In a cage on the grazing isles.

I did it for a year, and three months, and a week, and how I did it that long I do not now know. Then I went to Betsy. "You'll have to wait," said her butler. "Miss Zoll is engaged just now."

"I'll wait," I said, and I did, for an hour and more in her "morning room." It was a bright and cheery place, high over the foredeck and its gardens. May had no gardens. May had four comfortable rooms all to herself, and whatever she liked to eat and all the video disks and books she asked for, but except for me and the servants she had them all to herself. Three visitors were allowed. I was

one. Betsy was another, but she had the grace never to go there, and the third, who would have been the most welcome of all but never came, was Jimmy Rex. Betsy had designed May's jail herself. It had bright, large windows, but they looked on nothing but the sea. It had one door, and there was an armed guard outside it always. At a push of a button the door would lock and steel shutters would slam across the windows, but there was never any need for the button. There was nowhere for May to go.

So I waited the time in Betsy's morning room as patiently as I could, and then she emerged in a robe, drowsily yawning and stretching, absently petting the hairy shoulder of the scoutship pilot who was her favorite of the moment. "Well, old man? What do you want now? Isn't May happy in her home? Would she like a little trip to relieve the monotony—say, a week or two in Miami with her drug pushers and arms runners?"

I would not let her anger me. "I've come to sell you my stock," I said.

She frowned at me in silence for a moment. Then she slapped the pilot's rump and pointed to the door. When he was gone, she said, "What's the trick, Jay?" There was no feeling to her voice at all. It might have been a machine talking, with a machine's requirement for more data on which to base the emotionless, compassionless decision of a machine. I felt myself chilled.

"I don't like what you do," I said. "I can't stop you, but I don't have to be an accomplice."

She rubbed thoughtfully at her lips, which were bruised and swollen, and then clapped her hands. At once her maid appeared in the door, peering through with an armed guard looking alertly over her shoulder. Betsy gestured drinking from a cup of coffee, and the maid produced a service for her at once. "You're not lying to me, I think," she said then, "but there's some kind of truth you're not telling me. What do you want to do with the money?"

"Go away."

"Leave your precious May?"

I kept my voice steady. "I have to get out of here for

a while, Betsy. I'll come back later and go on being a prison guard, but I need some time off. And I need to plan for my future." She looked unconvinced. I said the rest of it: "You're the tyrant here, Betsy. It has pleased you to let May live, but some day you'll be drunk, or doped, or in a rage at whoever is sharing your bed that day. And you'll take it out on her. When I can't help May anymore, I want to see what I can do for me."

She sipped the coffee, studying me over the lip of the cup, and then shrugged. "I'll accommodate you, Jay. I'll give you ten million dollars for your stock."

When I had turned down fifty! "Twenty-five," I bargained, and she shook her head and said:

"Nine."

And nine it was.

May could see at once that I had something to tell her, but she played the hostess and asked after my health and inquired wistfully after Jimmy Rex. She let me come to it in my own time. So, with a glass of wine in my hand, I said, "I'm going to New Zealand for a bit."

"Oh?"

"Just for a while, May. A few weeks maybe. Then I'll be back, I promise."

"Of course you will, Jay, dear. But you're absolutely right. You should get out of this for a while. And New Zealand's a lovely place—I remember, the skiing is first-rate!" And then, her eyes longingly on the open window and the emptiness beyond it, she said in a tone that wanted to be light, "I'd love to be there again. I couldn't do Betsy any harm there." She knew that every word was heard as well as I did, and I suppose she was talking to Betsy as much as to me, though she knew how little good that would do. "I would give my word not to," she said, "and I've never broken it."

I left her before the tears began to trickle down my cheek. I knew that May's word was good. I also knew that Betsy, the mother of lies, would never believe it.

And, oh! my Mary, oh Mary, my May,
Blest was the hope and accursed the day,
Curst was the day when I brought you away,
Away from the grazing isles.

New Zealand was not an idle choice. It had three things
going for it. First, it was lightly populated and far from
rest of the miserable landlocked world. Second, their
geothermal springs made them poor customers for the
Fleet, and so less likely to want to keep in Betsy's good
graces. Third, I had a friend there.

Betsy's eyes did not stop at the hull of the oaty-boat.
So on the first day in Auckland I visited six different banks
to talk about investing my nine million dollars. On the
second day I toured the sheeplands by air, on the pretext
of buying a ranch, and that night I allowed myself to have
two or three more drinks than usual in the guests' lounge
at the little hotel. To anyone who would listen I explained
what a vindictive bitch Betsy Zoll was, and how I had at
last given up hope that my sweet May would ever be free
again. I did not know which of the ranchers or barmen
or guests would be passing the word on to Betsy, but I
had no doubt she would know everything I said.

And on the third day I went to visit an offshore oatie
and there, in the low-pressure turbine room, I met Sam
Abramowitz, as we had arranged on the first. "No one
can hear us here," he said over the hiss and groan of the
generators. "What do you want me to do?" And then,
when I told him, "You're insane!"

I agreed that it was an insane world all over. "Still,"
I said, "what I need is a scout vessel with a pilot, and an
aircraft willing to take the chance of being fired on, for a
million dollars."

He pursed his lips. He didn't answer at first, but turned
and gazed around the booming, gasping turbine room as
though he were suddenly less sure that we couldn't be
spied on. Then he said, "I couldn't set it up overnight,
you know."

"I don't want it overnight, Sam. I want some time to pass, so Betsy will relax a little. At least a month. Six would be better. Just send me a message when you've got it set up—something about investing in a new sheep-shearing machine, maybe—and the pilot must wear something I'll recognize, so I'll know he's there."

He shook his head slowly, not to refuse, only to say it was an outlandish idea. "A million dollars, did you say? It may cost more."

"I've got more," I said. He sighed. It meant yes. I reached out and grasped his hand in both of mine. "You're a good friend, Sam. It's not just for me, you know. It's for the finest lady who ever drew breath."

He looked away and didn't answer. There was a strain in the set of his jaw that I didn't understand and didn't much like. But the important thing was that he had agreed. Then and there I wrote a power of attorney for him, to draw what he liked and spend as he chose. If there was nothing left of the nine million when he was done, well, then I would be a penniless old man. But I would be free, and so would May.

And so should May have been, for it was a good plan and Sam Abramowitz a better friend than I deserved. He was also careful and cunning. When at last the signal came and the scoutship showed up, it was from one of the new Argentinian boats, and the pilot came to Betsy with a fine, false tale of locating unsuspected patches of deep cold that he was willing to sell for a price. And the pilot wore the green scarf that identified him. I could not talk to him, for he was closeted with Betsy, driving his bargain and delivering his goods, but I went down to the sternways and studied the vessel with care. A scoutship has no more beauty of line than an egg. Speed is not important, nor looks. What is important is the strength of hull to withstand whatever pressures it may encounter as it dives deep and sends its probes deeper still to measure the bottom water. It looked solid. Once in it and well away, we had our chance. It would be a run for the bottom to hide under the thermoclines and the scattering layers, and then away, well out of reach of

any of Betsy's eyes or guns. We had range enough to make
it to Australia or Hawaii or Japan, or anywhere between. I
had settled on Manila. Of all destinations that was the most
dangerous for us, since the islands were small and sea visitors frequent, but therefore the one where Betsy would be
least likely to look while we did what we had to do to change
our appearance and find our way to a new home.

All that was needed was the aircraft.

And so, as soon as it was dark, I went down to May's
room. She was sewing as interminably she did, pausing
to read for a while and then to return to the needle. "It's
a hot night," I said, stepping to the port and gazing at the
warm sea, twenty meters below. By leaning out and cran-
ing my neck I could see the scoutboat moored to the
sternways, just past the gate in the mesh. There was a
man in a long green scarf where he was supposed to be.
He was paying for the fuel he had bought, and his orders
were to stall until the aircraft arrived.

Which would not be long.

I said, "I wish we could go for a swim." May gave me
a sharp glance. "Look," I said, catching her hand and
drawing her to the port. "It's not much of a dive. And on
a night like this we could swim to Hawaii if we chose,
and see the palms and the black beaches again." It was
foolish talk, and I was grinning foolishly as I raised her
hand to my lips and kissed it. When I let her hand go, it
was curled around the scrap of paper I'd written out before. It said:

"When I say jump we both jump, and there will be a
boat to take us free."

"Have a drink, dear Jay," May said gently, nodding
me to the bar. And a while later she excused herself to
the bathroom, and when she came out she went back to
her sewing, only looking up to gossip about the fine fresh
pineapple they'd served her for dinner and the strange
dream she'd awakened with that morning.

Half an hour later we were still chattering away, when
the first-level aircraft-warning bells began to ring. I as-

sumed an expression of surprise and curiosity, and pulled May toward the port to look out.

And May's door opened, and little Jimmy Rex walked in.

He was eight years old then, spoiled rotten by Betsy for the past three, and for that matter born with his father's family's rotten blood in him. You must know that in three years the boy had visited his mother just twice. It was Betsy who had sent him, of course. His eyes were bright with an eight-year-old's deviltry. "Are you going to do something foolish, mother May?" he asked, the voice clear, the face pure, the heart made up of equal parts brat and bully. I stood between them.

"What makes you ask a question like that?" I demanded.

He pouted up at me. "Betsy says it's very strange," he complained, "that you've become a drunk, and sold your stock, and stopped asking me to visit here. And there's a plane from the Soviet fleet that showed up on our screens a few minutes ago, claiming that they've lost their electronics and don't know if we're their home boat or not."

I had not expected Betsy to make so quick a connection. But outside the door the guard was paying no attention to us. He was listening to the ship's intercom, his scarred, mean face envious as he heard the challenges to the Russian VTOL. The Russian was earning his pay, for he knew as well as I that the boat's surface-to-air missiles were homing in on him at that very second. I opened my mouth to answer Jimmy Rex, but May caught my arm.

"Can't we take him, Jason?" she begged.

"We can *not*," I cried. "And we have no time to argue!" For if Betsy was suspicious enough to send him here, we had minutes, maybe seconds, and the diversion of the aircraft would not puzzle her for long.

There was no weakness in May's brain. She understood me well. She knew I spoke truth. But she was also

a mother, whose only child had been lost to her. She gazed on him one moment more before she sobbed and turned to the port.

That was one moment too many. "No!" shrilled little Jimmy Rex, and did the only thing he could do to stop her. He darted out into the corridor and jerked the handle that would seal May's cabins off and keep her from getting through.

He did not keep all of her inside.

The door slammed . . . and the terrible strong shutters slashed closed upon my May.

There I was, alone with what was left of May. And minutes later the steel outer door grudgingly slid open again, and there was Betsy storming in, with Jimmy Rex crowding behind her. Betsy looked furious and triumphant and outraged all at once . . . and then, when she saw that it was only May's headless body that lay bleeding in my arms, more than anything else, relieved.

For Jimmy Rex I will say this much. He wept beside his mother's decapitated corpse. He screamed and sorrowed, and I believe he truly grieved—for ten minutes or so.

Even Betsy was shaken, though not as long as that, for he was still shrieking when she turned to me with an expression of awe and delight. "You old fool," she said admiringly, "I knew you'd do something dashing and stupid to solve all my problems. I ought to thank you."

"If you do," I said as steadily as I could, "there'll be two dead women in this room." And there would have, though by then her goons were holding me fast.

The room was mad, with medics covering May's poor body and a guard leading Jimmy Rex away and blood everywhere—everywhere! But Betsy looked only at me, and this time I could not read her expression at all. If I had not known her so well, I would have thought there was pity in it.

At last she sighed and shook her head. "Old man," she said roughly, "keep your loony illusions. Get off my boat."

She nodded to the guards, and twenty minutes later the great OT was disappearing behind me as the scoutship that should have carried May to freedom instead carried only me to—I am not sure what.

> And so the queen she met her end.
> The axe was raised by her dearest friend.
> Her son, no son, made the blade descend
> To finish the queen of the isles.
> The fair, sweet queen, the sorrowful queen,
> Oh, pity the queen of the isles!

For more than a year after that I woke shaking every night from a dream of the great steel shutter chopping May's dear head off. It was bad, and what I woke to was perhaps even worse. What "illusions" made nasty Betsy pity me?

I never found an answer to that question. Perhaps I did not want one.

THE HIGH TEST

Of all the science-fiction writers who inspired and delighted my youth, the one who most completely saturated the pleasure centers of my brain was the late Edward Elmer Smith, Ph.D. I wasn't the only one who felt that. Doc Smith invented the "space opera," the high-tech deep-space adventuring that set the style for everything from John Campbell's first stories to *Star Wars* and beyond. It's a crying shame that Doc's *The Skylark of Space* has never been made into a movie; it's as thrilling and colorful as the best of them, and a lot more intelligently imagined. One of the joys of growing up to be an editor was that I was able to get Doc to write new stories for me ("Skylark DuQuesne" was the most important of them), so that I could carry on into middle age the joys of my youth. When Doc died, I mourned deeply. His daughter and son-in-law, Verna and Albert Trestrail, are long-term and well-loved friends and when, a summer or two ago, I stayed for a few days at their comfortable home in central Indiana, I was enchanted to find that Verna still owned Doc's own personal typewriter, a four-square old Woodstock as

big as a breadbasket. Could I write a story on it? I begged. Of course, Verna answered, and kindly kept my coffee cup filled and fresh ashtrays within reach as, over two long days, I wrote the first draft of "The High Test." The former cabin boy had grown to command the *Q.E. 2*! Of course, "The High Test" is not exactly a Doc Smith story. But it's not exactly a typical Fred Pohl story, either, and I expect the reason is that I was thinking of Doc all the time I was writing it.

2213 12 22 1900UGT

Dear Mom:

As they say, there's good news and there's bad news here on Cassiopeia 43-G. The bad news is that there aren't any openings for people with degrees in quantum-mechanical astrophysics. The good news is that I've got a job. I started yesterday. I work for a driving school, and I'm an instructor.

I know you'll say that's not much of a career for a twenty-six-year-old man with a doctorate, but it pays the rent. Also it's a lot better than I'd have if I'd stayed on Earth. Is it true that the unemployment rate in Chicago is up to eighty percent? Wow! As soon as I get a few megabucks ahead I'm going to invite you all to come out here and visit me in the sticks so you can see how we live here—you may not want to go back!

Now, I don't want you to worry when I tell you that I get hazardous duty pay. That's just a technicality. We driving instructors have it in our contracts, but we don't really earn it. At least, usually we don't—although there are times like yesterday. The first student I had was this young girl, right from Earth. Spoiled rotten! You know the kind, rich, and I guess you'd say beautiful, and really used to having her own way. Her name's Tonda Aguilar— you've heard of the Evanston Aguilars? In the recombi- nant foodstuff business? They're really rich, I guess. This one had her own speedster, and she was really sulked

that she couldn't drive it on an Earth license. See, they have this suppressor field; as soon as any vehicle comes into the system, zap, it's off, and it just floats until some licensed pilot comes out to fly it in. So I took her up, and right away she started giving me ablation: "Not so much takeoff boost! You'll burn out the tubes!" and "Don't ride the reverter in hyperdrive!" and "Get out of low orbit— you want to rack us up?"

Well, I can take just so much of that. An instructor is almost like the captain of a ship, you know. He's the boss! So I explained to her that my name wasn't "Chowderhead" or "Dullwit!" but James Paul Madigan, and it was the instructors who were supposed to yell at the students, not the other way around. Well, it was her own speedster, and a really neat one at that. Maybe I couldn't blame her for being nervous about somebody else driving it. So I decided to give her a real easy lesson. Practicing parking orbits—if you can't do that, you don't deserve a license! And she was really rotten at it. It looks easy, but there's an art to cutting the hyperdrive with just the right residual velocity, so that you slide right into your assigned coordinates. The more she tried, the farther off she got. Finally she demanded that I take her back to the spaceport. She said I was making her nervous. She said she'd get a different instructor for tomorrow or she'd just move on to some other system where they didn't have benefacted chimpanzees giving driving lessons.

I just let her rave. Then the next student I had was a Fomalhautian. You know that species, they've got two heads and scales and forked tails, and they're always making a nuisance of themselves in the United Systems? If you believe what they say on the vidcom, they're bad news—in fact, the reason Cassiopeia installed the suppressor field was because they had a suspicion the Fomalhautians were thinking about invading and taking over 43-G. But this one was nice as pie! Followed every instruction. Never gave me any argument. Apologized when he made a mistake and got us too close to one of the mini-

black holes near the primary. He said that was because
he was unfamiliar with the school ship, and said he'd
prefer to use his own space yacht for the next lesson. He
made the whole day better, after that silly, spoiled rich
brat!

I was glad to have a little cheering up, to tell you the
truth. I was feeling a little lonesome and depressed. Probably it's because it's so close to the holidays. It's hard to
believe that back in Chicago it's only three days until
Christmas, and all the store windows will be full of holo-
decorations and there'll be that big tree in Grant Park and
I bet it's snowing . . . and here on Cassiopeia 43-G it's sort
of like a steam bath with interludes of Niagara Falls.

I do wish you a merry Christmas, Mom! Hope my gifts
got there all right.

                                        Love,
                                        Jim Paul

                                2213 12 25 LATE

Dear Mom:

Well, Christmas Day is just about over. Not that it's
any different from any other day here on 43-G, where the
human colonists were mostly Buddhist or Moslem and
the others were—well! You've seen the types that hang
around the United Systems building in Palatine—smelled
them, too, right? Especially those Arcturans. I don't know
whether those people have any religious holidays or not,
and I'm pretty sure I don't *want* to know.

Considering that I had to work all day, it hasn't been
such a bad Christmas at that. When I mentioned to Torklemiggen—he's the Fomalhautian I told you about—that
today was a big holiday for us, he sort of laughed and
said that mammals had really quaint customs. And when
he found out that part of the custom was to exchange
gifts, he thought for a minute. (The way Fomalhautians
think to themselves is that their heads whisper in each
other's ear—really grotesque!) Then he said that he had

been informed it was against the law for a student to give
anything to his driving instructor, but if I wanted to fly
his space yacht myself for a while he'd let me do it. And
he would let it go down on the books of the school as
instruction time, so I'd get paid for it. Well, you bet I
wanted to! He has some swell yacht. It's long and tapered,
sort of shark-shape, like the TU-Lockheed 4400 series,
with radar-glyph vision screens and a cruising range of
nearly 1,800 l.y. I don't know what its top speed is—
after all, we had to stay in our own system!

We were using his own ship, you see, and of course
it's Fomalhautian-made. Not easy for a human being to
fly! Even though I'm supposed to be the instructor and
Torklemiggen the student, I was baffled at first. I couldn't
even get it off the ground until he explained the controls
to me and showed me how to read the instruments. There's
still plenty I don't know, but after a few minutes I could
handle it well enough not to kill us out of hand. Torklemiggen kept daring me to circle the black holes. I told
him we couldn't do that, and he got this kind of sneer on
one of his faces, and the two heads sort of whispered
together for a while. I knew he was thinking of something
cute, but I didn't know what at first.

Then I found out!

You know that CAS 43, our primary, is a red giant star
with an immense photosphere. Torklemiggen bragged that
we could fly right through the photosphere! Well, of course
I hardly believed him, but he was so insistent that I tried
it out. He was right! We just greased right through that
thirty-thousand-degree plasma like nothing at all! The hull
began to turn red, then yellow, then straw-colored—you
could see it on the edges of the radar-glyph screen—and
yet the inside temperature stayed right on the button of
$40°$ Celsius. That's 43-G normal, by the way. Hot, if you're
used to Chicago, but nothing like it was outside! And
when we burst out into vacuum again there was no thermal shock, no power surge, no instrument fog. Just beautiful! It's hard to believe that any individual can afford a

ship like this just for his private cruising. I guess Fomalhaut must have some pretty rich planets!

Then when we landed, more than an hour late, there was the Aguilar woman waiting for me. She had found out that the school wouldn't let her change instructors once assigned. I could have told her that; it's policy. So she had to cool her heels until I got back. But I guess she had a little Christmas spirit somewhere in her ornery frame, because she was quite polite about it. As a matter of fact, when we had her doing parking orbits, she was much improved over the last time. Shows what a first-class instructor can do for you!

Well, I see by the old chronometer on the wall that it's the day after Christmas now, at least Universal-Greenwich Time it is, though I guess you've still got a couple of hours to go in Chicago. One thing, Mom. The Christmas packages you sent didn't get here yet. I thought about lying to you and saying they'd come and how much I liked them, but you raised me always to tell the truth. (Besides, I didn't know what to thank you for!) Anyway, merry Christmas one more time from—

Jim Paul

2213 12 30 0200UGT

Dear Mom:

Another day, another kilobuck. My first student today was a sixteen-year-old kid. One of those smart-alecky ones, if you know what I mean. (But you probably don't, because you certainly never had any kids like that!) His father was a combat pilot in the Cassiopeian navy, and the kid drove that way, too. That wasn't the worst of it. He'd heard about Torklemiggen. When I tried to explain to him that he had to learn how to go slow before he could go fast, he really let me have it. Didn't I know his father said the Fomalhautians were treacherous enemies of the Cassiopeian way of life? Didn't I know his father said

they were just waiting their chance to invade? Didn't I know—

Well, I could take just so much of this fresh kid telling me what I didn't know. So I told him he wasn't as lucky as Torklemiggen. He only had one brain, and if he didn't use all of it to fly this ship, I was going to wash him out. That shut him up pretty quick, you bet!

But it didn't get much better, because later on I had this fat lady student who just oughtn't to get a license for anything above a skateboard. Forty-six years old, and she's never driven before—but her husband's got a job asteroid mining, and she wants to be able to bring him a hot lunch every day. I hope she's a better cook than a pilot! Anyway, I was trying to put her at ease, so she wouldn't pile us up into a comet nucleus or something, so I was telling her about the kid. She listened, all sympathy—you know, how teenage kids were getting fresher every year—until I mentioned that what we were arguing about was my Fomalhautian student. Well, you should have heard her then! I swear, Mom, I think these Cassiopeians are psychotic on the subject. I wish Torklemiggen were here so I could talk to him about it—somebody said the reason CAS 43-G put the suppressor system in in the first place was to keep them from invading, if you can imagine that! But he had to go home for a few days. Business, he said. Said he'd be back next week to finish his lessons.

Tonda Aguilar is almost finished, too. She'll solo in a couple of days. She was my last student today—I mean yesterday actually, because it's way after midnight now. I had her practicing zero-G approaches to low-mass asteroids, and I happened to mention that I was feeling a little lonesome. It turned out she was, too, so I surprised myself by asking her if she was doing anything tomorrow night, and she surprised me by agreeing to a date. It's not romance, Mom, so don't get your hopes up. It's just that she and I seem to be the only beings in this whole system who know that tomorrow is New Year's Eve!

                                        Love,
                                        Jim Paul

2214 01 02 2330UGT

Dear Mom:

I got your letter this morning, and I'm glad that your leg is better. Maybe next time you'll listen to Dad and me! Remember, we both begged you to go for a brand-new factory job when you got it, but you kept insisting a rebuilt would be just as good. Now you see. It never pays to try to save money on your health!

I'm sorry if I told you about my clients without giving you any idea of what they looked like. For Tonda, that's easy enough to fix. I enclose a holo of the two of us which we took this afternoon, celebrating the end of her lessons. She solos tomorrow. As you can see, she is a really good-looking woman, and I was wrong about her being spoiled. She came out here on her own to make her career as a dermatologist. She wouldn't take any of her old man Aguilar's money, so all she had when she got here was her speedster and her degree and the clothes on her back. I really admire her. She connected right away with one of the best body shops in town, and she's making more money than I am.

As to Torklemiggen, that's harder. I tried to make a holopic of him, but he got really upset, you might even say nasty. He said inferior orders have no right to worship a Fomalhautian's image, if you can believe it! I tried to explain that we didn't have that in mind at all, but he just laughed. He has a mean laugh. In fact, he's a lot different since he came back from Fomalhaut on that business trip. Meaner. I don't mean that he's different physically. Physically he's about a head taller than I am, except that he has two of them. Two heads, I mean. The head on his left is for talking and breathing, the one on his right for eating and showing expression. It's pretty weird to see him telling a joke. His jokes are pretty weird all by themselves, for that matter. I'll give you an example. This afternoon he said, "What's the difference between a mammal and a roasted hagensbiffik with murgry sauce?" And when I said I didn't even know what those things were,

much less what the difference was, he laughed himself foolish and said, "No difference!" What a spectacle. There was his left-hand head talking and sort of yapping that silly laugh of his, deadpan, while the right-hand head was all creased up with giggle lines. Some sense of humor. I should have told you that Torklemiggen's left-hand head looks kind of like a chimpanzee's, and the right one is a little bit like a fox's. Or maybe an alligator's, because of the scales. Not pretty, you understand. But you can't say that about his ship! It's as sweet a job as I've ever driven. I guess he had some extra accessories put on it while he was home, because I noticed there were five or six new readouts and some extra hand controls. When I asked him what they were for, he said they had nothing to do with piloting and I would find out what they were for soon enough. I guess that's another Fomalhautian joke of some kind?

Well, I'd write more, but I have to get up early in the morning. I'm having breakfast with Tonda to give her some last-minute run-throughs before she solos. I think she'll pass all right. She surely has a lot of smarts for somebody who was a former Miss Illinois!

Love,
Jim Paul

2214 01 03 LATE

Dear Mom:

Your Christmas package got here today, and it was really nice. I loved the socks. They'll come in real handy in case I come back to Chicago for a visit before it gets warm. But the cookies were pretty crumbled, I'm afraid — delicious, though! Tonda said she could tell that they were better than anything she could bake, before they went through the CAS 43-G customs, I mean.

Torklemiggen is just about ready to solo. To tell you the truth, I'll be glad to see the last of him. The closer he gets to his license, the harder he is to get along with.

This morning he began acting crazy as soon as we got into high orbit. We were doing satellite-matching curves. You know, when you come in on an asymptotic tractrix curve, just whistling through the upper atmosphere of the satellite and then back into space. Nobody ever does that when they're actually driving, because what is there on a satellite in this system that anybody would want to visit? But they won't pass you for a license if you don't know how.

The trouble was, Torklemiggen thought he already did know how, better than I did. So I took the controls away to show him how, and that really blew his cool. "I could shoot better curves than you in my fourth instar," he snarled out of his left head, while his right head was looking at me like a rattlesnake getting ready to strike. I mean, mean. Then, when I let him have the controls back, he began shooting curves at one of the mini-black holes. Well, that's about the biggest no-no there is. "Stop that right now," I ordered. "We can't go within a hundred thousand miles of one of those things! How'd you pass your written test without knowing that?"

"Do not exceed your life station, mammal," he snapped, and dived in toward the hole again, his forehands on the thrust and roll controls while his hindhands reached out to fondle the buttons for the new equipment. And all the time his left-hand head was chuckling and giggling like some fiend out of a monster movie.

"If you don't obey instructions," I warned him, "I will not approve you for your solo." Well, that fixed him. At least he calmed down. But he sulked for the rest of the lesson. Since I didn't like the way he was behaving, I took the controls for the landing. Out of curiosity I reached to see what the new buttons were. "Severely handicapped mammalian species!" his left head screeched, while his right head was turning practically pale pink with terror, "do you want to destroy this planet?"

I was getting pretty suspicious by then, so I asked him straight out: "What is this stuff, some kind of weapons?"

That made him all quiet. His two heads whispered to each other for a minute, then he said, very stiff and formal, "Do you speak to me of weapons when you mammals have these black holes in orbit? Have you considered their potential for weaponry? Can you imagine what one of them would do, directed toward an inhabited planet?" He paused for a minute, then he said something that really started me thinking. "Why," he asked, "do you suppose my people have any wish to bring culture to this system, except to demonstrate the utility of these objects?"

We didn't talk much after that, but it was really on my mind.

After work, when Tonda and I were sitting in the park, feeding the flying crabs and listening to the singing trees, I told her all about it. She was silent for a moment. Then she looked up at me and said seriously, "Jim Paul, it's a rotten thing to say about any being, but it almost sounds as though Torklemiggen has some idea about conquering this system."

"Now, who would want to do something like that?" I asked.

She shrugged. "It was just a thought," she apologized. But we both kept thinking about it all day long, in spite of our being so busy getting our gene tests and all—but I'll tell you about that later!

                                        Love,
                                        Jim Paul

                    2214 01 05 2200UGT

Dear Mom:

Take a good look at this date, the fifth of January, because you're going to need to remember it for a while! There's big news from CAS 43-G tonight...but first, as they say on the tube, a few other news items.

Let me tell you about that bird Torklemiggen. He so-loed this morning. I went along as check pilot, in a school ship, flying matching orbits with him while he went through

the whole test in his own yacht. I have to admit that he was really nearly as good as he thought he was. He slid in and out of hyperdrive without any power surge you could detect. He kicked his ship into a corkscrew curve and killed all the drives, so he was tumbling and rolling and pitching all at once, and he got out of it into a clean orbit using only the side thrusters. He matched parking orbits—he ran the whole course without a flaw. I was still sore at him, but there just wasn't any doubt that he'd shown all the skills he needed to get a license. So I called him on the private TBS frequency and said, "You've passed, Torklemiggen. Do you want a formal written report when we land, or shall I call in to have your license granted now?"

"Now this instant, mammal!" he yelled back, and added something in his own language. I didn't understand it, of course. Nobody else could hear it, either, because the talk-between-ships circuits don't carry very far. So I guess I'll never know just what it is he said, but honestly, Mom, it surely didn't sound at all friendly. All the same, he'd passed.

So I ordered him to null his controls, and then I called in his test scores to the master computer on 43-G. About two seconds later he started screeching over the TBS, "Vile mammal! What have you done? My green light's out, my controls won't respond, is this some treacherous warm-blood trick?"

He sure had a way of getting under your skin. "Take it easy, Torklemiggen," I told him, not very friendlily— he was beginning to hurt my feelings. "The computer is readjusting your status. They've removed the temporary license for your solo, so they can lift the suppressor field permanently. As soon as the light goes on again you'll be fully licensed, and able to fly anywhere in this system without supervision."

"Hah," he grumbled, and then for a moment I could hear his heads whispering together. Then—well, Mom, I was going to say he laughed out loud over the TBS. But

it was more than a laugh. It was mean, and gloating. "Depraved retarded mammal," he shouted, "my light is on—and now all of Cassiopeia is mine!"

I was really disgusted with him. You expect that kind of thing, maybe, from some spacehappy sixteen-year-old who's just got his first license. Not from an eighteen-hundred-year-old alien who has flown all over the galaxy. It sounded sick! And sort of worrisome, too. I wasn't sure just how to take him. "Don't do anything silly, Torklemiggen," I warned him over the TBS.

He shouted back: "Silly? I do nothing silly, mammal! Observe how little silly I am!" And the next thing you know he was whirling and diving into hyperspace—no signal, nothing! I had all I could do to follow him, six alphas deep and going fast. For all I knew we could have been on our way back to Fomalhaut. But he only stayed there for a minute. He pulled out right in the middle of one of the asteroid belts, and as I followed up from the alphas I saw that lean, green yacht of his diving down on a chunk of rock about the size of an office building.

I had noticed, when he came back from his trip, that one of the new things about the yacht was a circle of ruby-colored studs around the nose of the ship. Now they began to glow, brighter and brighter. In a moment a dozen streams of ruby light reached out from them, ahead toward the asteroid—and there was a bright flare of light, and the asteroid wasn't there anymore!

Naturally, that got me upset. I yelled at him over the TBS: "Listen, Torklemiggen, you're about to get yourself in real deep trouble! I don't know how they do things back on Fomalhaut, but around here that's grounds for an action to suspend your license! Not to mention they could make you pay for that asteroid!"

"Pay?" he screeched. "It is not I who will pay, functionally inadequate live-bearer, it is you and yours! You will pay most dreadfully, for now we have the black holes!" And he was off again, back down into hyperspace, and one more time it was about all I could do to try to keep up with him.

There's no sense trying to transmit in hyperspace, of course. I had to wait until we were up out of the alphas to answer him, and by that time, I don't mind telling you, I was *peeved*. I never would have found him on visual, but the radar-glyph picked him up zeroing in on one of the black holes. What a moron! "Listen, Torklemiggen," I said, keeping my voice level and hard, "I'll give you one piece of advice. Go back to base. Land your ship. Tell the police you were just carried away, celebrating passing your test. Maybe they won't be too hard on you. Otherwise, I warn you, you're looking at a thirty-day suspension, plus you could get a civil suit for damages from the asteroid company." He just screeched that mean laughter. I added, "And I told you, keep away from the black holes!"

He laughed some more and said, "Oh, lower than a smiggstroffle, what delightfully impudent pets you mammals will make now that we have these holes for weapons—and what joy it will give me to train you!" He was sort of singing to himself more than to me, I guess. "First reduce this planet! Then the suppressor field is gone, and our forces come in to prepare the black holes! Then we launch one on every inhabited planet until we have destroyed your military power. And then—"

He didn't finish that sentence, just more of that chuckling, cackling, *mean* laugh.

I felt uneasy. It was beginning to look as though Torklemiggen was up to something more than just high jinks and deviltry. He was easing up on the black hole and kind of crooning to himself, mostly in that foreign language of his but now and then in English: "Oh, my darling little assault vessel, what destruction you will wreak! Ah, charming black hole, how catastrophic you will be! How foolish these mammals who think they can forbid me to come near you—"

Then, as they say, light dawned. "Torklemiggen," I shouted, "you've got the wrong idea. It's not just a traffic regulation that we have to stay away from black holes. It's a lot more serious than that!"

But I was too late. He was inside the Roche limit before I could finish.

I almost hate to tell you what happened next. It was pretty gross. The tidal forces seized his ship, and they stretched it.

I heard one caterwauling astonished yowl over the TBS. Then his transmitter failed. The ship ripped apart, and the pieces began to rain down into the Schwarzschild boundary and plasmaed. There was a quick, blinding flash of fall-in energy from the black hole, and that was all Torklemiggen would ever say or do or know.

I got out of there as fast as I could. I wasn't really feeling very sorry for him, either. The way he was talking there toward the end, he sounded as though he had some pretty dangerous ideas.

When I landed it was sundown at the field, and people were staring and pointing toward the place in the sky where Torklemiggen had smeared himself into the black hole. All bright purplish and orangey plasma clouds—it made a really beautiful sunset, I'll say that much for the guy! I didn't have time to admire it, though, because Tonda was waiting, and we just had minutes to get to the Deputy Census Director, Division of Reclassification, before it closed.

But we made it.

Well, I said I had big news, didn't I? And that's it, because now your loving son is

                              Yours truly,

                              James Paul Aguilar-Madigan,
                              the newlywed!

SPENDING A DAY AT THE LOTTERY FAIR

All writers have favorite themes and return to them over and over—even when they don't intend to and perhaps, as in my own case, don't realize quite how often they've done so until it comes time to put a collection of stories together. Their excuse (which I do dearly hope you will find justified in the present examples) is that a new treatment, a new setting, a new angle of attack can refresh an argument—especially an argument that seems worth making in the first place. At any rate, this story came about in the summer of 1982, when curiosity led me to Knoxville to see how they were doing with their first-ever world's fair. I am no great connoisseur of world's fairs; I'd only been to three before Knoxville—the pair in New York City a generation apart and the 1970 event in Osaka, Japan. Knoxville was a much smaller spectacle. Still, it had a lot of interesting exhibits and a holiday-carnival atmosphere; I had a good time. The locals I talked to seemed to be enjoying it a lot less, and when I asked them why so glum, they reported that it was losing money by the fistful and pot. What

then (I wondered) was the reason for having it? Echo
gave me an answer, and so I went back to my hotel
room and began writing this story.

THEY WERE THE BAXTER FAMILY, RANDOLPH AND MIL-
licent the parents, with their three children, Emma and
Simon and Louisa, who was the littlest; and they didn't
come to the fair in any old bus. No, they drove up in a
taxi, all the way from their home clear on the other side
of town, laughing and poking each other, and when they
got out, Randolph Baxter gave the driver a really big tip.
It wasn't that he could really afford it. It was just because
he felt it was the right thing to do. When you took your
whole family to the Lottery Fair, Baxter believed, you
might as well do it in style. Besides, the fare was only
money. Though Millicent Baxter pursed her lips when she
saw the size of the tip, she certainly was not angry; her
eyes sparkled as brightly as the children's, and together
they stared at the façade of the Lottery Fair.

Even before you got through the gates there was a
carnival smell, buttered popcorn and cotton candy and
tacos all together, and a carnival sound of merry-go-round
organs and people screaming in the rollercoaster, and bands
and bagpipes from far away. A clown stalked on tall stilts
through the fairgoers lining up at the ticket windows,
bending down to chuck children under the chin and making believe to nibble the ears of teenage girls in bright
summer shorts. Rainbow fountains splashed perfumey
spray. People in cartoon-character costumes, Gus the
Ghost and Mickey Mouse and Pac-Man, handed out free
surprise packages to the kids; when Simon opened his it
was a propeller beanie, a fan for Emma, for little Louisa
cardboard glasses with a Groucho Marx mustache. And
crowded! You could hardly believe such crowds! Off to
one side of the parking lot the tour buses were rolling in
with their loads of foreign visitors, Chinese and Argen-

tines and Swedes; they had special entrances and were
waved through by special guards who greeted them, some
of the time anyway, in their own native languages—
"Willkommen!" and *"Bon jour!"* and *"Ey there, mate!"*
—as long as they didn't speak anything like Urdu or Serbo-
Croatian, anyway. For the foreign tourists didn't have to
pay in the usual way; they bought their tickets in their
country of origin, with valuable foreign exchange, and
then everything was free for them.

Of course it wasn't like that for the regular American
fairgoers. They had to pay. You could see each family
group moving up toward the ticket windows. They would
slow down as they got closer and finally stop, huddling
together while they decided how to pay, and then one or
two of them, or all of them, would move on to the window
and reach into the admissions cuff for their tickets. Randolph Baxter had long before made up his mind that there
would be no such wrangles on this day for his family. He
said simply, "Wait here a minute," and strode up to the
window by himself. He put his arm into the cuff, smiled
at the ticket attendant, and said grandly, "I'll take five,
please."

The ticket seller looked at him admiringly. "You know,"
she offered, "there aren't that many daddies who'll take
all the little fellows in like that. Sometimes they make
even tiny babies get their own tickets." Baxter gave her
a modest I-do-what-I-can shrug, though he could not help
that his smile was a little strained until all five tickets had
clicked out of the roll. He bore them proudly back to his
family and led them through the turnstiles.

"My, what a crowd," sighed Millicent Baxter happily
as she gazed around. "Now, what shall we do first?"

The response was immediate. "See the old automobiles," yelled Simon, and, "No, the animals!" and, "No,
the stiffs!" cried his sisters.

Randolph Baxter spoke sharply to them—not angrily
but firmly. "There will be no fighting over what we do,"
he commanded. "We'll *vote* on what we do, the demo-

cratic way. No arguments and no exceptions. Now," he
added, "the first thing we're going to do is that you kids
will stay right here while your mother and I get tickets
for the job lottery." The parents left the children arguing
viciously among themselves and headed for the nearest
lottery booth. Randolph Baxter could not help a tingle of
excitement, and his wife's eyes were gleaming, as they
studied the prize list. The first prize was the management
of a whole apartment building—twenty-five thousand dollars a year salary and a free three-room condo thrown in!

Millicent read his thoughts as they stood in line. "Don't
you just wish!" she whispered. "But personally I'd settle
for any of the others. Look, there's even a job for an
English teacher!" Randolph shook his head wordlessly.
It was just marvelous—five full-time jobs offered in this
one raffle, and that not the biggest of the day. The last
one, after the fireworks, always had the grandest of prizes.
"Aren't you glad we came?" Millicent asked, and her
husband nodded.

But in fact he wasn't, altogether, at least until they
safely got their tickets and were on their way back to the
children, and then he was quickly disconcerted to see that
the kids weren't where they had been left. "Oh, hell,"
groaned Randolph. It was early in the day for them to get
lost.

But they weren't very far. His wife said sharply, "There
they are. And look what they're doing!" They were at a
refreshment stand. And each one of them had a huge cone
of frozen custard. "I *told* them not to make any purchases
when we weren't with them!" Millicent cried, but in fact
it was worse than that. The children were talking to a pair
of strange grownups, a lean, fair, elderly woman with a
sharp, stern face and a round, dark-skinned man with a
bald head and immense tortoise-shell glasses.

As the Baxters approached, the woman turned to them
apologetically. "Oh, hullo," she said, "you must be the
parents. I do hope you'll forgive us. Mr. Katsubishi and
I seem to have lost our tour, and your children kindly
helped us look for it."

"It's all right, Dad," Simon put in swiftly. "They're on this foreign tour, see, and everything's free for them anyway. Dad? Why can't we get on a tour and have everything free?"

"We're Americans," his father explained, smiling tentatively at the tall English-looking woman and the tubby, cheerful Japanese—he decided that they didn't *look* like depraved child molesters. "You have to be an international tourist to get these unlimited tickets. And I bet they cost quite a lot of money, don't they?" he appealed to the man, who smiled and shrugged and looked at the woman.

"Mr. Katsubishi doesn't speak English very well," she apologized. "I'm Rachel Millay. Mrs. Millay, that is, although my dear husband left us some years ago." She glanced about in humorous distress. "I don't suppose you've seen a tour leader carrying a green and violet flag with a cross of St. Andrew on it?"

Since Randolph Baxter had no idea what a cross of St. Andrew looked like, it was hard to say. In any case, there were at least twenty tour parties in sight, each with its own individual pennant or standard, trudging in determined merriment toward the pavilions, the rides, or the refreshment stands. "I'm afraid not," he began, and then paused as his wife clutched his arm. The P.A. system crackled, and the winners of the first drawing were announced.

Neither of the Baxters was among them. "Well, there are six more drawings," said Millicent bravely, not adding that there were also six more sets of raffle tickets to buy if they wanted any hope of winning one of them. Her husband smiled cheerfully at the children.

"What's it to be?" he asked generously. "The life exhibit? The concert—"

"We already voted, Dad," cried Emma, his elder daughter. "It's the animals!"

"No, the stiffs!" yelled her baby sister.

"The old autos," cried Simon. "Anyway, there won't be any stiffs there until later, not to speak of!"

Baxter smiled indulgently at the foreigners. "Chil-

dren," he explained. "Well, I do hope you find your group."
And he led the way to the first democratically selected
adventure of the day, the space exhibit.

Baxter had always had a nostalgic fondness for space,
and this was a pretty fine exhibit, harking back to the
olden, golden days when human beings could spare enough
energy and resources to send their people and probes out
toward the distant worlds. Even the kids liked it. It was
lavish with animated 3-D displays showing a human being
walking around on the surface of the Moon, and a spacecraft slipping through the rings of Saturn, and even a
probe, though not an American one, hustling after Hal-
ley's Comet to take its picture.

But Randolph Baxter had some difficulty in concen-
trating on the pleasure of the display at first because, as
they were getting their tickets, the tall, smiling black man
just ahead of him in line put his arm into the admissions
cuff, looked startled, withdrew his arm, started to speak,
and fell over on the ground, his eyes open and staring, it
seemed, right into Randolph Baxter's.

When you have a wife and three kids and no job, living
on welfare, never thinking about tomorrow because you
know there isn't going to be anything in tomorrow worth
thinking about, a day's outing for the whole family is an
event to be treasured. No matter what the price—especially if the price isn't in money. So the Baxter family did
it all. They visited six national pavilions, even the Para-
guayan. They lunched grandly in the dining room at the
summit of the Fair's great central theme structure, the
Cenotaph. And they did the rides, all the rides, from
the Slosh-a-Slide water chutes through the immense Fer-
ris wheel with the wind howling through the open car and
Simon threatening to spit down on the crowds below to
the screaming, shattering rollercoaster that made little
Louisa wet her pants. Fortunately her mother had brought
clean underwear for the child. When she sent the little
girl off with her sister to change in the ladies' room, she

followed them anxiously with her eyes until they were
safely past the ticket collector and then said, "Rand, honey.
You paid for all those rides yourself."

He shrugged defensively. "I want everybody to have
a good time."

"Now, don't talk that way. We agreed. The children
and I are going to pay our own way all the rest of the
day, and the subject is closed." She proved the point by
changing it. "Look," she said, "there are those two foreigners who lost their tour group again." She waved, and
Mrs. Millay and Mr. Katsubishi came up diffidently.

"If we're not intruding?" said Mrs. Millay. "We never
did find our tour guide, you see, but actually we're getting
on quite well without. But isn't it hot! It's never like this
in Scotland."

Millicent fanned herself in agreement. "Do sit down,
Mrs. Millay. Is that where you're from, Scotland? And
you, Mr. Kat— Kats—"

"Katsubishi." He smiled, with an abrupt deep bow.
Then he wrinkled his face in concentration for a moment
and managed to say: "I, too—Sukottaland."

Millicent tried not to look astonished but evidently did
not succeed. Mrs. Millay explained, "He's from around
Kyle of Lochalth, you know." Since Millicent obviously
didn't know, she added, "That's the Japanese colony in
northern Scotland, near my own home. In fact, I teach
English to Japanese schoolchildren there, since I know
the language—my parents were missionaries in Honshu,
you see. Didn't you know about the colony?"

Actually, Millicent and Randolph did know about the
colony. Or, at least, they almost did, in the way that
human beings exposed to forty channels of television and
with nothing much to do with their time have heard of,
without really knowing much about, almost every concept, phenomenon, event, and trend in human history. In
just that way they had heard of the United Kingdom's
pact with Japan, allowing large Japanese immigration into
an enclave in the north of Scotland. The Japanese made

the area bloom both agriculturally and economically. The United Kingdom got a useful injection of Japanese capital and energy, and the Japanese got rid of some of their surplus population without pain. "I wish we'd thought of that," Millicent observed in some envy, but her husband shook his head.

"Different countries, different ways," he said patriotically, "and actually we're doing rather well. I mean, just look at the Lottery Fair! That's American ingenuity for you." Observing that Mrs. Millay was whispering a rapid-fire translation into Mr. Katsubishi's ear, he was encouraged to go on. "Other countries, you see, have their own way of handling their problems. Compulsory sterilization of all babies born in even-numbered years in India, as I'm sure you're aware. The contraceptive drugs they put in the water supply in Mexico—and we won't even talk of what they're doing in, say, Bangladesh." Mrs. Millay shuddered sympathetically as she translated, and the Japanese beamed and bowed then spoke rapidly.

"He says one can learn much," Mrs. Millay translated, "from what foreign countries can do. Even America."

Millicent, glancing at the expression on her husband's face, said brightly: "Well! Let's not let this day go to waste. What shall we do next?" At once she got the same answers from the children: "Old cars!" "Animals!" "No," whined Baby Louisa, "I wanna see the stiffs!"

Mr. Katsubishi whispered something in staccato Japanese to Mrs. Millay, who turned hesitantly to Millicent Baxter. "One doesn't wish to intrude," she said, "but if you are in fact going to see the Hall of Life and Death as your daughter suggests . . . well, we don't seem to be able to find the rest of our tour group, you see, and we would like to go there. After all, it is the theme center for the entire fair, as you might say—"

"Why, of course," said Millicent warmly. "We'd be real delighted to have the company of you and Mr. Kats— Kats—"

"Katsubishi," he supplied, bowing deeply and showing

all his teeth in a smile, and they all seven set off for the Hall of Life and Death, with little Louisa delightedly leading the way.

The hall was a low, white marble structure across the greensward from the Cenotaph, happy picnicking families on the green, gay pavilions all around, ice cream vendors chanting along the roadways, and a circus parade, horses and a giraffe and even an elephant, winding along the main avenue with a band leading them, diddley-boom, diddley-boom, diddley-bang! bang! bang!—all noise, and color, and excitement. But as soon as they were within the Hall they were in another world. The Hall of Life and Death was the only free exhibit at the fair—even the rest rooms were not free. The crowds that moved through the Hall were huge. But they were also reverential. As you came in you found yourself in a great, domed entrance pavilion, almost bare except for seventy-five raised platforms, each spotlighted from a concealed source, each surrounded by an air curtain of gentle drafts. At the time the Baxters came in more than sixty of them were already occupied with the silent, lifeless forms of those who had passed on at the Fair that day. A sweet-faced child here, an elderly woman there, there, side by side, a young pair of newlyweds. Randolph Baxter looked for and found the tall, smiling black man who had died in the line before him. He was smiling no longer, but his face was in repose and almost joyous, it seemed. "He's at peace now," Millicent whispered, touching her husband's arm, and he nodded. He didn't want to speak out loud in this solemn hall, where the whisper of organ music was barely audible above the gentle hiss of chilled air curtains that wafted past every deceased. Hardly anyone in the great crowd spoke. The visitors lingered at each of the occupied biers; but then, as they moved toward the back of the chamber, they didn't linger. Some didn't even look, for every tourist at the Fair could not help thinking, as he passed an empty platform, that before the Fair closed that night it would be occupied . . . by someone.

But the Rotunda of Those Who Have Gone Before was only the anteroom to the many inspiring displays the Hall had to offer. Even the children were fascinated. Young Simon stood entranced before the great Timepiece of Living and Dying, watching the hands revolve swiftly to show how many were born and how many died in each minute, with the bottom line always showing a few more persons alive in every minute despite everything the government and the efforts of patriotic citizens could do—but he was more interested, really, in the mechanism of the thing than in the facts it displayed. Millicent Baxter and Mrs. Millay were really thrilled by the display of opulent caskets and cerements, and Randolph Baxter was proud to point out to Mr. Katsubishi the working model of a crematorium, with all of its escaping gases trapped and converted into valuable organic feedstocks. And the girls, Emma and Louisa, stood hand in hand for a long time, shuddering happily as they gazed at the refrigerated display cases that showed a hideous four-month embryo next to the corpse of a fat, pretty two-year-old. Emma moved to put her arm around her mother and whispered, "Mommy, I'm *so* grateful you didn't abort me." And Millicent Baxter fought back a quick and tender tear.

"I'd never let you die looking like *that*," she assured her daughter, and they clung together for a long moment. But Randolph Baxter was becoming noticeably ill at ease. When they finally left the Hall of Life and Death his wife took him aside and asked in concern, "Is something the matter, hon?"

He shrugged irritably at the foreigners, who were talking together in fast, low-toned Japanese. "Just look at their faces," he complained. And indeed both Mr. Katsubishi and Mrs. Millay's expressions seemed to show more revulsion than respect.

Millicent followed her husband's eyes and sighed—there was a little annoyance in the sigh, too. "They're not Americans," she reminded her husband. "I guess they just don't understand." She smiled distantly at the foreign

pair, and then looked around at her offspring. "Well, children, who wants to come with me to the washrooms, so we can get ready for the big fireworks?"

They all did, even Randolph, but he felt a need stronger than the urging of his bladder. He remained behind with the foreigners. "Excuse me," he said somewhat formally, "but may I ask what you thought of the exhibit?"

She glanced at the Japanese. "Well, it was most interesting," she said vaguely. "One doesn't wish to criticize, of course—" And she stopped there.

"No, no, please go on," Randolph encouraged.

She said, "I must say it did seem odd to, well, *glorify* death in that way."

Randolph Baxter smiled, and tried to make it a forgiving smile, though he could feel that he was upset. He said, "Perhaps you miss the point of the Hall of Life and Death— in fact, of the whole Lottery Fair. You see, some of the greatest minds in America have worked on this problem of surplus population—think tanks and government agencies—why, three universities helped design this Fair. Every bit of it is scientifically planned. To begin with, it's absolutely free."

Mrs. Millay left off her rapid-fire sotto voce Japanese translation to ask, "You mean, free as far as money is concerned?"

"Yes, exactly. Of course, one takes a small chance at every ticket window, and in that sense there is a price for everything. A very carefully computed price, Mrs. Millay, for every hotdog, every show, every ride. To get into the Fair in the first place, for instance, costs one decimill—that's one percent of a point zero zero zero one probability of receiving a lethal injection from the ticket cuff. Now, that's not much of a risk, is it?" He smiled. "And of course it's absolutely painless, too. As you can see by just looking at the ones who have given their lives inside."

Mr. Katsubishi, listening intently to Mrs. Millay's translation in his ear, pursed his lips and nodded thought-

fully. Mrs. Millay said brightly, "Well, we all have our own little national traits, don't we?"

"Now, really, Mrs. Millay," said Randolph Baxter, smiling with an effort, "please try to understand. Everything is quite fair. Some things are practically free, like the park benches and the rest rooms and so on; why, you could use some of them as much as a million times before, you know, your number would come up. Or you can get a first-class meal in the Cenotaph for just about a whole millipoint. But even that means you can do it a thousand times, on the average."

Mr. Katsubishi listened to the end of Mrs. Millay's translation and then struggled to get out a couple of English words. "Not—us," he managed, pointing to himself and Mrs. Millay.

"Certainly not," Baxter agreed. "You're foreign tourists. So you buy your tickets in your own countries for cash, and of course you don't have to risk your lives. It wouldn't help the American population problem much if you did, would it?" He smiled. "And your tour money helps pay the cost of the Fair. But the important thing to remember is that the Lottery Fair is entirely voluntary. No one has to come. Of course," he admitted with a self-deprecatory grin, "I have to admit that I really like the job lotteries. I guess I'm just a gambler at heart, and when you've spent as much time on welfare as Mrs. Baxter and I have, those big jobs are just hard to resist! And they're better here than at the regular city raffles."

Mrs. Millay cleared her throat. Good manners competed with obstinacy in her expression. "Really, Mr. Baxter," she said, "Mr. Katsubishi and I understand that—heavens, we've had to do things in our own countries! We certainly don't mean to criticize yours. What's hard to understand, I suppose, is, actually, that fetus." She searched his face with her eyes, looking for understanding. "It just seems strange. I mean, that you'd prefer to see a child born and then perhaps die in a lottery than to abort him ahead of time."

Mr. Baxter did his very best to maintain a pleasant expression, but he knew he was failing. "It's a difference in our national philosophies, I guess," he said. "See, we don't go in for your so-called 'birth control' here. No abortion. No contraception. We accept the gift of life when it is given. We believe that every human being, from the moment of conception on, has a right to a life—although," he added, "not necessarily a *long* one." He eyed the abashed foreigners sternly for a moment, then relented. "Well," he said, glancing at his watch, "I wonder where my family can be? They'll miss the fireworks if they don't get back. I bet Mrs. Baxter's gone and let the children pick out souvenirs—the little dickenses have been after us about them all day. Anyway, Mrs. Millay, Mr. Katsubishi, it's been a real pleasure meeting the two of you and having this chance to exchange views—"

But he broke off, suddenly alarmed by the expression on Mr. Katsubishi's face as the man looked past him. "What's the matter?" he demanded roughly.

And then he turned, and did not need an answer. The answer was written on the strained, haggard, tear-streaked face of his wife as she ran despairingly toward him, carrying in her hands a plastic cap, a paperweight, and a helium-filled balloon in the shape of a pig's head, but without Emma and without Simon and even without little Louisa.

SECOND COMING

All the good science-fiction editors I knew when I was trying to learn the trade spent a lot of their time thinking of tricks, devices, and subtle manipulations designed to get writers to write stories for them that might not otherwise have got written. You might think they didn't have to do that. After all, writers are in the business of writing; why not just let them get on with it and take what comes as it comes? Because they might be spending their time writing something unsuitable, for one reason. Because they might be writing it for Someone Else is the other. So John Campbell, Horace Gold, Bob Lowndes, Don Wollheim—and I—would pass out story ideas, mail off Xeroxes of covers that needed stories written around them, dream up "theme" issues—anything at all that would prod a lazy writer into producing a story instead of whatever else he had planned to do with his time that day. The art has not been lost. Ellen Datlow, fiction editor of *Omni*, wasn't even born when John Campbell began practicing that art, but she has thought of devices even the Master never knew. Not long ago, for instance, she called up

half a dozen of her favorite writers to announce that
she was going to publish a special fiction issue containing a story by each of them, all limited to a maximum
of five hundred words. Five hundred words! It takes me
five hundred words to answer the phone! However,
these little behavior-modification tricks do work their
magic, and so I sat down to try. I tried at least half a
dozen story ideas without luck, because after the first
page and a half each one of them convinced me that
it wanted to be a full-sized story if not indeed a three-
volume novel sequence. Then my son, Fred the Fourth,
out of the kindness of his heart, gave me an opening
sentence, and the other 469 words followed easily after.

I GUESS, JUST AS WITH THE KENNEDY ASSASSINATION,
everybody can remember exactly where he was and what
he was doing on the day the space people brought Jesus
back to Earth.

I was aboard Air Force One with the President—I'm
Secret Service—and when Major Manley radioed the un-
believable message from the orbiting space shuttle we
turned right around and headed straight for California.
Beat the shuttle down, and waited, parked at the end of
the landing strip, watching TV.

Of course, business had stopped all over the world.
Everybody was watching the pictures from the big telescope on Mauna Kea—what a brute that spaceship was,
half a mile long!—and listening to replays of Manley's
message.

Well, the shuttle made its turn and came down, and
they got the crew out and into Air Force One while the
ground people were still purging the fuel vapors. "You
sure it's Jesus?" the President demanded.

"That's what they say, Mr. President. I took a picture
of Him—see for yourself." And he passed over a Pola-
roid.

The President winced. "I didn't think He'd look like *that*."

"Well, He's Jewish, you know—"

"No, I mean He's so *young*. It's been nearly two thousand years!"

Major Manley explained, "They were traveling at light speed almost all this time—you know, time dilatation? After they rolled away the stone and took Him out of the cave—"

"They *kidnapped* Jesus?"

"They don't look at it that way, Mr. President. He was not in very good shape. They figured we were through with Him. So they took Him to their planet, where they have a place to keep specimens of life forms from all over the galaxy—"

"They put *Jesus* in a *zoo*?" Manley shrugged. "What's He doing now?" the President asked.

"They say He's watching TV mostly. Doesn't much like what He sees, they say, but I didn't talk to Him myself—I don't speak Aramaic. Anyway, I was glad to get out of there, because that ship's pretty scary. You just wouldn't *believe* all the nasty kinds of weapons they've got!"

The President's eyes gleamed, and the secretary of defense exulted. "New weapons! What a bargaining chip!"

The President glanced around the room, and the expressions of delight were unanimous. There remained only one thing to do. He crooked a finger and his secretary turned on her recorder. "Take a decree, Mabel. I, the President, and so on, do hereby proclaim that Jesus Christ is come again, and—uh—"

"And He's ours!" the secretary finished. And then, raptly, "Thank God."

It looked pretty good there. Of course, the other countries were screeching their heads off. *Pravda* raged. The Chicoms canceled a trip by their soccer team, and the Israeli ambassador practically had a heart attack trying

to argue that He was, after all, one of their nationals by birth. That didn't matter; we were first, and NASA cleared the Canaveral runways for His landing. But He requested all three networks to provide thirty minutes for a prime-time telecast, and that was when it all went sour. Never mind He didn't look right. Never mind He spoke in Aramaic, which practically nobody understood. It was what He said that was the bad part—that, and the fact that before we got the translation, there was a priority call from the Mauna Kea telescope people to say the ship was breaking out of orbit and heading back out into space. "But what did He *say?*" moaned the President, and the translator, sweating, shook his head.

"Something about He doesn't like the way we've spoiled His planet," he croaked. "Says He told us what to do, and we haven't done it—we've messed everything up—"

"Hell," shouted the President, "we can fix that up. Call Him back. We can make a deal. We'll give Him His own TV station so He can preach to the multitudes, let pilgrims come visit Him—anything He wants!"

But the translator was shaking his head again. "He doesn't want that. He says He's going back with the space people. They've got a better-class zoo."

ENJOY, ENJOY

Terry Carr is one of the true gentlemen of the science-fiction field. Editors have trouble being beloved; what they do cuts too close to the writers' bones for comfort. I do not believe there is an editor in the world who some writer, somewhere, does not wish dead. On those grounds I feel sure that there must therefore be some people who hate Terry Carr, but I've never met one. Perhaps the reason is that he has never been in charge of a major magazine or boss of a large book publishing company; he has put in his editorial time as editorial consultant, anthologist, assistant to other editors, proprietor of a special line of his own within a larger group, and these are not the exposed mountaintops where the ravaging lightnings strike. However, they are good places for someone to be whose biggest interest is in finding and showcasing bright new talent. That's something Terry does extremely well. Devotees still fondly remember the Carr "Ace Special" series of a decade and a half ago, when Terry took his chances on such unknowns as Ursula K. LeGuin, Joanna Russ, R. A. Lafferty, and a lot of others whose subsequent careers

show how good an editor he really is. So when Terry Carr asks me for something, I try to deliver; and when he told me he was putting together a new anthology of original stories called *Fellowship of the Stars*, I was pleased to offer him this one—and delighted when he accepted it.

BOOZE, BROADS, BIG CARS, THE FINEST OF FOOD, WAterbeds filled with vintage champagne. Those were some of the things that went with Tud Cowpersmith's job. The way he got the job was by going to a party in Jackson Heights. The way he happened to be at the party was that he had no choice.

It wasn't a bad party, for a loft in Jackson Heights. It wasn't a bad loft. The windows at one end looked out on the tracks of the IRT el, but they had been painted over with acrylics to look like stained glass. Every twenty minutes you got a noise like some very large person stumbling by with garbage-can lids for shoes, but except for that the el might as well not have been there. Anyway, at that end of the loft the stereo speakers stood four feet high on the floor, so the noise didn't matter all that much. You couldn't possibly talk at that end. Cowpersmith wanted, eventually, to talk, as soon as the person he wanted to talk to showed up, so he drifted to the other end.

There the noise was more or less bearable, and there the windows were still clear. They were even clean. He could see through them down on a sort of communal garden, three or four backyards for three or four different old apartment buildings thrown together: a tiny round plastic swimming pool, now iced over with leaves and boughs frozen into it; bare trees that probably had looked very nice in the summer. To get to the windows at that end you had to thread your way through a sort of indoor jungle, potted plants presumably carried in from the garden for the cold weather. And there, on a chrome-rimmed,

chrome-legged kitchen table, the host and hostess were
rolling joints. They greeted Cowpersmith—

"Want a hit?"

"Thanks."

—but the pot did not ease him. He was looking for
somebody. That was the reason he was there.

The person he was looking for was named Murray.
Murray was an old, old...friend? Something like that.
What he basically was was somebody who owed Cowpersmith fifty dollars, from a time when fifty hadn't seemed
like an awful lot. Cowpersmith had heard, the day before,
that Murray was in town, and tracked him down to a hotel
on Central Park South.

After some deliberation he had telephoned Murray. He
really hated doing it. He needed the fifty, but in his view
the odds against getting it were so bad that he didn't like
the risk of investing a dime in a phone call. The dime
was, after all, real money. There was no way to flash a
revoked American Express card at the phone booth, as
he had done with the last two restaurants and the airline
that had brought him back from Chicago, where the last
of his bankroll had melted away. But the odds had paid
off! Murray was in, and obliging—

"What fifty?"

"Well, don't you remember, you met that Canadian
girl—"

"Oh, Christ, sure. Was it only fifty? Must be some
interest due by now, Tud. Tell you what—"

—and the way it worked out they were to meet at this
party, and Cowpersmith would collect not fifty but a
hundred dollars.

That required some decision making, too, because there
was the investment for a subway token to be considered.
But Murray had sounded prosperous enough for a gamble.
Only no Murray. Cowpersmith took another hit from a
girl wearing batik bellbottoms and a halter top and glared
around the room. Through the roar of Alice Cooper he
realized she was talking to him.

"What?"

"I said, is your name Ted?"

"Tud."

"Turd?"

"Tud Cowpersmith," he yelled over the androgynous rock. "It's a family name, Tudsbury."

She reached up close to his ear—she was not more than five feet tall—and shouted, "If you're a friend of Murray's he's looking for you." He allowed her to lead him around the buttress of the stairwell, for the first time noticing that her armpits were unshaven, the hair on her head stuck out in tiny, tied witch curls, and she was quite pretty.

And there was Murray, knotting his wild red eyebrows hospitably. "Hey, Tud. Looking great, man! Long time."

"You're looking fine too," said Cowpersmith, although it wasn't really true. Murray looked a little bit fine and a lot prosperous; the medallion that hung over his raw-silk shirt was clearly gold, and he wore a very expensive-looking, though ugly, thick wristwatch. The thing was he also looked about fifteen years older than he had eighteen months before. They sat in two facing armchairs, one a broken lounger, the other so overstuffed that the stuffing was curling out of it. The girl sat cross-legged between them on the floor, and Murray idly played with her tied curls.

Cooper had changed to the New York Queens and somebody had turned the volume down, or else the shelter of the stairwell did the same thing for them. Cowpersmith got several words of what Murray was saying.

"A job?" Cowpersmith repeated. "What kind of a job?"

"The finest fucking job in all the world," said Murray, and laughed and laughed, poking the girl's shoulder. When he had calmed down, he said, "What do you work for, Tud?"

Cowpersmith said angrily, "God, *you* know. I worked for the advertising agency until they took cigarette ads off TV, then I was with the oil company until—"

"No, no. For what *purpose*."

Cowpersmith shrugged. "Money?"

"Sure, but what do you do with the money?"

"Pay bills?" he guessed.

"No, no, damn it! *After* you do all the lousy stuff like that. What do you do with the *extra* money? Like when you were still pulling down twenty-five K at the agency and everything was on the expense account anyway?"

"Oh, sure." It had been so long ago Cowpersmith had almost forgotten. "Fun. Good food. Plays. Girls. Cars—"

"Right on," cried Murray, "and that's what everyone else works for, too. Everybody but me! That's what my job *is*. I don't have to work *for* those things, because I work *at* them. I don't imagine you're going to believe this, Tud, but it's true," he added as an afterthought.

Cowpersmith looked down at the girl and swallowed hard. A dismal vision flashed through his mind, of the five crumpled twenties in his pocket turning out to be joke money that, turned over, might say *April Fool* or, held for ten minutes, might evaporate their ink, leaving bare paper and ruin. "I don't have any idea of what you're talking about," he said to Murray, but still looking at the girl.

"You think I'm stoned," Murray said accurately.

"Well—"

"I don't blame you. Look. Well, let's see. Shirley," he said, half laughing, "how do we explain this? Try it this way," he went on, not waiting for her help, "suppose you had all the money in the world. Suppose you had more money than you even wanted, right?"

"I follow you. I mean, as a theoretical thing."

"And then suppose you had like an accident. Crash-bang; you're in a car accident or a piano falls on you. Quadriplegic. Can't have any fun anymore. Got that?"

"Bad scene," said Cowpersmith, nodding.

"All right, but even though you can't do much yourself anymore, there's a way you can have *some* fun vicariously. Like you're not going to Ibiza yourself, but you're seeing slides of it, or something. You can't get the kicks

a normal person can, but you can get something, maybe not much but better than nothing, out of what other people do. Now, in that position, Tud, what would you do?"

"Kill myself."

"No you wouldn't, for Christ's sake. You'd hire other people to have fun for you. And then with this process—" he patted the ugly thing that looked like a wristwatch, but Cowpersmith now realized was not—"you can play back their fun, and maybe it isn't much, but it's all the jollies you can ever get. Right, Shirley?"

She shook her head and said sweetly, "Shit."

"Well, anyway, it's *something* like that. I guess. It's kind of secret, I think probably because it's someone like Howard Hughes or maybe one of the Rockefellers that's involved. They won't say. But the job's for real, Tud. All I have to do is have all the fun I can. They pick up the tab, it all goes on the credit card, and they get the bill, and they pay it. As long as I wear this thing, that's all I have to do. And every Friday, besides all that, five hundred in cash."

There was a pause, while Bette Midler flowed over and around them from the speakers and Cowpersmith looked from the girl to his friend, waiting for the joke part. At last he said, "But *nobody* gets a job like that."

"Wrong, friend," said Shirley. "You did. Just now. If you want it. I'll take you there tomorrow morning."

Behind the door stenciled *E.T.C. Import-Export Co., Ltd.* there was nothing more than a suite of offices sparsely occupied and eccentrically furnished. Hardly furnished at all, you might say. There was nobody at the reception desk, which Shirley walked right past, and no papers on the desk of the one man anywhere visible. "I've got a live one for you, Mr. Morris," Shirley sang out. "Friend of Murray's."

Mr. Morris looked like a printing salesman, about fifty, plump, studying Cowpersmith over half glasses. "Good producer," he agreed reluctantly. "All right, you're hired."

And he counted out five hundred dollars in bills of various sizes and pushed them across the desk to Cowpersmith.

Cowpersmith picked up the money, feeling instantly stoned. "Is that all there is to it?"

"No! Not for me, I've got all the paperwork now, your credit card, keeping records—"

"I mean, like, don't you want me to fill out an application form?"

"Certainly not." He opened his desk drawer and pulled out a wristwatch-shaped thing. Cowpersmith could not see all of the inside of the drawer from his angle, but he was nearly sure there was nothing else in it. He handed it to Cowpersmith and said, "Once you put it on it won't come off by itself, but we'll unlock it any time you want to quit. That's all. Go have fun. By which," he added, "I don't actually mean screwing, because we've got plenty of records of that already."

"What then?" asked Cowpersmith, disconcerted.

"Hell, man! Up to you. Water skiing, skin diving, breaking the bank at Monte Carlo. What do you dream about, when things look bad? You do dream, don't you?"

"Well, sure, but—" Cowpersmith hesitated, thinking. "I always wanted to eat at La Tour d'Argent. And, uh, there's this crazy poison fish they have in Japan—"

"Sounds good," the man said without enthusiasm. "I'll have your card delivered to you at your hotel tomorrow."

"Yes, but wait a minute. What's the catch?"

"No catch, Tud," said Shirley, annoyed. "Jesus, what does it take to convince you?"

"Nothing like this ever happened to me before. There has to be something wrong with it."

"No there doesn't," said Mr. Morris, "and I have to get busy on your card."

Cowpersmith found himself standing up. "No, wait," he said. "How—how long does the job last?"

Shrug. "Until you get bored, I guess."

"Then what?"

"Then you turn in your recordings. And you take your last week's pay and go look for another job."

"Recordings?" Cowpersmith looked down at his wrist, where, without thinking about it, he had clasped on the metal object. "Is this a tape recorder?"

"I'm not into that part of it," Mr. Morris said. "I only know my job, and I've just done it. Good-by."

And that was all she wrote. At Shirley's urging, Cowpersmith checked into a small but very nice hotel on the Upper East Side, went to a massage parlor, ice-skated at Rockefeller Center, and met Shirley for a late drink in a Greek bar in Chelsea. "Good start," she said. "Now you're on your own. Got any plans?"

"Well," he said experimentally, "I think I can still make the Mardi Gras in Rio. And I heard about a safari tour to Kenya—"

"Travel, huh. Why not?" She finished her drink. "Well, we'll keep in touch—"

"No, take it easy," he said. "I don't understand some things."

"There isn't any reason for you to understand. Just enjoy."

"I tried to call Murray, but he's gone off somewhere—"

"And you're going too, right? Look," she said, "you're going to ask some probably very important questions, to you, but all I know's my own job—"

"Which is?"

"—which is none of your business. Go enjoy. When Mr. Morris wants to be in touch with you he'll be in touch with you. No. Don't ask how he'll find you. He'll find you. And so good night."

And so, for eight dynamite months, Tud Cowpersmith enjoyed. He did everything he had ever wanted to do. He made the carnival in Rio and discovered hearts-of-palm soup in a restaurant overlooking the Copacabana beach. He rode a hydrofoil around Leningrad and toured the

Hermitage, bloated on fresh caviar. Gypsy violins in Soho, pounded abalone on Fisherman's Wharf, a nude-encounter weekend at Big Sur, high-stakes gambling in Macao. First-class stewardesses on half a dozen airlines began to recognize him, in half a dozen languages. Shirley turned up once, in his suite at the George Cinq, but only to tell him he was doing fine. Another time he thought he saw Murray pushing a scooter at the Copenhagen airport, but he was going one way and Murray another, and there was no way for Cowpersmith to get off the moving person carrier to catch him. He took up motorcycle racing and tried to enjoy listening to the harpsichord and, in spite of what Morris had said, repeatedly and enthusiastically enjoyed a great deal of sex. It was at the time of his second case of gonorrhea that he began to feel enough was very nearly enough, and then one morning his phone rang.

"Cowpersmith?" said Mr. Morris' tinny little voice, very far away. "You don't seem to be having a lot of fun right now. Are you about ready to quit?"

Although the pleasure had not been quite as much pleasure lately, the prospect of losing it was very much pain. "No!" yelped Cowpersmith. "What are you talking about? Hell, man, you should see the girl I just—" He looked around; he was alone in the big bed. "I mean, I've got this date—"

"No," whispered the small voice, "that's not good enough. Your EI's been down for three weeks now. Not below the threshold yet. We can still get a little good stuff from you. But the quality's definitely down, Cowpersmith, and something's got to be done about it."

Dismayed, Cowpersmith sat up and swung his feet over the side of the bed. "How do you know about—what is it, my EI?"

"Emotional index? Well, what do you think, man? We continuously monitor the product, and it just isn't what we want."

"Yeah," Cowpersmith conceded. "Look, I just woke up and I'm a little fuzzy, but—" He got out of bed, car-

rying the phone, and sat in a chair by the window. Outside was Grosvenor Square, with a demonstration going on in front of the American Embassy, so he knew he was in the Europa in London.

"But what, Cowpersmith?"

"But I'll think of something. Hold on."

By this time the staff of the hotel had learned to value him and understand his likes, so the floor waiter, alerted by the incoming phone call, was bringing in his black coffee, American style, with two large glasses of fresh orange juice. Cowpersmith swallowed a little of one and a little of the other and said, "Listen, can you give me an idea of what he likes?"

"Who likes?"

"Whoever it is is paying for all this stuff."

"I can't discuss our clients," said Mr. Morris. "They told me not to."

"Well, can you give me some idea?"

"No. I don't know what you've been doing; the monitor doesn't show that. It shows where you are and how you're feeling. That's it. We won't know exactly what you've been up to until the debriefing, when they study the recordings. Me, I'll never know. Not my department."

"Well, don't you have *any* idea what kind of stuff they like?"

"Mostly, any kind of stuff they haven't had before."

"Hah!" Cowpersmith thought wildly. "Listen, how's this? Has anybody just sort of sat and meditated for you?"

Pause. "You mean like religious meditation? Like some kind of guru?"

"Well, yes. Or just sitting and thinking, like, you know, Thoreau at Walden Pond."

"I give it forty-eight hours," said Mr. Morris.

"Or—well, how about skin diving? Again. The doctor told me to lay off for a little while until my ear healed up after Bermuda, but I heard about this neat stuff at the Great Barrier Reef, and—"

"Cowpersmith," said the tiny voice, "you know what

you're costing? Not counting the half a thousand a week in cash. Your charge has been running over forty-eight hundred a week, on the average. You got to show more than some spearfishing maybe a couple weeks from now. You got to show *today*. *And* tomorrow. And every day. So long."

So Cowpersmith kept at it. The meditation didn't seem to be going well after the first hour, so he hired a new travel consultant and for a while things looked bright. Or bright enough. Maybe. He backpacked across the Trinity Mountains and flew to Naples for a swim in the Blue Grotto. He ate couscous and drank akvavit and smoked Acapulco gold, all in their native environment. Then he took a pack mule through the Montana hills, and flew back to Naples for four hours of clambering around the ruins of Pompeii, and hit Paris for nightclubs and Waikiki for surfing...

...But a couple of wipeouts at Diamond Head made his ear feel worse, and one nightclub turned out to be an awful lot like another, except that where the toilet jokes were in French he couldn't understand them. He knew the phone was going to ring again. He didn't need the little machine on his wrist to tell him he was down. He *felt* down.

So he came to a decision, and just sat in his hotel room, sullenly waiting. He had already put eleven thousand dollars in a numbered bank account in Bern and paid off all his old debts, and if it was over it was over.

But he didn't want it to be over.

The more he thought about it, the more he didn't want it to be over.

It was, after all, the finest fucking job in all the world, and everything Murray had said about it was true. No more headwaiters falling all over themselves? No more pretty women to take to the clubs, to the tracks, to bed? He ordered up a couple of bottles of brandy and worked himself up to a weeping drunk and when, the next morn-

ing, it was inevitably followed by a dry-mouthed, burning-bellied hangover, he sat wallowing in the misery of his thousand-franc-a-day suite, shaking and enfeebled, barely moving to order up food, and more booze, and more food. The longer he sat, the worse he felt. And the next day. And the next day. And—

And by the fifth day, after most of a week of solid, sullen misery, he realized that his phone had not rung.

Why not? He certainly wasn't enjoying.

He didn't understand why, but when it came through to his mind that it was so, he didn't really care why. Hope was back. The magic money machine had not turned itself off! So he cleaned himself up. He got himself dressed. He waved off the floor waiter and the major-domo and the concierge and went out for a walk, a perfectly dull, uninteresting, unexciting walk, up the Champs Elysees to the Lido Arcade. He ate a quiche and drank a beer and dropped in on a flick. It was an old Barbra Streisand with French subtitles; he had seen it before, and he didn't care. It bored the ears off him. He enjoyed being bored very much.

But when he got back to the hotel, New York was on the line.

"For homey pleasures," said Mr. Morris' small, distant voice, "you don't get paid this kind of money. You want a McDonald's hamburger, quit and come back."

"I had this feeling you'd call," Cowpersmith acknowledged. "What can I say? I've had it with joy. It is no fun anymore."

"So quit. This was your second warning anyhow, and you don't get but three."

"All right," said Cowpersmith, after a moment of digesting that bit of information. "But tell me one thing. Last week I was *really* down; how come you didn't fire me then?"

"Last week? Last week you were *great*. I thought you knew, pleasure isn't the only sensation they like."

"You mean you'll pay me for misery?"

"One of our best units," said the little voice in his ear, "was terminal stomach cancer. They paid him five grand a week plus full medical every week he didn't take pain-killers."

That took a moment to digest too, and it went down hard, but Cowpersmith began to see hope. "Well, I don't want to go that far—"

"Whatever you were doing last week was far enough, I'd say."

"Then maybe I could—"

"Sure," said Mr. Morris. "Nice talking to you. Third strike is out."

Ensued some of the most depressing weeks of Cowpersmith's life. Not miserable. At least not reliably miserable; he could not even be sure, from day to day, that he was quite bugged enough to register a decent misery on his wristband, and that in itself was discouraging. He tried everything he could think of. Inspiration struck, and he made a quick list of all the things he had been putting off because they were awful: went to the dentist, had a barium enema, got tattooed. That took care of three days, and, looking back at them honestly, he had to admit they were not memorably bad, merely lousy. He flew back to Washington and spent two afternoons in the Senate gallery—merely tedious; after the first half hour he stopped hearing what was being said and caught himself drowsing off. He flanged together two stereo systems and poured thirty watts of acid rock into one earpiece and Mahler into the other and came out with only a headache. He invented excuses to go in and out of Kennedy airport, with special emphasis on the Customs line and the hackstands, but after a while even that anger diminished. Food. Remembering all the enjoyment he had had from good food, he looked for dyspepsia and displeasure from bad. He ate a haggis in Glasgow, flew to Heathrow and had brawn for dinner, caught a commuter flight to Paris and had an American breakfast at Orly. None of it worked very well. It proved to be harder to make oneself unhappy than to find joy, which had, after all, lasted for the best

part of a year. The other thing was that deliberately making oneself unhappy made one, well, unhappy. It was not a way he liked to live. He discovered that twenty cups of coffee a day, sixty cigarettes, and a maximum of three hours of sleep gave him a perpetual headachy feeling that made everything an annoyance, but the other side of the coin was that nothing was much *more* than an annoyance; he was simply too beat to care. In desperation he returned to the States and delved into copies of the underground press, answering all the ads he could find for "instruction," "discipline," and so on, but that mostly got him a large number of FBI men and postal inspectors, and the S-M experiences were basically, he thought, pretty God-awful anyway. So he was not all that surprised when, less than five weeks from the second warning, his phone rang again. He was in Waikiki, where he had been nerving himself up to trying to get his ear hurting again in the surf, and he was frankly grateful to be spared it.

"Third time's the charm," said the little voice. "Come home, come home for debriefing."

"I'm fired, right?"

"Well," said distant Mr. Morris judiciously, "you stop working for us as soon as you're debriefed. But you get a year's severance pay, which comes to, let's see, twenty-six K."

"Wow!" cried Cowpersmith. And then, "Uh. Say. Was that, you know, just to give me a high?"

"No, although you did register a beaut. No, it's real. You just have to turn over the recording, and you're on your own."

"Well," said Cowpersmith, picking up the phone and walking out onto the lanai. "Well," he said, surrendering a dream, "I guess that's about it, then. Isn't it? I'll catch the first plane tomorrow—"

"No," said Mr. Morris, "you won't do that, you'll catch the next plane right now. We've arranged for your tickets; they'll be at the desk when you check out. Which should be in fifteen minutes."

And five minutes after he hung up, the Ilikai bellman

was at the door, eager for Cowpersmith's one beaten bag.

Mr. Morris had been very thorough. They not only had Cowpersmith's ticket at the desk, they had an envelope with two twenty-dollar bills and ten singles, for tips and miscellaneous. And they also had their instructions about his credit card. "I'm very sorry," said the clerk politely, "but as of the time you settle your account with us your card is canceled. And we have to pick it up. It's part of our contract with the company—"

"Well, fine," said Cowpersmith. "Tell you what. I forgot to pick up a couple little things in the shops, so let me have the card for a minute *before* I finish settling up."

"So sorry," said the clerk. "You already have."

And now, when it was all over, Cowpersmith spent his time in the taxi to the airport thinking of things he could have done but had not. He got onto the plane in a daze of missed menus and untried wines, and had to be prodded sharply by the stewardess before he realized he was in the wrong part of the airplane. "Sorry," he mumbled, allowing himself to be led aft. He glanced around with some wonder. He had almost forgotten that there were parts of a 707 where people sat three abreast.

At Kennedy he was met: Shirley.

He stared at her through gummed eyelids. By the sun it was late afternoon, but by the clock of his body it was eight in the morning after a night with no more sleep than a man can get sitting in a coach seat between a fat plumber on a group tour and a small boy who alternated snoring and leaping about. "Had fun?" she asked, steering him toward a chauffeur-driven Bentley.

"You know better than I," he said bitterly, trying to take the wristband off and slap it in her palm. The gesture failed, because it still would not come open.

"You'll feel better when we get going," she said. "I've got a Thermos of coffee. It's about an hour's drive."

"I know, I know," grumped Cowpersmith, who had, after all, been in and out on the Kennedy-Manhattan run more times than he could count. But when the chauffeur

took a right-hand turn where there had always been a left, he realized he did not know. It did not seem important, and he drowsed until the car stopped, doors opened—

"Here's your boy, Morrie."

"Looks like we'll have to carry him in."

—and he opened his eyes to see Mr. Morris and the chauffeur tugging at him.

"I'm all right," he said with dignity, and halfway up the pebbled walk looked around and said, "Where is this place, anyway?" Porticoed porch, ivied walls, he had not seen it before.

"Where you get debriefed," said Shirley, pausing at the door. "So long, Tud."

He hesitated. "You're not coming in? Will I see you again?"

"I'll see you," she said, patted his shoulderblade and returned to the car.

Sensory impressions smote him: An entrance hall, with a staircase winding up under a huge canvas-shrouded painting in a gilt frame. A library of glassed-in shelves, mostly empty, with drop-clothed chairs around a cold and swept fireplace. A dining hall, and beyond it a closed door.

"Does he live in this place, whoever he is?" asked Cowpersmith, staring about.

Mr. Morris sighed. "There is no 'he,'" he said patiently. "There are 'they.' They are here, some of them ... This is the part I hate," he added morosely.

"Why?"

"Well, you're going to ask a lot of questions again. You all do. And you're going to figure you've done your bit, now you have a right to know. Right? And maybe in a sense you do, although it's pretty pointless ... Anyway. What we do now, we take the recordings from you, and when we've got enough to make a shipment, we send them off. I don't know where, exactly. I don't know what they do with them, exactly. But it's a big business with them."

"Big business?" Misconceptions and erroneous as-

sumptions were splintering in Cowpersmith's brain.

"Well, like a TV network. I mean, I think they kind of broadcast them, sort of like a *National Geographic* television special: sensory impressions from all over, strange pleasures of the aborigines—"

"I *never*," said Cowpersmith positively, apprehensions dissolving the sleep from his mind, "heard any broadcast like that."

"No. Not on this planet, no."

Cowpersmith swallowed, choking on apprehensions and the splinters of former certainties.

"The mistake you made," said Mr. Morris sympathetically, "is that you assumed the people who hired you were human beings. They're not. No. You wouldn't think so if you'd seen one. They, uh ... Well, they look a little bit like fish and a little bit like the devil. All red, you see. And not very big—"

"But Murray said—"

"Oh, Christ," said Mr. Morris, "how could Murray know? If it's any consolation to you, when he was debriefed he was as surprised as you are. It gets everybody the same way."

"Bloody charming," said Cowpersmith bitterly. "Now I'm an agent of a foreign power. I wouldn't be surprised if the FBI picks me up about this."

"I would," said Mr. Morris. "In there, go on."

"Where?"

"There. Through the door."

"What do we do in there?" Cowpersmith demanded, truculent because the only alternative was being terrified.

"You turn over the recording to them and that's that," said Mr. Morris.

Cowpersmith swallowed again, choking this time on plain panic. He wished that the car hadn't gone away. Still, he thought, they had to be somewhere on Long Island. Maybe Sands Point? Maybe Patchogue. And he still had most of the fifty dollars, plus whatever had been left in his coat, plus, of course, that Swiss bank account. There would be a taxi ...

"Okay," he said, tugging at the wristband. "Let's get it over with and I'll get out of here."

"Oh," said Mr. Morris, annoyed, "what are you doing? That's not the recording. That's only the monitor, so we could tell how you were doing and where you were. You turn over the recording in there."

And he opened the door behind the dining hall.

Two men in white stepped through. They were not smiling. They were without expression, like saloon bouncers or dog catchers.

The room behind them looked like an operating chamber: bright lights over a flat white table. Rows of transparent jars lined the shelves around the room. They came in two sizes:

In the large (there were two of them) red and hideous things stirred uneasily, looking out toward Cowpersmith with great pale eyes.

In the smaller jars, of which there were more than a dozen—

Were the floating objects in them *really* human heads? And that one there, next to the brighter of the two red creatures, the one with the wild red eyebrows—wasn't it very familiar?

It was too late to turn; the men were reaching out for him as Mr. Morris said from behind him, sadly, disclaimingly, "What better recording could they have than the one in your own brain?"

GROWING UP IN EDGE CITY

Among the closest friends I had in the thirty years I lived in Red Bank, New Jersey, was a family named Waterman, Bob and Dorothy and their offspring, who were much of an age with my own. It was a great loss when they moved nearly a hundred miles away, to the antique New Jersey resort city of Cape May, which is about as far south as you can get in the state without swimming. So, when I could, I drove down to visit them with as much of my family as could be collected for the purpose. All the way down the Garden State Parkway, on one visit, a story was nibbling at my mind—not just a set of characters and situations but a particular way of telling the story that I had just invented and wanted to try out. After we'd all caught up on old times over lunch, and the kids had gone off to the boats or the shopping centers or the boardwalk and beach, I mentioned to Dorothy Waterman that I had just realized the right place to set the story was right in Cape May. "Well," she said, "I've got a typewriter I'm not using—" And so, sitting

on the Watermans' porch, between lunch and our dinner date at one of the best seafood restaurants in the
world, this came out.

IN THE EVENINGS AFTER SCHOOL CHANDLIE PLAYED PRI-
vate games. He was permitted to do so. His overall index
of gregariousness was high enough to allow him to choose
his own companions, or no companion at all but a Pal, when
he wanted it that way. On Tueday and Fourthday he generally spent his time with a seven-year-old female named
Marda, quick and bright, with a chiseled, demure little face
that would have beseemed a pretty woman of twenty, apt
at mathematical intuitions and the stringing of beads. The
proctors logged in their private games under the heading of
"sensuality sensitivity training," but they called them "You
Show Me Yours and I'll Show You Mine." The proctors,
in their abstract and deterministic way, approved of what
Chandlie did. Even then he was marked for special chal-
lenge, having been evaluated as Councilman potential, and
when on most other evenings Chandlie went down to the
machine rooms and checked out a Pal, no objections were
raised, no questions were asked, and no follow-up warn-
ings were flagged in the magnetic cores of his record-fiche.
He went off freely and openly, wherever he chose. This was
so even though there was a repeating anomaly in his log.
Almost every evening for an hour or two, Chandlie's personal transponder stopped broadcasting his location fix.
They could not tell where he was in Edge City. They accepted this because of their own limitations. It was recorded in the proctors' basic memory file that there were
certain areas of the City in which old electromagnetic ef-
fects interfered with the radio direction finding signals. They
were not strategically important areas. The records showed
nothing dangerous or forbidden there. The proctors noted
the gap in the log but attached no importance to it. As a
matter of routine they opened up the Pal's chrome-steel

tamper-proof course-plot tapes from time to time, but it was only spot-checking. They did the same for everyone's Pal. They never found anything significantly wrong in Chandlie's. If they had been less limited, they might have inquired further. A truly good program would have cross-referenced Chandlie's personality profile, learned from it that he was gifted in man-machine interactions, and deduced from this the possibility that he had bugged the Pal. If they had then checked the Pal's permanent record of instructions, they would have learned that it was so. They did not do that. The proctors were not particularly sophisticated computer programs. They saw in their inputs no reason to be suspicious. Chandlie's father and mother could have told the programs all about him, but they had been Dropouts since he was three.

At the edge of Edge City, past the school sections, near the hospital and body-disposal units, there was a dark and odorous place. Ancient steel beams showed scarred and discolored. They bore lingering radioactivity, souvenir of an old direct hit from a scrambler missile. It was no longer a dangerous place, but it was not an attractive one, either, and on the master location charts it was designated for storage. It was neither very useful nor very much used. What could be stored there was only what was not very much valued, and there were few such things kept in Edge City. If they were remembered. The air was dank. Spots of mildew and rust appeared and swelled on whatever was there. However often the Handys came in to scrub and burn and polish, the surfaces were never clean. It was environmentally interesting, in a city where there was no such thing as environment, for at times it was pervaded by a sound like a distant grumbling roar, and at times it grew quite cold or quite hot. These were the things that had first interested Chandlie in it. What capped his interest was discovering by accident, one evening when he had just returned from wandering in the strange smells and sounds, that the proctors had not known where he was. He determined to spend more

time there. The thought of doing something the proctors did not know all about was both scary and irresistible. His personal independence index had always been very high, almost to the point of remedial action. On his second visit, or third, he discovered the interesting fact that some of the closed doors were not locked on a need-to-enter basis. They were merely closed and snapped. Turning a knob would open them. Anyone could do it. He opened every door he passed. Most of them led only to empty rooms, or to chambers that might as well be empty for all he could make of the gray metal cylinders or yellowed fiber cartons that were stacked forgotten inside them. Some of the doors, however, led to other places, and some of the places were not even marked on the city charts. With his Pal romping and humming its shrill electronic note by his side, Chandlie penetrated the passages and stairways he found right up to the point at which he became certain he was not permitted to be there. A buckled guide rail that gouged at his flesh told him that. These areas were dangerous. Having reached that conclusion, he returned to his studies and spent a week learning how to reprogram the Pal to go into sleep mode on voice command from himself. He then returned to the dangerous area, left the Pal curled up inside one of the uninteresting doors, and went on into the unknown, down a broad and dusty flight of stairs.

In the pits under Edge City the air was damper and danker even than in the deserted places above. It was not at all cold. Chandlie was astonished to discover that he was sweating. He had never known what it was like to sweat before in his life, except as a natural consequence of exercise or, once or twice, while experiencing an illness surrogate. It took some time for him to realize that the reason for this was that the air about him was quite warm, perhaps as much as ten degrees over the 28°C at which he had spent his life. Also, the grumbling roaring noise was sharper and nearer, although not as loud as he had sometimes heard it before. He looked about himself wonderingly and uncertainly. There

were many things here that were strange, unfamiliar, and, although he had not had enough of a background of experience to be sure of correctly identifying the sensation, frightening. For example, this part of the City was not very well lighted. Every other public place he had ever seen had been identically illuminated with the changing skeins of soft brilliance from their liquid crystal walls. Here it was not like that. Light came from discrete points. There was a bright spot enclosed in a glass sphere here, another there, another five meters away. Objects cast shadows. Chandlie spent some time experimenting with making shadows. Sometimes there were considerable gaps between the points of light, with identical glass spheres that looked like the others but contained no central glowing core, as though they had stopped working and for some reason the Handy machines had not made them work again. Where this happened the shadows merged to produce what he recognized as darkness. Sometimes as a little boy during the times when his room light was sleep-reduced he had pulled the coverlid over his head to see what darkness was like. Warm and cozy. This was not cozy. Also, there were distant thumping, creaking sounds. Also, he remembered that not far above him and beyond him was the corpse-disposal area, and while he had no unhealthy fear of cadavers, he did not like them. Chandlie felt to some degree ill at ease. To some degree he wished that he had not countercommanded his Pal to stay behind. It was exciting to be all on his own, but it was also worrisome. It would have been a comfort to have the Pal gamboling and humming beside him, to see its bright milky-blue eyes following him, to know that in the event of any unprogrammed event it would automatically relay a data pulse to the proctors for evaluation and, if need be, action. What action? he thought. Like rescuing a little boy from goblins, he joked to himself, remembering a story from his preprimary anthropology talk-times. Joking to himself helped him put aside the cobwebby fears. He still felt them, but he did not feel any of them strongly enough to turn back. His index of curiosity, also, was very high.

* * *

   All of this was taking place on a Wonday, after sched-
uled hours, which meant that Chandlie had received his
weekly therapies that day and was chockful of hormones,
vitamins, and confidence. Perhaps it was that which made
him so bold. On such accidents of timing so many things
depend. But he went on. After a time he discovered that the
new world he was exploring was no longer getting darker.
It was getting lighter. Simultaneously it was becoming even
more hot. Sweat streamed from his unpracticed pores. Salty
moisture drenched the long hair at his temples, dampened
his chest, rolled in beads from his armpits and down his back.
He became aware that he himself had an odor. The light was
brighter before him than it was behind, and rounding a corner, he saw a yellow radiance that made him squint. He
stopped. Reinventing the Eskimo glare-reducer on the spot,
he stared through his half-spread fingers. Then, heedless,
he ran down a flight of ancient steps, almost falling as one
slid loosely away beneath him but righting himself and running on. He stopped on an uneven surface of grayish-yel-
lowish gritty grains that he recognized, from Earth Sciences,
as sand. The great distant noise was close now, grave and
impersonal rather than threatening; he saw what it came
from. Rolling hillocks of water humped themselves slowly
up out of a flat blue that receded into infinity before him.
They grew, peaked, bent forward, and crashed in white wet
spray, and the noise was their serial collision with themselves and with the sand. The heat was unbearable, but
Chandlie bore it. He was entranced, thrilled, consternated,
delighted almost out of his skull. This was a "beach!" That
was "sea!" He was "outdoors!" No such things had ever
happened to any young person he had ever known or heard
of. No such things happened to anyone but Dropouts. He
had never expected any such thing to happen to him. It was
not that he was unaware that there were places not in the
Cities. Earth Sciences had taught him all that, as they taught
him about the sluggishly molten iron core at the Earth's heart
and the swinging distant bodies that were called "Moon"

and "planets" and "stars." He had even known, by implication and omission rather than by ever hearing it stated as a fact, that somewhere in the world between the Cities were places like the places where people had lived generations and, oh, ages ago, when people were dull and cruel, and that it was at least in theory possible for a person from a city to stand in such a place and not at once become transformed into a Dropout, or physically changed, or killed. But he had never known that such places could be found near Edge City.

All that very painful brightness came from one central brightness which, as Chandlie knew, was the "Sun." It cost him some pain and several minutes of near blindness to learn that it could not be looked at directly without penalty. Its height, he recalled, meant "midday," which was puzzling until he deduced and remembered enough to understand that City time was world time. He had known that solar time differed as one went east or west, but it had never mattered before. As he became able to see again he looked about him. When he looked before him, he saw the rolling sweep of the ocean, dizzyingly big. When he looked behind him, he saw the skirted and stilted bulk of Edge City rising away like the Egyptian tetrahedral tombs for the royal dead. To his right was a stretch of irregular sand and sea that curved around out of sight under a corner of the city. But to his left, to his left, there was something quite strange. There were buildings. Buildings, plural. Not one great polystructure like a proper City, buildings. People moved among them. He breathed deeply to generate courage and walked toward them. Plodding through the sand was new to him, difficult, like walking with five-kilogram anklets on a surface that slid and slipped and caved irregularly away under his foot-gloves. The people saw him long before he was close enough to speak or hear, even a shout, over the wind and the breaking waves. They spoke to each other, and then gestured toward him. He could see that they were smiling. He knew at once that they were Dropouts. As he came closer to them, and a few of them walked toward him, he could see that

some of them were not very clean, and all of them were straggly-haired, the women just on their scalps, the men wherever men could grow hair, beards, sideburns, mustaches, one barrel of a man thatched front and back with a bear's pelt. They all seemed quite old. Surely not one was under twenty. Physically they were deviant in accidental and unwholesome ways. On school trips to the corpse-disposal areas Chandlie had been struck by the unkemptness of the dead, but these people were living and unkempt. Some were gray and balding. Some women's breasts hung like sucked-dry fruits. Some wore glass disks in frames before their eyes. The faces of some were seamed and darkened. Some stood stooped, or bent, or walked limping. The clothes they wore did not hug and constrain them as right clothing should. The things they wore were smocks or shorts or sweaters. Or anything at all. As Chandlie had never seen an ugly person, he did not recognize what he felt as revulsion; and as he did not recognize it, it was not that, it was only disquiet. He looked at them curiously and seekingly. It occurred to him that his father and his mother might be among these people. He did not recognize them, but then he had very little memory of what his father and mother looked like.

As a very little boy Chandlie had experienced a programming malfunction in one of his proctors. It had taken the form of giving him incomplete answers and sometimes incomplete questions. The parts it left out were often the direct statements. The parts it gave him were then only the supplementary detail: "Proctor, what is the shape of the Earth?" "—which is why your transparency buildups show a ship disappearing from the bottom up as it reaches the horizon." He had required remedial confidence building after that. And may have had an overdose. It was a little like that with the Dropouts. They made him welcome, speaking to him from very close up so that he turned his head to avoid their breaths. They offered him disgusting sorts of food, which he ate anyway, raw fruits and cooked meats. Some of them actually touched him or tried to kiss

him. "What we want to give you," they said, "is love." This
troubled him. He did not want to conceive a child with any
of them, and some of the speakers, also, were male. They
said things like, "You are so young to come to us, and so
pretty. We welcome you." They showed him everything
they did and offered him their pleasures. On a walkway made
of wood with the beach below them and surf spraying up
onto his face they took him into a round building with a round
turntable. Some of the younger, stronger men pushed at
poles and stanchions and got it revolving slowly and wob-
blingly. It bore animal figures that moved as it turned, and
they invited him to ride them. "It is a merry-go-round," they
cried. To oblige them he sat on one of the horses for a revolution or two, but it was nothing compared to a Sleeter or
Jumping Pillows. "We live freely and without constraint,"
they said. "We take what the world gives us and harm no
one. We have joys the City has forgotten." Causing him to
detach the lower part of his day garment so that his feet and
legs were naked to the codpiece, they walked with him along
the edge of the water. Waves came up and bathed his ankles
and receded again. Grit lodged between his toes. His thighs
itched from drying salt. They said to him: "See over here,
where the walls have corroded away." They led him under
the skirt of the City to an in-port. Great cargo carriers were
rolling in from the agrocommunes, pouring grain and frozen foods into the hoppers, from which three of the young-
est Dropouts were scooping the next day's meals into canvas
pouches. "The City does not need all of this," they said,
"but if they knew we took it, they would drive us away."
They warmed berries between their grimy palms and gave
them to Chandlie until he could eat no more. "Stay with
us," they pleaded. "You are a human being, or you would
not have come here alone! The City is not a life for human
beings." He began to feel quite ill. He was conscious, too,
of the passage of time. As the sun disappeared behind the
gray pyramid and the wind from the sea became cold, they
said: "If you must go back, go back. But come again. We
do not have many children here ever. We like you. We want
to love you." He allowed some of them to touch him, then

turned and retraced his steps. He did not like the way he felt and did not understand the way he smelled. It was the first time in his life that Chandlie had been dirty.

When he reactivated his Pal, the machine immediately went into receiving mode. It then turned to Chandlie with its milky-blue eyes gleaming and spoke: "Chandlie, you must report at once to the proctors." "All right," he said. He had been expecting it. Although he was good at re-programming machines, he had not expected to be gone so long and had not prepared for it.

The proctors received him in the smallest of the Inter-view Halls. He entered through a door that closed behind him and immediately became only one more square in a checkerboard of mirrors and gray metal panels. Behind some of the mirrors the proctors were scanning him. Be-hind others there might be members of the council, or ap-prentices, or interested citizens, anyone. He could not see, he could only see himself reflected into infinity wherever he looked. He stood under the heatless bright lights, blink-ing stubbornly. The proctors did not ask him any questions. They did not make any threats, either. They merely made a series of statements as follows: "Chandlie. First, you have interfered with the operation of your Pal. Second, you have absented yourself without authorization. Third, you have visited an area of the City where you have no occasion to go. Fourth, you have failed to report your activities in the proper form." They were then silent for a time. It was at this time that he was permitted to offer any corrections or supplementary information if he wished to do so. He did not. He stood mute, and after the appropriate time had passed, the proctors instructed him to withdraw. One square of mirror swung forward and became a door again, and he left the room. He returned to his dormitory. His peers were all in their own rooms and presumably asleep; it was very late. Chandlie bathed carefully, attempted to vomit, failed, rinsed his mouth carefully, and put on a sleeping blouse. The food the Dropouts had given him did not satisfy him,

but he was afraid to eat until it had gone through his system. All that night he tossed and turned, waking up enough to know where he was and remember where he had been and then falling back to sleep again, unsatisfied and unresolved.

For some days Chandlie continued his normal life, but he was aware that the matter would not stop there. Prudence suggested to him that he should behave at least normally, if possible exemplarily. Curiosity overrode prudence. In free-study times he dialed for old books that were known to be of interest to Dropouts, *Das Kapital* and *Walden* and silly, sexy satires by people like Voltaire and Swift. He played old ballads by people like Dylan Thomas and Joan Baez. He read poetry: Wordsworth, Browning, Ginsberg. He studied old documents that, so said his books, had once been electrically important, and was baffled by contextual ignorance ("A well-regulated militia being necessary to the security of a free State, the right of the people to keep and bear arms shall not be infringed." "Militia"? "State"? "Bear"—in the sense of bearing a child, perhaps? But only the arm parts?), until he reached the decision to ask for clarification from the preceptors for Social Studies. Then he was baffled to understand why these things were important. They were gritty days for Chandlie. His age-peers detected that something was wrong almost at once, deduced that he was in trouble with the proctors and, naturally enough, anticipated the punishment of the proctors with punishments of their own. In Living Chess he was played only as a pawn, though usually he had been a bishop and once a rook. His Tai Chi movements were voted grotesque, and he was not invited to exercise with the rest of his group. They did not speak of his situation to him directly, except for Marda. She sat down next to him in free time and said, "I'll miss you if you go away, Chandlie." He pored mulishly over a series of layover transparency prints. "Why do you look at them when I'm here?" she cried. He said crushingly, "Your genitalia are juvenile. These are adult, much more interesting." She grew angry. "I don't think I want to con-

ceive with you ever," she said. He put down the cassette of transparencies, stood up, and rapped on the door of an older girl. It was the first time he had ever seen tears. The second time was the following Fiveday, when he was called before the council of decision-making persons and saw his own.

The council, which was charged with the responsibility for making decisions in all cases not covered by standing instructions to the proctors, met when it needed to, where it chose to. Chandlie was of some interest to them, for whatever personal reasons each of them had for concerning himherself, and so there were nearly twenty-five persons present when he was admitted. The room they chose to use this time was rather like the drawing room of a gentlemen's club. There were small tables with inlaid chessboards, sideboards with coffee, candies, refreshments of all kinds, stereopaints of notables of the City's history squirming on the walls. The head of the council, as of that hour, indicated a comfortable seat for Chandlie and gave him a cup of chilly sweet foam that was flavored with fruits and mint. He was a man. He looked about thirty, with neat bangs, wide-spaced tawny eyes, diffraction-grating rings on his fingers that moved hypnotically as he gestured. "Chandlie," he said, "we have a full file of reports. Beach sand, bits of weathered wood and caked salt have been found on your garments and on your skin, after evaporating wash water. Stool analysis shows consumption of nearly raw vegetable foods. We then ordered a spectral study of your skin and found compensatory pigmentation of your arms, face, neck, and lower body compatible with exposure to unfiltered sunlight. There is no point in wasting our time, Chandlie. It is clear that you have been outside the City." The boy nodded and said, "Yes, I have been outside the City." He had thought carefully of what he should say when he was asked questions, for he was aware of the risks involved. Risks to himself, to some extent. His ambitions were not fully formed at that time, but they excluded being downgraded as a po-

tential Dropout. Risks to the Dropouts themselves in a much
more immediate way, of course. "What did you see outside?" asked the head of the council in a friendly and curious way, and all of the twenty-five, or almost all, stopped
talking or reading to listen. "I saw a beach," cried Chandlie.
"It was very strange. The Sun was so hot, the wind so strong.
There were waves a meter and a half high that came in and
crashed on the sand. I walked in the water, I found berries.
They did not taste very good, but I ate them. There were
buildings made of wood and, I think, plaster?" He was asked
to describe the buildings; he did so. He was asked why he
was there; he told them it was curiosity. Finally he was
asked, very gently. "And did you see any people?" At once
he replied: "Of course, there were some women in the
corpse-disposal area. I think someone they knew had died.
And a man adjusting some Handys." "No," said the head
of the council, "we mean outside. Did you see anyone
there?" Chandlie looked astonished. "How could anyone
live there?" he asked. "No. I didn't see anyone." The head
of the council, after a while, looked around at the others.
He held up seven fingers inquiringly. Most of them nodded,
some shrugged, a few were paying no attention at all. "You
have seven demerits, Chandlie," he said, "and you will work
them off as the proctors direct." At once Chandlie was en-
raged. "Seven!" he cried. "How unfair!" It was maddening
that they should have believed him and still awarded so harsh
a punishment, seven days without free time, or seven weeks
with no optional-foods privileges, or seven of whatever the
proctors judged would be most punitive, and therefore most
likely to discourage repetition of the infractions, for him.
Before he left he was in tears, which only resulted in two
additional demerits. He was then returned to his peer group,
who gradually accepted him again as before.

For more than twenty years Chandlie kept the secret of
the Dropout colony outside Edge City. He did not return
there in all that time. But he did not speak of it, not even to
Marda, by whom he did indeed conceive a child at the ap-

propriate time. As a child he accumulated very few further demerits, and as a young adult none. His conduct was a model to the entire city and particularly, almost offensively, to his peer group, who reluctantly but inevitably elected him their age representative when he was almost thirty. It was then, with a seat on the council, that he achieved his intention. He disclosed the full truth of his expedition outside the City. He denounced the former councilpersons for their failure to recognize when a little boy was lying. He accused them of suspecting that there was indeed a Dropout colony at the edge of Edge City, and proposed that he himself be given the authority to deal with it. Angrily the ones he had denounced left, refusing to vote. Resentfully the ones who remained gave him the authority. He then in person, in person, he himself, went outside, himself directing the armed Pals with their lasers and serrated steel fangs. The weathered buildings burned sullenly but surely as the heat of the lasers drove out the long accumulation of brine. The Dropouts screamed and ran before the Pals snapping at them. Some escaped, but not very many. A crew of Handys was set to repairing and strengthening the walls around the food input areas, so that in the event any Dropouts returned they would be unable to continue their pilferage. When Chandlie reentered the City, there was nothing left outside that was alive, or useful. The following year he was elected head of the council years before his turn, and several times again. This had been his intention. He knew that he could not have achieved this so soon if it had not been for the Dropouts. In a sense he remained forever grateful to them. Sometimes he wondered if any of them were still alive in whatever part of the scarred and guarded Earth they had fled to. In a way he hoped some were. It would have been useful to know of another Dropout colony, although he really had no particular interest in harrying them, unless, of course, he could see a way in which it would benefit his career.

We Purchased People

Jack Williamson and I have collaborated on eight or nine novels over the years. I've collaborated with a number of other writers, and so I know what I'm talking about when I proclaim that working with Jack, who is a wise and gentle human being, is as nearly painless as writing ever gets. Especially collaborative writing. Still, there are times when our interests diverge a little. As in all writing, there are occasions when one of us thinks up a scene or a situation that is too attractive to throw away but doesn't fit properly into the joint effort. When Jack and I were writing our novel *Farthest Star*, we each came up with one of those displaced bits. Jack's was a lovely sequence that dealt with an immense mountain called Knife in the Sky. The episode he had in mind did not fit into the novel, but he made it into a short story for *Boy's Life*. Mine was this one: "We Purchased People." There are some themes that I seem to come back to over and over. The only way I realize that is by thinking the process over afterward,

when it's history; I'm not usually conscious of it while I'm doing it. One of those themes is overpopulation—a theme on which, you will observe, I have played variations at least twice in this collection alone. Another is the idea of "possession." That appears not only in the two novels with Jack Williamson, *Farthest Star* and its sequel, *Wall Around a Star*, but in my solo novel *Plague of Pythons* (lately revised and rereleased as *The Demon in the Skull*) and several short stories—including this one. Why is this theme so permanently appealing to me over decades? I have a suspicion that there is a psychological basis for it. I wonder if it does not represent a metaphor for a deep-seated fear of manipulation from outside, of control by external forces that overrule our basic, instinctual decency and common sense ... but I guess I will leave the resolution of that question to my shrink.

ON THE THIRD OF MARCH THE PURCHASED PERSON NAMED Wayne Golden took part in trade talks in Washington as the representative of the dominant race of the Groombridge star. What he had to offer was the license of the basic patents on a device to convert nuclear power plant waste products into fuel cells. It was a good item, with a ready market. Since half of Idaho was already bubbling with radioactive wastes, the Americans were anxious to buy, and he sold for a credit of $100 million. On the following day he flew to Spain. He was allowed to sleep all the way, stretched out across two seats in the first-class section of the Concorde, with the fastenings of a safety belt gouging into his side. On the fifth of the month he used up part of the trade credit in the purchase of fifteen Picasso oils on canvas, the videotape of a flamenco performance, and a fifteenth-century harpsichord, gilt with carved legs. He arranged for them to be preserved, crated,

and shipped in bond to Orlando, Florida, after which the items would be launched from Cape Kennedy on a voyage through space that would take more than twelve thousand years. The Groombridgians were not in a hurry and thought big. The Saturn Five booster rocket cost $11 million in itself. It did not matter. There was plenty of money left in the Groombridge credit balance. On the fifth of the month Golden returned to the United States, made a close connection at Logan Airport in Boston, and arrived early at his home kennel in Chicago. He was then given eighty-five minutes of freedom.

I knew exactly what to do with my eighty-five minutes. I always know. See, when you're working for the people who own you, you don't have any choice about what you do, but up to a point you can think pretty much whatever you like. That thing you get in your head only controls you. It doesn't change you, or anyway I don't think it does. (Would I know if I were changed?)

My owners never lie to me. Never. I don't think they know what a lie is. If I ever needed anything to prove that they weren't human, that would be plenty, even if I didn't know they lived 86 zillion miles away, near some star that I can't even see. They don't tell me much, but they don't lie.

Not ever lying, that makes you wonder what they're like. I don't mean physically. I looked that up in the library once, when I had a couple of hours of free time. I don't remember where, maybe in Paris at the Bibliothèque Nationale, anyway I couldn't read what the language in the books said. But I saw the photographs and the holograms. I remember the physical appearance of my owners, all right. Jesus. The Altairians look kind of like spiders, and the Sirians are a little bit like crabs. But those folks from the Groombridge star, boy, they're something else. I felt bad about it for a long time, knowing I'd been sold to something that looked as much like a cluster of maggots on an open wound as anything else I'd ever

seen. On the other hand, they're all those miles away, and all I ever have to do with them is receive their fast-radio commands and do what they tell me. No touching or anything. So what does it matter what they look like?

But what kind of freaky creature is it that never says anything that is not objectively the truth, never changes its mind, never makes a promise that it doesn't keep? They aren't machines, I know, but maybe they think I'm kind of a machine. You wouldn't bother to lie to a machine, would you? You wouldn't make it any promises. You wouldn't do it any favors, either, and they never do me any. They don't tell me that I can have eighty-five minutes off because I've done something they like, or because they want to sweeten me up because they want something from me. Everything considered, that's silly. What could they want? It isn't as if I had any choice. Ever. So they don't lie, or threaten, or bribe, or reward.

But for some reason they sometimes give me minutes or hours or days off, and this time I had eighty-five minutes. I started using it right away, the way I always do. The first thing was to check at the kennel location desk to see where Carolyn was. The locator clerk—he isn't owned, he works for a salary and treats us like shit—knows me by now. "Oh, hell, Wayne boy," he said with that imitation sympathy and lying friendliness that makes me want to kill him, "you just missed the lady friend. Saw her, let's see, Wednesday, was it? But she's gone." "Where to?" I asked him. He pushed around the cards on the locator board for a while, he knows I don't have very much time ever so he uses it up for me, and said: "Nope, not on my board at all. Say, I wonder. Was she with that bunch that went to Peking? Or was that the other little fat broad with the big boobs?" I didn't stop to kill him. If she wasn't on the board, she wasn't in eighty-five-minute transportation range, so my eighty-five minutes—seventy-nine minutes—wasn't going to get me near her.

I went to the men's room, jerked off quickly, and went out into the miserable biting March Chicago wind to use

up my seventy-nine minutes. Seventy-one minutes.
There's a nice Mexican kind of restaurant near the kennel,
a couple of blocks away past Ohio. They know me there.
They don't care who I am. Maybe the brass plate in my
head doesn't bother them because they think it's great
that the people from the other stars are doing such nice
things for the world, or maybe it's because I tip big. (What
else do I have to do with the money I get?) I stuck my
head in, whistled at Terry, the bartender, and said: "The
usual. I'll be back in ten minutes." Then I walked up to
Michigan and bought a clean shirt and changed into it,
leaving the smelly old one. Sixty-six minutes. In the drug-
store on the corner I picked up a couple of porno paper-
backs and stuck them in my pockets, bought some
cigarettes, leaned over and kissed the hand of the cashier,
who was slim and fair-complexioned and smelled good,
left her startled behind me, and got back to the restaurant
just as Alicia, the waitress, was putting the gazpacho and
the two bottles of beer on my table. Fifty-nine minutes.
I settled down to enjoy my time. I smoked, and I ate, and
I drank the beer, smoking between bites, drinking between puffs. You really look forward to something like
that when you're working, and not your own boss. I don't
mean they don't let us eat when we're working. Of course
they do, but we don't have any choice about what we eat
or where we eat it. Pump fuel into the machine, keep it
running. So I finished the guacamole and sent Alicia back
for more of it when she brought the chocolate cake and
American coffee, and ate the cake and the guacamole in
alternate forkfuls. Eighteen minutes.

If I had had a little more time I would have jerked off
again, but I didn't, so I paid the bill, tipped everybody,
and left the restaurant. I got to the block where the kennel
was with maybe two minutes to spare. Along the curb a
slim woman in a fur jacket and pants suit was walking
her Scottie away from me. I went up behind her and said,
"I'll give you fifty dollars for a kiss." She turned around.
She was all of sixty years old but not bad, really, so I

kissed her and gave her the fifty dollars. Zero minutes, and I just made it into the kennel when I felt the tingling in my forehead and my owners took over again.

In the next seven days of March Wayne Golden visited Karachi, Srinagar, and Butte, Montana, on the business of the Groombridgians. He completed thirty-two assigned tasks. Quite unexpectedly he was then given 1,000 minutes of freedom.

That time I was in, I think it was, Pocatello, Idaho, or some place like that. I had to send a TWX to the faggy locator clerk in Chicago to ask about Carolyn. He took his time answering, as I knew he would. I walked around a little bit, waiting to hear. Everybody was very cheerful, smiling as they walked around through the dusty, sprinkly snow that was coming down, even smiling at me as though they didn't care that I was purchased, as they could plainly see from the golden oval of metal across my forehead that my owners use to tell me what to do. Then the message came back from Chicago: "Sorry, Wayne baby, but Carolyn isn't on my board. If you find her, give her one for me."

Well. All right. I have plenty of spending money, so I checked into a hotel. The bellboy brought me a fifth of Scotch and plenty of ice, fast, because he knew why I was in a hurry and that I would tip for speed. When I asked about hookers, he offered anything I liked. I told him white, slim, beautiful asses. That's what I first noticed about Carolyn. It's special for me. The little girl I did in New Brunswick, what was her name—Rachel—she was only nine years old, but she had an ass on her you wouldn't believe.

I showered and put on clean clothes. The owners don't really give you enough time for that sort of thing. A lot of the time I smell. A lot of times I've almost wet my pants because they didn't let me go when I needed to.

Once or twice I just couldn't help myself, held out as long as I could and, boy, you feel lousy when that happens. The worst was when I was covering some kind of a symposium in Russia, a place with a name like Akademgorodok. It was supposed to be on nuclear explosion processes. I don't know anything about that kind of stuff, and anyway I was a little mixed up because I thought that was one of the things the star people had done for us, worked out some way the different countries didn't have to have nuclear weapons and bombs and wars and so on any more. But that wasn't what they meant. It was explosions at the nucleus of the galaxy they meant. Astronomical stuff. Just when a fellow named Eysenck was talking about how the FG prominence and the EMK prominence, whatever they were, were really part of an expanding pulse sphere, whatever that is, I crapped my pants. I knew I was going to. I'd tried to tell the Groombridge people about it. They wouldn't listen. Then the session redactor came down the aisle and shouted in my ear, as though my owners were deaf or stupid, that they would have to get me out of there, please, for reasons concerning the comfort and hygiene of the other participants. I thought they would be angry, because that meant they were going to miss some of this conference that they were interested in. They didn't do anything to me, though. I mean, as if there was anything they *could* do to me that would be any worse, or any different, from what they do to me all the time, and always will.

When I was all clean and in an open-necked shirt and chinos I turned on the TV and poured a mild drink. I didn't want to be still drunk when my thousand minutes were up. There was a special program on all the networks, something celebrating a treaty between the United Nations and a couple of the star people, Sirians and Capellans it seemed to be. Everybody was very happy about it, because it seemed that now the Earth had bought some agricultural and chemical information, and pretty soon there would be more food than we could eat. How much

we owed to the star people, the Secretary General of the UN was saying, in Brazilian-accented English. We could look forward to their wise guidance to help Earth survive its multitudinous crises and problems, and we should all be very happy.

But I wasn't happy, not even with a glass of John Begg and the hooker on her way up, because what I really wanted was Carolyn.

Carolyn was a purchased person, like me. I had seen her a couple of dozen times, all in all. Not usually when either of us was on freedom. Almost never when both of us were. It was sort of like falling in love by postcard, except that now and then we were physically close, even touching. And once or twice we had been briefly not only together, but out from under control. We had had about eight minutes once in Bucharest, after coming back from the big hydropower plant at the Iron Gate. That was the record, so far. Outside of that it was just that we passed, able to see each other but not to do anything about it, in the course of our duties. Or that one of us was free and found the other. When that happened, the one of us that was free could talk, and even touch the other one, in any way that didn't interfere with what the other was doing. The one that was working couldn't do anything active, but could hear, or feel. We were both totally careful to avoid interfering with actual work. I don't know what would have happened if we had interfered. Maybe nothing? We didn't want to take that chance, though sometimes it was a temptation I could almost not resist. There was a time when I was free and I found Carolyn, working but not doing anything active, just standing there, at TWA Gate 51 at the St. Louis airport. She was waiting for someone to arrive. I really wanted to kiss her. I talked to her. I patted her, you know, holding my trenchcoat over my arm so that the people passing by wouldn't notice anything, or at least wouldn't notice anything much. I told her things I wanted her to hear. But what I wanted was to kiss her, and I was afraid to. Kissing her on the

mouth would have meant putting my head in front of her eyes. I didn't think I wanted to chance that. It might have meant she wouldn't see the person she was there to see. Who turned out to be a Ghanaian police officer arriving to discuss the sale of some political prisoners to the Groombridgians. I was there when he came down the ramp, but I couldn't stay to see if she would by any chance be free after completing the negotiations with him, because then my own time ran out.

But I had had three hours that time, being right near her. It felt very sad and very strange, and I wouldn't have given it up for anything in the world. I knew she could hear and feel everything, even if she couldn't respond. Even when the owners are running you, there's a little personal part of you that stays alive. I talked to that part of her. I told her how much I wished we could kiss, and go to bed, and be with each other. Oh, hell. I even told her I loved her and wanted to marry her, although we both know perfectly well there's not ever going to be any chance of that ever. We don't get pensioned off or retired; we're *owned*.

Anyway, I stayed there with her as long as I could. I paid for it later. Balls that felt as though I'd been stomped, the insides of my undershorts wet and chilly. And there wasn't any way in the world for me to do anything about it, not even by masturbating, until my next free time. That turned out to be three weeks later. In Switzerland, for God's sake. Out of season. With nobody in the hotel except the waiters and bellboys and a couple of old ladies who looked at the gold oval in my forehead as though it smelled bad.

It is a terrible but cherished thing to love without hope.

I pretended there was hope, always. Every bit of freedom I got, I tried to find her. They keep pretty careful tabs on us, all two or three hundred thousand of us purchased persons, working for whichever crazy bunch of creepy crawlers or gassy ghosts happens to have bought us to be their remote-access facilities on the planet they

themselves cannot ever visit. Carolyn and I were owned by the same bunch, which had its good side and its bad side. The good side was that there was a chance that some day we would be free for quite a long while at the same time. It happened. I don't know why. Shifts change on the Groombridge planet, or they have a holiday or something. But every once in a while there would be a whole day, maybe a week, when none of the Groombridge people would be doing anything at all, and all of us would be free at once.

The bad side was that they hardly ever needed to have more than one of us in one place. So Carolyn and I didn't run into each other a lot. And the times when I was free for a pretty good period, it took most of that to find her, and by the time I did she was like half a world away. No way of getting there and back in time for duty. I did so much want to fuck her, but we had never made it that far and maybe never would. I never even got a chance to ask her what she had been sentenced for in the first place. I really didn't know her at all, except enough to love her.

When the bellboy turned up with my girl, I was comfortably buzzed, with my feet up and the Rangers on the TV. She didn't look like a hooker, particularly. She was wearing hip-huggers cut below the navel, bigger breasted than I cared about but with that beautiful curve of waist and back into hips that I like. Her name was Nikki. The bellboy took my money, took five for himself, passed the rest to her, and disappeared, grinning. What's so funny about it? He knew what I was, because the plate in my head told him, but he had to think it was funny.

"Do you want me to take my clothes off?" She had a pretty, breathless little voice, long red hair, and a sweet, broad, friendly face. "Go ahead," I said. She slipped off the sandals. Her feet were clean, a little ridged where the straps went. Stepped out of the hip-huggers and folded them across the back of Conrad Hilton's standard armchair, took off the blouse and folded it, ducked out of the medallion and draped it over the blouse, down to red lace

bra and red bikini panties. Then she turned back the bed-
clothes, got in, sat up, snapped off the bra, snuggled down,
kicked the panties out of the side of the bed, and pulled
the covers over her. "Any time, honey," she said. But I
didn't lay her. I didn't even get in the bed with her, not
under the covers; I drank some more of the Scotch, and
that and fatigue put me out, and when I woke up it was
daylight, and she had cleaned out my wallet. Seventy-one
minutes left. I paid the bill with a check and persuaded
them to give me carfare in change. Then I headed back
for the kennel. All I got out of it was clean clothes and a
hangover. I think I had scared her a little. Everybody
knows how we purchased people came to be up for sale,
and maybe they're not all the way sure that we won't do
something bad again, because they don't know how reliably our owners keep us from ever doing anything they
don't like. But I wished she hadn't stolen my money.

The overall strategies and objectives of the star people,
particularly the people from the Groombridge star who
were his own masters, were unclear to the purchased
person named Wayne Golden. What they did was not hard
to understand. All the world knew that the star people
had established fast radio contact with the people of Earth,
and that in order to conduct their business on Earth they
had purchased the bodies of certain convicted criminals,
installing in them tachyon fast-radio transceivers. Why
they did what they did was less easy to comprehend. Art
objects they admired and purchased. Certain rare kinds
of plants and flowers they purchased and had frozen at
liquid-helium temperatures. Certain kinds of utilitarian
objects they purchased. Every few months another rocket
roared up from Merritt Island, just north of the Cape, and
another cargo headed for the Groombridge star, on its
twelve-thousand-year voyage. Others, to other stars, peo-
pled by other races in the galactic confraternity, took
shorter times—or longer—but none of the times was short
enough for those star people who made the purchases to

come to Earth to see what they had bought. The distances were too huge.

What they spent most of their money on was the rockets. And, of course, the people they purchased, into whom they had transplanted their tachyon transceivers. Each rocket cost at least $10 million. The going rate for a healthy male paranoid capable of three or more decades of useful work was in the hundreds of thousands of dollars, and they bought them by the dozen.

The other things they bought, all of them—the taped symphonies and early-dynasty *ushabti*, the flowering orchids, and the Van Goghs—cost only a fraction of one percent of what they spent on people and transportation. Of course, they had plenty of money to spend. Each star race sold off licensing rights on its own kinds of technology. All of them received trade credits from every government on Earth for their services in resolving disputes and preventing wars. Still, it seemed to Wayne Golden, to the extent that he was capable of judging the way his masters conducted their affairs, a pretty high-overhead way to run a business, although of course neither he nor any other purchased person was ever consulted on questions like that.

By late spring he had been on the move for many weeks without rest. He completed sixty-eight tasks, great and small. There was nothing in this period of eighty-seven days that was in any way remarkable except that on one day in May, while he was observing the riots on the Place de la Concorde from a window of the American Embassy on behalf of his masters, the girl named Carolyn came into his room. She whispered in his ear, attempted unsuccessfully to masturbate him while the liaison attaché was out of the room, remained in all for some forty minutes, and then left, sobbing softly. He could not even turn his head to see her go. Then on the sixth of June the purchased person named Wayne Golden was returned to the Dallas kennel and given indefinite furlough, subject to recall at fifty minutes notice.

* * *

Sweetest dear Jesus, nothing like that had ever happened to me before! It was like the warden coming into Death Row with a last minute reprieve! I could hardly believe it.

But I took it, started moving at once. I got a fix on Carolyn's last reported whereabouts from the locator board and floated away from Dallas in a cloud of Panama Red, drinking champagne as fast as the hostesses could bring it to me, en route to Colorado.

But I didn't find Carolyn there.

I hunted her through the streets of Denver, and she was gone. By phone I learned she had been sent to Rantoul, Illinois. I was off. I checked at the Kansas City airport, where I was changing planes, and she was gone from Illinois already. Probably but they weren't sure, they thought, to the New York district. I put down the phone and jumped on a plane, rented a car at Newark, and drove down the Turnpike to the Garden State, checking every car I passed to see if it was the red Volvo they thought she might be driving, stopping at every other Howard Johnson's to ask if they'd seen a girl with short black hair, brown eyes, and a tip-tilted nose and, oh, yes, the golden oval in her forehead.

I remembered it was in New Jersey that I first got into trouble. There was the nineteen-year-old movie cashier in Paramus, she was my first. I picked her up after the 1 A.M. show. And I showed her. But she was really all wrong for me, much too old and I much too worldly. I didn't like it much when she died.

After that I was scared for a while, and I watched the TV news every night, twice, at six and eleven, and never passed a newsstand without looking at all the headlines in the papers, until a couple of months had passed. Then I thought over what I really wanted very carefully. The girl had to be quite young and, well, you can't tell, but as much as I could be sure, a virgin.

I sat in a luncheonette in Perth Amboy for three whole days, watching the kids get out of the parochial school, before I found the second. It took a while. The first one that looked good turned out to be a bus kid, the second was a walker but her big sister from the high school walked with her. The third walked home alone. It was December, and the afternoons got pretty dark, and that Friday she walked but she didn't get home. I never molested any of them sexually, you know. I mean, in some ways I'm still kind of a virgin. That wasn't what I wanted, I just wanted to see them die. When they asked me at the pretrial hearing if I knew the difference between right and wrong, I didn't know how to answer them. I knew what I did was wrong for them. But it wasn't wrong for me, it was what I wanted.

So, driving down the Parkway, feeling discouraged about Carolyn, I noticed where I was and cut over to Route 35 and doubled back. I drove right to the school, past it, and to the lumberyard where I did the little girl. I stopped and cut the motor, looking around. Happy day. Now it was a different time of year, and things looked a little different. They'd piled up a stack of two-by-twelves over the place where I'd done her. But in my mind's eye I could see it the way it had been then. Dark gray sky. Lights from the cars going past. I could hear the little buzzing feeling in her throat as she tried to scream under my fingers. Let's see. That was, oh, good heavens, nine years ago.

And if I hadn't done her she would have been twenty or so. Screwing all the boys. Probably on dope. Maybe knocked up or married. Looked at in a certain way, I saved her a lot of sordid miserable stuff, menstruating, letting the boys' hands and mouths on her, all that...

My head began hurting. That's one thing the plate in your head does, it doesn't let you get very deeply into the things you did in the old days, because it hurts too much. So I started up the car and drove away, and pretty soon the hurting stopped.

I never think of Carolyn, you know, that way.

They never proved that little girl on me. The one they caught me for was the nurse in Long Branch, in the parking lot. And she was a mistake. She was so small, and she had a sweater over her uniform. I didn't know she was grown up until it was too late. I was very angry about that. In a way I didn't mind when they caught me, because I had been getting very careless. But I really hated that ward in Marlboro where they put me. Seven, Jesus, seven years. Up in the morning, and drink your pink medicine out of the little paper cup. Make your bed and do your job—mine was sweeping in the incontinent wards, and the smells and the sights would make you throw up.

After a while they let me watch TV and even read the papers, and when the Altair people made the first contact with Earth I was interested, and when they began buying criminally insane to be their proxies I wanted them to buy me. Anything, I wanted *anything* that would let me get out of that place, even if it meant I'd have to let them put a box in my head and never be able to live a normal life again.

But the Altair people wouldn't buy me. For some reason they only took blacks. Then the others began showing up on the fast radio, making their deals. And still none of them wanted me. The ones from Procyon liked young women, wouldn't ever buy a male. I think they have only one sex there, someone said. All these funnies are peculiar in one way or another. Metal, or gas, or blobby, or hard-shelled and rattly. Whatever. And they all have funny habits, like if you belong to the Canopus bunch you don't ever eat fish.

I think they're disgusting, and I don't really know why the USA wanted to get involved with them in the first place. But the Chinese did, and the Russians did, and I guess we just couldn't stay out. I suppose it hasn't hurt much. There hasn't been a war, and there's a lot of ways in which they've helped clean things up for us. It hasn't hurt me, that's for sure. The Groombridge people came

into the market pretty late, and most of the good healthy criminals were gone; they would buy anybody. They bought me. We're a hard-case lot, we Groombridgians, and I do wonder what Carolyn was in for.

I drove all the way down the coast. Asbury Park, Brielle, Atlantic City, all the way to Cape May, phoning back to check with the locator clerk, and never found her.

The one thing I did know was that all I was missing was the shell of her, because she was working. I could have had a kiss or a feel, no more. But I wanted to find her anyway. Just on the chance. How many times do you get an indefinite furlough? If I'd been able to find her, and stay with her, sooner or later, maybe, she would have been off too. Even if it were only for two hours. Even thirty minutes.

And then in broad daylight, just as I was checking into a motel near an Army base, with the soldiers' girls lined up at the cashier's window so their boy friends could get back for reveille, I got the call: Report to the Philadelphia kennel. Soonest.

By then I was giddy for sleep, but I drove that Hertz lump like a Maserati, because soonest means soonest. I dumped the car and signed in at the kennel, feeling my heart pounding and my mouth ragged from fatigue, and aching because I had blown what would have to be my best chance of really being with Carolyn. "What do they want?" I asked the locator clerk. "Go inside," he said, looking evilly amused. All locator clerks treat us the same, all over the world. "She'll tell you."

Not knowing who "she" was, I opened the door and walked through, and there was Carolyn.

"Hello, Wayne," she said.

"Hello, Carolyn," I said.

I really did not have any idea of what to do at all. She didn't give me a cue. She just sat. It was at that point that it occurred to me to wonder at the fact that she wasn't wearing much, just a shortie nightgown with nothing under it. She was also sitting on a turned-down bed. Now,

you would think that considering everything, especially the nature of most of my thinking about Carolyn, that I would have instantly accepted this as a personal gift from God to me of every boy's all-American dream. I didn't. It wasn't the fatigue, either. It was Carolyn. It was the expression on her face, which was neither inviting nor loving, was not even the judgment-reserving look of a girl at a singles bar. What it especially was not was happy.

"The thing is, Wayne," she said, "we're supposed to go to bed now. So take your clothes off, why don't you?"

Sometimes I can stand outside of myself and look at me and, even when it's something terrible or something sad, I can see it as funny; it was like that when I did the little girl in Edison Township, because her mother had sewed her into her school clothes. I was actually laughing when I said, "Carolyn, what's the matter?"

"Well," she said, "they want us to ball, Wayne. You know. The Groombridge people. They've got interested in what human beings do to each other, and they want to kind of watch."

I started to ask why us, but I didn't have to; I could see where Carolyn and I had had a lot of that on our minds, and maybe our masters could get curious about it. I didn't exactly like it. Not exactly; in fact in a way I kind of hated it, but it was so much better than nothing at all that I said, "Why, honey, that's great!"—almost meaning it; trying to talk her into it; moving in next to her and putting my arm around her. And then she said:

"Only we have to wait, Wayne. *They* want to do it. Not us."

"What do you mean, wait? Wait for what?" She shrugged under my arm. "You mean," I said, "that we have to be plugged in to them? Like they'll be doing it with our bodies?"

She leaned against me. "That's what they told me, Wayne. Any minute now, I guess."

I pushed her away. "Honey," I said, half crying, "all this time I've been wanting to—Jesus, Carolyn! I mean,

it isn't just that I wanted to go to bed with you. I mean—"

"I'm sorry," she cried, big tears on her face.

"That's lousy!" I shouted. My head was pounding, I was so furious. "It isn't fair! I'm not going to stand for it. They don't have any *right*!"

But they did, of course, they had all the right in the world; they had bought us and paid for us, and so they owned us. I knew that. I just didn't want to accept it, even by admitting what I knew was so. The notion of screwing Carolyn flipped polarity; it wasn't what I desperately wanted, it was what I would have died to avoid, as long as it meant letting *them* paw her with my hands, kiss her with my mouth, flood her with my juices; it was like the worst kind of rape, worse than anything I had ever done, both of us raped at once. And then—

And then I felt that burning tingle in my forehead as they took over. I couldn't even scream. I just had to sit there inside my own head, no longer owning a muscle, while those freaks who owned me did to Carolyn with my body all manner of things, and I could not even cry.

After concluding the planned series of experimental procedures, which were duly recorded, the purchased person known as Carolyn Schoerner was no longer salvageable. Appropriate entries were made. The Probation and Out-Service department of the Meadville Women's Reformatory was notified that she had ceased to be alive. A purchasing requisition was initiated for a replacement, and her account was terminated.

The purchased person known as Wayne Golden was assigned to usual duties, at which he functioned normally while under control. It was discovered that when control was withdrawn he became destructive, both to others and to himself. The conjecture has been advanced that that sexual behavior which had been established as his norm— the destruction of the sexual partner—may not have been appropriate in the conditions obtaining at the time of the

experimental procedures. Further experiments will be
made with differing procedures and other partners in the
near future. Meanwhile Wayne Golden continues to function at normal efficiency, provided control is not withdrawn at any time, and apparently will do so indefinitely.

experimental procedures. Further experiments will be
made with differing procedures and other partners in the
near future. Meanwhile Wayne Golded continues to give
musical performances without, of
course, any apparat..

REM THE REMEMBERER

I don't much like writing "'special occasion" stories for
particular purposes. To be saddled with somebody else's
theme or settings comports very poorly with the undis-
ciplined and stochastic way I think I am best able to
write; so it's hard work. If editors as a race had group
awareness, they wouldn't ask me, either, because all
too often I have dutifully done what some editor asked
me to do, only to find about the time I finished the story
that some higher-up had canceled the special issue or
the magazine or project itself; "Kiss of Death Fred" one
editor called me, and she was at least in this respect
right. This story is one such. It represents one of my
very few involvements with the United Nations, specifically with UNICEF. I got a call from a man who said
that UNICEF had decided to publish a book of what
the children of the next generation would make of their
world, in all the parts of the world the United Nations
covered, and would I care to write one for the United
States? I could not say no. With all its nasty and con-
spicuous faults, the United Nations has greatly bettered

the world we live in; and of all the things it does, UN-
ICEF is the most clearly, unequivocally good. So I wrote
this story . . . and hardly had I finished it when the word
came that high-level consultations had voted to torpedo
the whole plan, and the book would never appear.

SOMETIMES WHEN REM WOKE UP IN THE MORNING HE
was crying. Not for long. Just for a minute, out of a dream
he didn't like. When his mother, Peg, heard him, she came
into his small, cheerful room and stood in the doorway,
smiling at him until she was sure he was altogether awake.
She worried about him. He was ten years old, and she
thought he was too old for that. She gave him his breakfast
and sent him off to school on his bicycle. By then he was
cheerful again.

In the afternoons he helped the grownups. When Peg
was housecleaning, Rem mopped and brushed and helped
prepare the food. When Burt, his father, was working at
home on his analyses (Burt was something like a public
accountant, in charge of the Southern New York Regional
energy budgets), Rem checked his figures on a pocket
calculator. On Tuesdays and Fridays he went out in cat-
amarans with his Uncle Marc to help harvest mussels from
the Long Island Sound Nurseries. The mussels grew on
long, knotted manila lines that hung from floats. Each day
hundreds of cords had to be pulled up, and stripped of
the grown mussels, and reseeded with tiny mussel larvae,
and put back in the water. It was hard work. Rem was
too small to handle pulling up the ropes, but he could strip
and reseed, and pick up the mussels that fell in the bottom
of the boat so the men wouldn't crush them with their
feet, and generally be useful. It was tiring. But it felt good
to be tired after three hours in the catamaran, and the
water was always warm, even when the air coming down
off Connecticut was blustery and cold. In all but the worst
weather Marc would wink and nod toward the side, and

Rem would skin out of his outer clothes and dive overboard and swim down among the dangling cords, looking to see how the mussels were growing. Sometimes he took an air-pack and his uncle or one of the other men came with him, and together they would go clear down to the bottom to look for stray oysters or crabs or even lobsters that had escaped from the pens out around Block Island.

Then he would go home and meet his father, bicycling back from the Sands Point railroad station. If the weather was nice they'd dig in the garden or toss a ball around. Then they would have dinner—wherever they were having dinner that night; they rotated around from home to home most nights of the week so that each family had the job of cooking and cleaning up only two or three times a week. One of the grownups usually helped the children with their homework after dinner. Rem liked it when it was his father's turn, particularly when the homework assignment was about ecology. He was always popping up with questions. "Don't hog the floor, son," his father would say. "Give the others a chance."

"It's always the same dumb questions, too," his cousin, Grace, complained. She was eight, still pretty much a brat. "'Why don't we get sick from eating sewage?' What a dumb question!"

His father laughed. "Well, it's not all that dumb. The thing is, we don't eat sewage. We just use it to grow things. All the New York City sewage goes into the settling ponds and then the algae tanks. Who knows what algae is?"

Rem knew the answer, of course, but he was polite enough to let one of the younger ones answer. Even Grace. "What they make bread out of," she said.

"That's one thing algae is used for, yes. But most of the algae is piped into Long Island Sound. The mussels live on it. So do the fish, but the mussels are the big crop. We grow three-quarters of the protein for the whole United States here, just on that algae. And, of course, on the waste heat from the power generators around Hell Gate.

That warms up the Sound so the mussels grow all year round."

"And so do the potatoes," Grace crowed.

Rem's father said, "Yes, they do. That's a little different, though. They take the sludge from the algae tanks and spread it over the fields along the Island. Did you know they used to be covered with houses? Well, we got rid of the houses, and we began growing the best potatoes in the world there, again. But we use some of the warm water piped underground to keep the soil warm, and we get two crops a year."

Then Rem asked another question, always the same one or one like it: "But," he persisted, "aren't those bad things, sewage and sludge and all?"

"People used to think so. Then we learned that some bad things are actually good things, in the wrong place."

"*How* did we learn?"

His father looked at his watch. "That happened almost a hundred years ago. The people who lived then made some very good decisions."

Grace said indignantly, "They did *bad* things."

"In a way, but then they did better ones. We all know about the bad things. They drove around in cars that burned gasoline! They dumped sewage in the ocean, and ruined it for fifty years all up and down the coast. They used radioactive materials that poisoned places forever, just because they wanted more and more electric thises and automatic thats. But then they realized they were being too greedy. They learned—what did they learn?"

All the kids chanted, "Use it over! Put it back!"

"That's right. They learned not to waste things, and that decision made all the difference in the world. They decided not to be greedy. And now," he said, looking at his watch again, "it's time for everybody under the age of thirty-two to go to bed." He looked around the room with a surprised expression. "Why, that's all of you! Good night."

And Rem went back to his own room and to bed.

He didn't mind going to sleep. After all, he was pleasantly tired. He did mind the dreams. He remembered them clearly; and they were always the same, and always so real, not as though he were falling asleep but as though he were waking...

He woke up happy, with the vanishing clouds of a happy dream in his mind. Then the rattle and rasp of the air conditioner in his room chased the last of the dream away. By the time he got up and turned his little light on—he always needed one, even in the summer, because the skies were almost always dingy dark—he could remember the dream, but he couldn't feel it anymore.

His mother, Peg, worried about the way he always seemed to dream the same wishful dream, but when Rem realized that, he just stopped telling her about it. He did ask her if he could please leave the air conditioner off, at least in the winter, so that he could wake up more slowly and enjoy the dream more. "I wish you could, honey," she said, "but you know Dr. Dallinger said you had to have something filter the air, because of your asthma. I'm sorry about the noise. Maybe we can get you a new one— Although I don't know how, with the payments on the cars and the way heat's going up. And you wouldn't believe what I spent in the supermarket yesterday, just for three little bags of groceries." Then she laughed and hugged him and said, "A noisy air conditioner isn't so bad! What if you had to live in New York City?"

She was the one who drove him in to school every day. His father had to leave an hour earlier because of the traffic. School wasn't bad. Rem liked to learn, and he liked being with the other children. He even liked recess, at least in the winter, when the storm winds from Canada blew some of the sulfur-smelling smog away and the reek from the slow, iridescent waves of Long Island Sound was not so strong. He didn't mind the cold. He did mind being kept inside so much of the time, when the air index was "Unsatisfactory" or "Dangerous to Health" or even,

which had happened two or three times the previous summer, "Condition Red! No burning! No driving!" On days like that everybody was stuck wherever he happened to be. Everything stopped. Rem and his mother would take turns in the shower and then sit, playing cards, or talking, or just resting, waiting for the time to pass. If his father was lucky, he would be doing the same thing in his office in the city. If he wasn't, he might be caught in the long unmoving snarl of cars on the freeways, waiting for permission to start again. That was how Rem's uncle Marc had died, two years before, when he had another heart attack sitting at the wheel and got out of the car for help, and died there.

But then after a while the rain would come. It was worse than the dry heat at first, because the drops would come down as sticky black blobs that stained all the houses, dirtied the windows, and killed the grass, where there was any grass. But after a while there might be a real storm, with luck even a hurricane, and then for a few days Long Island might look queerly green and fresh for a while.

What Rem liked best was the one or two evenings a week when his father got home before his bedtime. They would talk about grown-up things.

Rem's father, Burt, was very proud of him. He told his wife, "Rem's really interested in things—important things; I think he's going to be somebody the world will be glad to have when he grows up." One of the "important things" was why the Sound was dead and unhealthy. Another was why everybody drove their own cars instead of riding trains or buses, or even working near where they lived. His father tried to answer them as well as he could. "Well, son," he said, "people *like* having their own cars. You'll see, when you grow up and get your own license. When you get behind the wheel, you're on your own. You can shut out all the unpleasant things—"

"What things, Dad?"

Burt looked suddenly remorseful. "Oh, not things like *here*, Rem! You and your mother—well, I wouldn't change

places with anybody in the world. But there are a lot of problems." Burt was a tax accountant for the New York State government. He shook his head. "We need so much," he said, "and it's hard to know where the money's going to come from. Let's see, what was the other question? Oh, about waste heat and sewage. Well, that's one of the problems, Rem. There's so much pollution, and it costs too much to get rid of it. I suppose that, of course, you could theoretically use the heat from the factories and power plants and so on to heat homes or even to warm up some sort of farms—they'd have to be greenhouses, actually—so you could grow more things. But the capital cost, Rem, would be immense." He hesitated, trying to find the words to explain economics to a ten-year-old. "We just don't have the money. Maybe if we'd started a long time ago— But we didn't. You can't drive cars without freeways to drive them on, do you see? I guess the government could have built piping systems and recirculation plants, but then where would the money have come from for the highways? We did the best we could. I think. We used up all the low-sulfur fuels first, and we kept on dumping sewage until it was too late to stop. And it got harder and harder to make the fertilizer to grow the food. I suppose," he said thoughtfully, "that if some people had made different decisions a century or so ago, the world would be quite a different place. Some ways, it would be pretty nice. But they didn't. And it's too late now." He smiled and squeezed Rem's shoulder. "Speaking of being late, it's about time for you to be off to bed."

So Rem would take his pills and drink his glass of soymilk and go off to sleep. He wasn't unhappy about that. He remembered the dream, and knew he would dream it again, and that was something to look forward to. It was so very pleasant, and so very real; he wasn't always sure which was the reality and which was the dream.

THE MOTHER TRIP

of friendships I still treasure ... and, later on, filling up
my daily pages in my office, this story

THE MOTHER TRIP

Putting this collection together has made me realize
that nearly every story in it was written, at least in
part, in some corner of the world far from my desk
and typewriter. That's not too surprising in some ways,
because I have this habit of doing at least four pages
worth of writing wherever I happen to be, every day,
and I do a lot of traveling. It is often easier to work
on a short story than a novel under such circumstances, if only because when you pack a couple of
novel manuscripts into a suitcase you don't have much
room left for clean socks. This one, however, was
written right at home. It's true that part of its setting
comes from a marvelous trip over the Cascade Mountains and much of its incident from a strange weekend
I spent with an encounter group in New Jersey, having
my sensitivities elevated and my inhibitions soaked
away in the blood-temperature pool. It was an un-
settling sort of experience, a dozen total strangers
opening to each other, but one I am glad I did
not miss. Among other things it brought me a couple

of friendships I still treasure ... and, later on, filling up
my daily pages in my office, this story.

IT COULD HAVE BEEN THIS WAY: THAT THE GET OF
Moolkri Mawkri could have landed in a faster-than-light
spaceship resembling an artichoke on the outskirts of
Jackson, Mississippi.

In this version Mawkri gathers her Get-cluster around
her broodingly, while Moolkri assumes the shape of a
man. The Get has studied all of the Earth's TV programs
while they were in orbit, and they have picked an average
person for Moolkri to be, not too tall, not too symmetrical,
not too *dyezhnizt* (a term in their language which relates
to the proportion between upper and middle circumfer-
ences). The Get is satisfied with Moolkri's appearance,
but all the same it is pretty funny-looking. They laugh as
he exits the spacecraft to explore.

Moolkri has well assimilated TV lore, and so he knows
how to behave in a way appropriate to his body. He hooks
his "thumbs" in his "belt," crosses a deserted bridge, and
strides swaggeringly down the light-saturated and totally
uninhabited street.

It does not seem unusual to Moolkri that there should
be no one gazing into the bright shop windows. He does not
have a very good grasp of what is usual or unusual for human beings. It is late at night, and so a human being (or at
least one from another city than Jackson) might find it
strange that everything was so brightly lit. Contrariwise, a
human might consider it odd that with every amenity turned
on for shoppers, there was not a single strolling person to
be seen. Moolkri does not realize this is strange. He is aware
that sometimes streets are deserted and sometimes not; he
is also aware that sometimes they are bright and sometimes
dark; he is simply not aware that deserted is not really compatible with well-lit, but then there is a lot he is not aware
of about the Earth.

So Moolkri swings, gunman wide, his "chaps" rustling
against each other and his "bandanna" bright against his

"neck." He slouches past the People's Cut Rate Pharmacy and Bette's New York Boutique and the Yazoo-Jackson Consolidated All-Faith Ashram, looking in the windows. He reads a typed notice about a lost Australian terrier. He inspects a naked black dummy with no hands, waiting for the window dresser to return in the morning and give her hands and ball gown. It is all interesting to him, and back in the spaceship Mawkri and her Get chatter excitedly among themselves, forgetting to be afraid as they receive his impressions.

It is not only his sense of vision that is active, it is also his sense of hearing, although that input does not produce much he considers worth noting. There are no voices, no footsteps. Overhead there is the sound of a motor, which he identifies easily enough as a helicopter. It is too far away for him to care much. He does not realize that it is quartering the city, alert for the sight of stray humans on the broad, bright street. He does not hear the radio message that the helicopter pilot transmits to the ground. Back in the spaceship the rest of the Get could have heard it, did in fact register the radio signal as an artifact originating nearby, but they did not associate the message with Moolkri.

Then the black-and-white slides silently around the corner. There is only one policeman in it. They are not expecting riots of mad killers, only the odd break-and-grab hoodlum or the hopeful would-be mugger. Moolkri hears the prowl car. First he hears the faint purr of the motor and whisper of tires, then, only in the last moment before it skids to a stop beside him, the quick bleat of its siren. He turns to look. The young cop leaps out. "Hands against the wall! Spread your feet! Hold it right there!" He does not say it like that precisely, there is brushwood and bayou in his accent, but Moolkri is not attuned to regional distinctions of dialect. Moolkri submits. It is unfortunate, but it is all right. He has been ready to submit to human violence, in case it should develop, ever since he accepted the assignment to explore. Now it appears that he will not return to the Get, but he does not mind that. The Get

will continue. He does not feel as though he were in danger. He only feels rage, and his rage races decisively, by means of his fourth and seventh senses, across the world and into the heavens.

In the spacecraft Mawkri mourns. The Get moves fearfully around her. She had wished to extend her motherhood to this planet, but it had rejected her. It was unfortunate since, among other things, it meant the end of sexual intercourse for her for the rest of her life, but she does not protest, only regrets.

Moolkri opens all the tactile inputs he has bothered to connect in order to perceive the policeman fully. He observes stimuli identified as pain, heat, body disorientation, and sex climax denied as the policeman's hand invades his body spaces. (There turns out to be nothing in the "pockets," nothing at all, Moolkri had never realized anything should be put there.)

Out of curiosity (he is overdeveloped in curiosity, that is why he is here), Moolkri increases his audio perception and, translating easily from the peckerwood English, hears the policeman radio in to see if there is a want on an unidentified white male pedestrian wearing a cowboy suit, about fifty, five feet seven, white beard, bald, blue eyes, no visible scars.

Listening in this way is only curiosity on Moolkri's part. It can no longer affect the outcome, since violence has already been done to him. He waits patiently, not very long. He hears headquarters report that there is no want on the described individual. The policeman tells Moolkri he can go. Moolkri adds to his file the datum that the violence has been withdrawn, but only out of neatness. The file is now complete. No more will be added.

The policeman cautions him against walking alone in the city at night, mentioning the risk of being robbed or harmed. He advises Moolkri to carry identification at all times. He gets back into his car, hesitates, then says, with half a smile and a cursory salute, "Y'all enjoy your stay in Jackson now, hear?"

But it is too late.

The automatic orbiting guardians have already reacted to Moolkri's broadcast danger of violence, as they were programmed to do. The spacecraft with Mawkri and the Get lifts and flees screaming into the sky. And the first planet busters begin to drop.

Fusion infernos blossom and burst. Cities slide into the already boiling sea. Mawkri's motherhood has punished the offense.

It is the end of the world of human beings, except as a blob of molten rock, and that is one way it could have been.

Or it could have been like this, that all of Moolkri Mawkri's Get remained in orbit, thundering down motherly orders to be obeyed:

Under pain of destruction!

Humans are commanded!

Alternative is the planet busters, and the end of your world!

In this version the Get prudently refrained from landing but after careful study of all radio and television transmissions elected to play a mother's arduous role from out in space. So they made a plan and ordered the world to carry it out. Six representatives of humankind were to present themselves, unarmed and tractable, in orbit: one each from China, the United States, Sweden, Rhodesia, Brazil, and the U.S.S.R.

The Get, here, too, had carefully studied all the EMF transmissions from Tokyo Tower and London's GPO and the American networks. The Get thought that most of them were very funny. Nevertheless they decoded them into aural and visual signals and analyzed them for meaning and implications.

Both Moolkri and Mawkri agreed that this complicatedly comic planet needed to be taken into the motherhood of Mawkri, and in this version they studied the means of manipulation nations and persons used upon each other. They were aware of the human custom of giving each other ultimatums: thus the commands from space. They

were not as aware of certain other human habits. They were taken quite by surprise when, united in a common purpose at last, all six of the nations that had a nuclear missile capability conferred through their secret hot lines, set a time, and fired simultaneously upon the orbiting spaceship of Moolkri Mawkri and the Get.

Of the resulting swarm of missiles it happened to be a cold-launched American Minuteman III that destroyed the ship, the Get, Moolkri, and Mawkri herself, and ended the first contact between their people and ours.

There is, however, a warmer and more loving version. In this version Moolkri spoke up:

"I do not think we can trust ourselves to these creatures," he said. "Neither do I think we should reveal ourselves to them, either for communication or to impose our helpful will on them. Let's cool it while we figure things out."

There was some resistance to this, particularly from a forensicist and a KP pusher in the Get. That was right and proper. It was their function to do that. The forensicist was charged with debating all devil's-advocate positions that no one really cared to espouse, and she was very good at it. The KP pusher (who was not really called that, but none of their words are much like ours) was detailed to making things happen. He *always* urged action, so that nothing desirable would fail to be done simply because no one bothered to make it occur. Nevertheless, in this version Moolkri prevailed upon the rest of the Get to lie low in orbit, and so they did while drones and far-watchers made a saturation study of one small area of the planet. It was near Arcata, California.

Moolkri became aware, in this version, as he had never otherwise been made aware during his sheltered life in the Get cluster, that the universe was a diversity of things. Oh, they had seen other races. They had been journeying for many subjective years, while the Get spawned and grew and matured; they were near the end of their journey now,

near the time when the Get would have to return to their home to disperse and mate. But these bipeds were unusual. Some of them were hairy, some were bald. Skeletally they were quite the same (bar the occasional malfunction or amputee), but in size and in weight they differed. Their fragrances, the drones reported, came in a wide variety of osmic frequencies, most of them not very nice.

It was in behavior, however, that the bipeds exhibited the most amazing diversity. It was not only that one biped differed from another. The same biped might behave in differing ways at differing times! They found and labeled one who was clearly a KP pusher; an hour later she was an empathizer!

Semantic analysis of their communications to each other was equally confusing. Some of the bipeds were aggressively mission-oriented within themselves:

"I'm a *woman*, not a *doll*." (Throwing a wastepaper basket at the male lying in the bed.) "I've got twenty-two years of *rage* inside me because of this mother trip you lay on me!" (Slamming a door.)

Moolkri played that tape five times to make sure he had understood it, marveling, for only a few minutes before it had seemed this pair were preparing to procreate.

Some of the bipeds were role playing; that is, their mission was assigned from context:

"Now, gentlemen, please!" (Big expression of the lips and corners of the eyes called "smile.") "*You* know that under the American system my client is entitled to the presumption of innocence." (Eyes turned directly into a television camera.) "You gentlemen can try this case in your newspapers all you like—and I'm not saying you shouldn't; you have a right to freedom of expression; and I approve that right!—but the State of California will decide my client's guilt or innocence, not you." (Decisive up and down movement of the chin and head.)

None of the Get understood any of this, and they stirred and muttered in their cluster. The forensicist proposed immediate annihilation of the planet. No one agreed, but still— But still, how could such persons live?

Among Moolkri Mawkri's people, person could not be separated from mission. They were the same thing. What a person was was what he did. It was the foreseen need for mission operators that determined how a person was nurtured; it was the nature of their aptitudes that decided which was chosen for what purpose. There was no such thing as a split personality in the Get. There was no one who was unhappy with his life. Moolkri could not play a role. He was always typecast. He could never attempt to change his image. He *was* his image.

The Get of Moolkri Mawkri came from a planet of the star Procyon, blue-white and burning. It was a deadly dangerous star, and it was only the dense, damp clouds in their atmosphere that kept the radiation from cremating every one of them at birth. Humans, of course, were physically repulsive to them. Humans did not have armored claws or vibrissae. Humans had only twelve senses, not nineteen, and two of the senses they did have ("pain" and "heat") seemed ridiculously unimportant to the Get. The Get clustered together, interlocking mouthhooks touching spiracles, and murmured to each other reassuringly and lovingly. (They didn't know it was lovingly; they had no way to relate to each other that was anything but loving.) They shuddered in apprehension at the physical qualities of humans. Humans seemed so *deformed*.

Of course, even the Get sometimes fell short of physical perfection. Moolkri himself had a birth defect that damaged his second instar. Their wisest evaluator lacked a limb, and so he would never be a breeder. (Therefore, he would never want to.) But all of the Get had the power to change their shape when they wanted to. Humans did not seem to have that power. They were condemned to inhabit forever the bodies they were born to, except for such rude mechanical devices as they used to replace teeth or assist sight or the daubs of paint and odor-producing substances that some humans employed to enhance their natural appearance. This seemed a terrible punishment to the Get.

But they tried not to judge. They had seen other races

and, compared to them, none seemed particularly attractive, and most were awful.

East of Arcata the road leaps rivers, looping through the foothills. There stands a long, low clapboard building with some of the windows replaced with plywood. It is more than a hundred years old. It wears its history in every scar. All day the logging trucks thunder down past it out of the Klamath Mountains, continuing their long-term systematic eradication of the redwood forests. Three of them have gone out of control and plunged through one corner of the building or another in the past thirty years.

No one wants to live in this house; it is like living next to the number one pin in a bowling alley. The porch stops short at the northwest corner. An eight-hundred-horsepower diesel tractor carried that piece of it away in 1968. The nine-foot log it was towing minced the driver's head; you can still see stains on the clapboard. The sign in front of the house now says:

> Klamath Valley Center
> for Development of
> Human Potential

One of Moolkri's drones had buzzed all around it for more than seven days, cataloguing the human creatures as well as the other fauna of the area (dragonflies, moths, rabbits, twenty-three kinds of birds, forty reptiles and amphibia, microorganisms past counting). There were sixteen of the humans, and they were playing a game.

The Get understood games. They enjoyed play. They even understood consciousness-raising games; those were the only games they ever played, except for athletic ones like vibrissa trilling and obstacle scuttling. They discovered the name of the human game was "Primal Weekend," which meant nothing to them, but watching the game itself

was a grand spectator sport. The cluster squirmed itself into such position that all several score of them could see clearly into one monitor or another. They studied the pictures the drone was transmitting with, for the first time since they had approached this messy little G-type star, a certain empathy and joy.

Some of the aspects of the game were peculiarly ludicrous to them. Not threatening. Just funny, and they laughed and laughed, in their way. (They did not know that some of the aspects would have been ludicrous to most humans, too . . . not necessarily the same aspects.) For instance, there was a game in which fifteen of the players locked arms and braced hips in a tight ring, while the sixteenth, sobbing and fighting, struggled to get into the group. How funny they thought the notion that any group might try to keep a member out! Another game involved a forty-one-year-old male player who rinsed out a pair of his underdrawers in a bucket while all the others squatted in a circle around him, calling out words of encouragement and love. (He had soiled himself in a passion of weeping and writhing a few minutes before.) The symbolism of this game was perfectly apparent to the Get, and they responded not with laughter but with understanding and joy.

But other games troubled the Get immensely.

The weekenders played the game called Psychodrama a lot. In one of the episodes two humans squatted facing each other, again in the circle of the ring. "I'm your wife," said one cheerfully. "I castrate you." Her voice grew more threatening. "You're not a real man!" She spat the words. "If you were half a man you'd beat me black and blue!"

"I want to, I want to," sobbed the male player. "I can't, I can't."

"Then I'm going to leave you," shrilled the female one, and, "You mustn't, you mustn't," wept the male.

The Get revolved uneasily, changing grips and communicating fearfully. They could not take their eyes off the monitors. They felt ill and damaged, in ways they had never felt before. They listened with sick fascination to

the translations of the audio track: "Kill her, Ben!" shouted the players in the ring. "Walk out on her! Kick her ass off! Hey, Ben, slap her with the plastic bat!"

Walk out on her?

The Get shivered. They could find no empathy whatever in the situation. Even their empathizers merely shook in fear. A mated couple planning to *split*? How could that *be*?

Among Moolkri and Mawkri's people, you see, such a thing is impossible. It is not statute or custom. It is natural law. When a seed planter like Moolkri intromits an egg ripener like Mawkri, the fertilization takes the form of a sort of allergic reaction. The Get that result are, in a sense, only hives.

Intromission plays more than a merely reproductive function with them, as screwing does with us. But the biology of it is ironclad. At first sexual encounter each partner builds up specific antigens. They cannot produce offspring without them. They can never have sexual intercourse with any other. The antigens produced from any other mating, or from intercourse with an unmated person, would kill them immediately in great, bloated, pustulant pain.

There is therefore no question of sexual morality among the Get or their planet-gotten. It is a boy-meets-girl world, a Cinderella planet on which when the prince discovers that She Is The One, they do indeed live happily together ever after, or else they do not live happily (or at all). They do not have the option of promiscuity. They have only one source of sexual pleasure. One partner for life.

And of course they only produce a Get once—subsequent intromissions are sterile, though a lot of fun—but as there are up to five hundred individuals in each get (more than half dying in the first half hour), the race goes on and grows.

So the Get were shocked and terrified, and some of them even made physically ill, by this inexplicable vice their specimens displayed. Their medical members were kept furiously busy, scuttling around the cluster to tend

the damaged ones, when they were not too damaged to function themselves.

Moolkri and Mawkri's people are no better than human beings. Their first reaction was total revulsion and a wish to destroy, like the stamp of a four-year-old foot on a spider. Their collective claws were trembling near the clasps for the planet busters, when one of the smallest of the Get, and usually one of the quietest, piped up, sobbing:

"But they can't help it."

Through a warped window both sides look strange to each other. Humans looked strange to Moolkri Mawkri's Get. Now consider how strange the Get look to us:

"They can't help it" is a concept none of them had ever heard before.

They chattered wonderingly for a while, and as they talked, the claws withdrew from the buster clasps. *They can't help it.* It was so strange a thought that it seemed to excuse almost any perversion, even promiscuity. And then an observer, restlessly examining the environment, cried, "Look what they're doing!" And they all quieted and stared at the monitors, still faithfully conveying what was happening at the Klamath Valley Center for the Development of Human Potential, and there they found an empathy they had not expected.

One corner of the building was an add-on shed of tarpaper and sheet metal, extending over a concrete pool.

A century and more before, some hungry and hopeful men had channeled a creek into a sluice in order to pick flakes of gold out of the water. They hadn't found much, but they had kept trying, relays of them for a couple of decades, and each one had deepened and widened the channel and the pool.

Now the gold was all gone, geologists having tracked the stream to its source and ripped out the auriferous rock that had given its flakes to the stream, but the pool was still there. The Center had cemented its bottom and covered its top and put in a heater. Now it was kept at hot blood temper-

ature (the Get liked that, it reminded them of home), and in it all sixteen of the humans (their coverings gone, only their hides still enclosing them) were knotted and seething together in the amniotic waters (the Get liked that too, it reminded them of their own cluster). The name of the game the people played in the water was Float. Naked and touching, they formed a chain. "Pass 'er down," cried the ones at the lower end, and at the top two humans picked up a third and slid her passively, relaxedly, half floating and half supported, touched and soothed and caressed, from hand to hand through the warm pool.

The Get chittered among themselves. It was almost like a Get cluster, the touching and the support. It was almost inviting enough to join; and perhaps it was not the fault of the humans that they did not have mouthhooks or spiracles so that they could join together properly.

"They can't be all bad," mused the little Get-sibling aloud. And he spoke for all of them.

"I think," said Moolkri, reaching over to glance at Mawkri for concurrence, "that we should study these people more. I do not know what to do," he added.

"We cannot stay very long," warned a rememberer. They all knew it was true. They had been a long time traveling. The Get was ripening, it was time to return home and seek partners.

And still they could not leave yet, they had to learn more. The drones were busy, busy, and the far-watchers turned their electronic sensors onto the world of human society (Washington, Moscow, Peking) and human science (Arecibo, Tyuratam-baikonur, and the Moon) and human relations (bedroom, bathroom, bus). Many things happened while they watched. A war broke out. It was in a part of the planet that none of the Get would really have thought worth fighting over, except that it held some large reserves of liquid hydrocarbon. ("But so easy to carry it somewhere else," marveled a commenter.) Nevertheless tens of thousands of humans died. Millions were hurt, or frightened, or impaired in some way. This part of the event amused the Get. It was

so *silly*. ("But I wonder if *they* think it's funny," queried the little one, laughing.) Drought and famine struck large patches of three continents. The Get observed this mass death with curiosity, but their emotions were not involved. After all, they were used to half their siblings dying before the rest of any get were old enough to preen themselves.

And then they turned off the far-watchers and recalled the drones, and they clustered and thought before they spoke.

"Human beings," said the Get member in charge of summarizing, "are clearly self-destructive. It is what their 'psychology' calls a 'death wish.' Unchecked, they will wipe themselves out."

"Talk sense," begged the little sibling. (Moolkri gave him a playful, partly disciplinary bite.) "No, I mean it," the little one went on. "They *act* as if they're going to destroy themselves. But, you know? They never have."

A judger responded: "That is true." A theorizer added, "What is causality for us may not be for them."

This concept caused consternation among the Get, but it seemed to fit the facts. "What then shall we do?" asked Moolkri. "We don't have very much time. Mawkri has stopped accepting intromission. She is near the time of her death, and I cannot be far."

"We'll miss you," said several of the Get together, sorrowful not for their parents but for themselves. "Let us then decide."

A proposer stated: "We have several choices. We can exterminate them." Instant contractile movements from all, signifying no. "We can help them to be more like us—but how? I have no proposal for this." Quivering movements from the cluster, signifying inability to respond, a request to go on. "Or," he said, "we can leave them alone."

"Stale, stale," murmured the Get. But the judger piped up:

"I think not. Let us hear more."

"We can go away without any further intervention at

all," went on the proposer. "We can leave one of our drones in orbit, programmed for Home. Then if one of their craft should someday find it, and if they wish, they can come to us. If not—not."

Mawkri cried feebly: "But a mother must care for all!"

"Mawkri," said the proposer, trembling, "your care has given us life. But the humans are not like us. They must make their mistakes if they will. It is how they learn."

And the judger confirmed wonderingly, "It is how they learn. We can do nothing to help. We can only wish them well . . . and wait."

And so the ship shaped like an artichoke turned on its axis, swallowed all its satellites but one, and retreated toward the constellation Canis Minor. And not an eye, not an interferometer, not a Schmidt ever saw it go.

There is still another version, in which Moolkri Mawkri's Get never reach Earth at all. In fact, they never leave their home planet. None of their people do. All the proliferating gets stay locked and squirming in their dense, damp viny nests until they ripen and seek partners. Technology? Yes, they build technology. They learn the workings of their own cellular biology and the devising of medicines. They learn to keep alive that half of every get which would otherwise die. They learn to tame the tangle vines, and finally to live without them, for there is then not enough space on their world for any kind of life at all, except their own. They learn to tunnel the planet's crust for living space and to harness the scattered heat of Procyon to drive engines to make new nests. They devise a sort of plastic—made from their excrement, their bodies once they have died, and the simple elements of the rocks—and they create new living spaces from it. They never reach out into space. They never taste the stars. They never got to Earth. They live forever (or until this version runs out of program) locked into their one small world; and nothing that happens anywhere else has anything to do with them. They do not kill, or spare, or help, or trust. And they do not receive any of those things from others.

But what is the use of a life that never reaches out to touch another? Never to hurt or help? Never to feel or even to see? No, it is not a very interesting version. We never play that one anymore.

A Day in the Life of Able Charlie

Like "Rem the Rememberer" (and also like "The Way It Was," both also in this volume), this story was written for a special purpose: It was to be part of an advertising campaign some visionary adman had dreamed up to run in the pages of *Scientific American*. True to form, about the time I finished the story I got a call from the adman to say, shamefacedly, that his boss had hated the campaign and so it was canceled as of that morning. This time the jinx did not stop there. About the time I was trying to decide whether I wanted to publish the story myself in *Galaxy* (which I was then editing) or offer it to some other publication, I discovered in the incoming manuscripts from authors a Stephen Goldin story called "Sweet Dreams, Melissa." To my horror, it was very like this one—worse, it was a good story. I could not honorably reject it; nor could I, I felt, allow my own to be published anywhere near it. So I tucked the story away for several years, until a magazine called *Creative Computing* asked me for something, and published it. So, unless you were a reader of computer magazines a

decade ago, there's no way you could have seen this
story before... and if it sounds at all familiar, it's probably because you've read "Sweet Dreams, Melissa."

THE TIME WAS 0900:00 A.M., AND CHARLIE WOKE UP.

The first thing he had to do was to find out who he
was that day, and so he explored his memory. He discovered that he was a white male American, thirty-two
years old, married, employed in the sales department of
a public utility company. He had two children, a boy and
a girl. He had made $17,400 in the year just past, and if
it hadn't been for Harriet's part-time teaching salary he
didn't know how they would have managed. He still owed
over $19,000 on their $38,000 house, $1,900 on the car,
and nearly a thousand on the loan for modernizing the
kitchen they had taken out two years before. Moreover,
his daughter, Florence, had unfortunately inherited his
bite, and so the orthodontist was going to cost him fifteen
hundred dollars very soon. Charlie discovered that many
of his thoughts were of money.

However, his memory contained many other things.
He became aware that he was a fan of the Los Angeles
Dodgers, and that he had volunteered as a Little League
coach against the day when his four-year-old son, Chuck,
was old enough to play. Charlie remembered that he was
inclined to favor Chuck over the girl. It was curious that
he could not remember what color Chuck's hair was, or
whether Florence was doing well in school, but Charlie
didn't realize that it was curious and so he continued to
explore his memory.

He was a heavy smoker, drank a can of beer now and
then, especially in hot weather, but didn't go much for
the hard stuff. Although he liked looking at other women,
he did not go beyond looking. Although he enjoyed a game
of poker twice a month, he did not care to gamble heavy
stakes. He drove a small foreign car (it was not clear

whether it was a Datsun, a VW, or a Fiat), on which he got 24.7 miles to the gallon in everyday use and nearly 29 miles a gallon on the road. (He did not know what color it was. It did not occur to him to wonder why.) Charlie remembered that he was active in his party's politics (he did not know whether it was Democrat or Republican) and that he thought the mayor of his town was a crook. But he could not have said the mayor's name.

All these things about himself Charlie apprehended in a very short time indeed. He then spent somewhat longer remembering what brand of cigarettes he smoked, where he bought them, what had happened when he tried to give them up (his wife complained of his short temper and begged him to start again), and what other brands he had tried. He rehearsed the services offered by his neighborhood filling station, and what he looked for when he needed gas on the road; what kind of Scotch impressed him when he was offered it at a friend's home; and why he had decided against switching from lather to an electric razor. Charlie inventoried every purchase he and his family had made for the past year, swiftly and without error. He recalled what TV programs he watched, what magazines he read and which of the thousands of commercials and advertisements they contained had affected any of the purchases.

At that point Charlie discovered that he had done everything he was required to do just then. He made a quick parity check on his instructions. When it revealed no gross error or failure on his part, he announced that he was ready for his next task and waited in standby mode for orders.

He waited what was for Charlie a very, very long time. All of this had taken Charlie a period measured only in fractions of a second. Now he rested, neither wondering nor moving, for a stimulus to further action. Without it he would do nothing, ever. He was not impatient. He knew what "patience" was in conceptual terms—he could relate it to his memory of himself waiting without "pa-

tience" for a traffic light to change—but it did not occur to him to feel that way now.

At 0901:30, give or take a few seconds, a young woman in a light gray dress, carrying a container of coffee, set the coffee down on her desk and seated herself before a large typewriter. She had heard the bell that announced Charlie was ready more than a minute before, but she was not quite ready for Charlie. She typed several rows of characters, checked them over, took a sip of her coffee, and stood up.

She glanced at the various lights and dials on Charlie's front panel, saw nothing to cause concern. Her typewriter had produced not only the visible row of characters on the sheet of paper it held but, on a spool connected electrically to the keys, a strip of magnetic tape. She snipped a four-foot length of it free, taped it to another reel, rewound it, and fed it into a scanning device. She removed the rubber band from a packet of perforated cards and dropped them into a hopper.

Then she pressed a button. Rubber-tipped fingers dealt the cards into sorting bins where, one by one, they were taken up again and read, like the music roll of an old player piano. The tape reel slid past its scanning head on a cushion of air and disappeared. The time was 0901:55.

Charlie began work—not at 0901:55, exactly, but at a time so near to it that the difference was measurable only in picoseconds.

His first problem, he was informed, had to do with cigarette package designs. He waited while the cards on that subject were scanned. There were forty-one alternate designs, and they were presented to him in pairs. First he was offered Package One and Package Two simultaneously; he compared them, made a value judgment based on what he knew of his own buying habits and preferences, and stated his preference. Then Package One and Package Three were offered to him, then Package One and Package Four, and so on until Package One had been compared with each of the others. Then he was offered

Package Two with Package Three, Package Two with Package Four; and on and on until each prospective design on the list had been compared with each other. (There were 861 combinations in all, taken two at a time.)

At that point Charlie went into a sort of reverie while another part of his mind—it could have been called his "subconscious"—tabulated the results of his cross-pairing and established an order of preference. He wrote down, in order, the ten package designs he had most favored. He wrote it in the form of impulses recorded on a magnetic tape (this caused a reel by the desk of the girl in gray to spin rapidly for a moment, which she noticed out of the corner of her eye). Then he hummed for a moment, waiting for the card reader to allow him to begin his next task.

Each of Charlie's value decisions had taken him only about four nanoseconds, but the evaluation and readout were much slower. It took him considerably longer to announce his results than to arrive at them, and so it was 0902:45 before he began his next job.

The next assignment was to assess the merits of some proposed shaving-cream formulations.

Here the task was considerably more difficult, for several reasons. The first part of his task was to rank his preferences among the fifty-five formulations as to their odors, textures, and visual appearances, each in combination with the other. Charlie did not, in fact, realize quite how difficult it was, since he had no idea that he possessed neither smell nor vision, and touch only in the sense that certain of his members were capable of probing a card or tape for punched holes. He then had to evaluate some twenty-four shapes and weights of pressure canisters in relation to each sort of lather. Here too, Charlie was unaware of his lacks. In fact he did not have thumb and fingers; the "grasp" and "weight" and "feel" of the canisters in his "hand" was in fact only a locating of certain binary statistics within the parameters of certain other quantities that were a part of his memory. In order for Charlie to be able to express an opinion on any of the matters on which his verdict was sought, many subter-

fuges had been devised by the programmers on the staff of the advertising agency that owned Charlie. They materially prolonged the time for each comparison. However, he was in no way concerned by this. He did what he had always done. He did the task that was assigned to him, and when it was done he looked for, and did, the task that was next.

In all of the hour and forty-odd minutes in which Charlie, husband of Harriet, father of Florence and Chuck, searched his responses to a wide range of offerings, he performed something over five thousand million separate operations, including parity checks and internal verifications. He faithfully reflected the customs and tastes of the average of a sample of some 4 million American males as they pertained to the purchase of tobacco, beer, gasoline, automotive accessories, soft drinks, airline tickets, motion picture admissions, sporting goods, hi-fi equipment, toilet articles, and power tools. When his final magnetic report was on the tape, he signaled by ringing a bell. That was the end of Charlie's working day. In a sense it was the end of his life.

The girl in the light-gray dress was in the assistant division chief's office when Charlie's bell rang, and so she didn't react at once. Charlie waited like a man on a benzedrine high, his mind clear and capable, but disengaged. It was nearly 1100 when the girl got back to her desk.

She took the spool of tape that held all his opinions and threaded it into a printer, where it began typing out plain copy at a rate of 350 words a minute. She replaced it with a blank spool, consulted her work sheet, and began to change Charlie with switch, with patch-cord, and with dial.

As she worked whole banks of memories dropped out of circuit. Chuck and Florence fell out of his personality without leaving a mark. His wife disappeared, his house, his car; the Los Angeles Dodgers went, with the Little League and the dunning letters from the bank.

She then checked the programming sheet and, follow-

ing its instructions, selected new personality ingredients for Charlie: an economic level, an age, a set of buying habits, a profile of interests. She began to charge Able Charlie with the sum of these habits and biases. He was not yet aware of what he was, since he had not yet received the command to learn himself. For that matter, he was no longer "he." Now Able Charlie was a teenage girl, her principal interests cosmetics, soft drinks, clothes, records, and boys.

When all the patches were complete and the new tapes were ready to roll, the girl in the gray dress double-checked, and pressed the "execute" button. Able Charlie, AC-770, began to take up his—her—its new life.

The girl in the gray dress idly examined the polish on her nails. Her mind was not far from standby mode, either; until the first readout came, or a trouble signal, she had nothing to do but wait for lunch.

Inside the AC-770 Charlie, or Charlotte, was swiftly sniffing colognes whose fragrance was only the simulation of magnetic patterns on iron-oxide tape and comparing shades of lipstick whose colors were only a point on a hypothetical scale. The girl programmer was comparing colors, too. She wished idly that she had a friend to chat with—Rose Pink, after all? Or Catalina Coral?—but when she thought she heard a low contralto sigh she dismissed it at once. She knew that she was alone.

THE WAY IT WAS

This is the third "kiss of death" story in this volume. This one I was maneuvered into by that secret master of us all, Harlan Ellison. He called me up one day to tell me there was a new magazine to be published by Bob Guccione—not *Omni*; it was long before *Omni*—whose editor, he said, was slavering to have a short article on the future written by me. Well, short articles on the future I sneeze out at the slightest request, and the money was good; when the editor called a little later, I told her I'd be glad to do it. We talked a little bit about subject matter, and I sat down to write it. I was typing happily along when the phone rang again. Had I understood, she wanted to know, that by "piece" she meant *fiction* piece—specifically, not an article but a short story? I had not. I wouldn't have started on the thing if I had. Still, in the course of thinking about the themes I wanted to touch on in the article I had dreamed up what seemed to me a brand-new aspect of a long-considered subject. So I said, all right, I'll do a story . . . and did . . . and then, what do you know, the new magazine

died stillborn. The story languished in Bob Guccione's files for a year or two until he started another new magazine. This one was called *Viva*, and my story appeared in its first issue. But this time the Pharaoh's curse had not yet finished its work. *Viva's* first issue was also its last, and this time I had slain not one but *two* magazines with a single story.

THIS IS THE WAY IT WAS WITH STAN AND EVANIE: THEY fell in love. When Stan came out of the waking-up room at Blue Balls, Evanie was there, pretty and new on the job and a little flustered, to give him his check and see that everything was all right. One thing led to another. An hour later they were lying in the long grass at the foot of a waterfall, gently stoned, skin bare on the warm, soft turf, listening to Rorschach Rock while sweet bunnies and gentle chipmunks peered at them from the edges of the lawn.

It was like the first time for both of them, only better, because they each knew every move the other was going to make and leapt to meet each other; there was never skin softer or smoother than Evanie's, never a breast as firm. Stan stayed hard inside her for fifty-four minutes, never impatient, bringing her with joy through gasps and shudders until both of them had had it all and they lay spent and contented among the violets. It was like the first time, because it was always like the first time; and, as always, the first they knew that it was over was when the waterfall stopped and the bunnies froze in midhop.

"Oh," said Evanie drowsily, "shit." She sat up and leaned away from him, scratching the inside of her thigh. "I guess I better get back to work, Sam."

"Stan."

"It was really nice, though, Stan."

"Yeah." Now that the breezes had stopped, too, Stan became aware of the way they smelled. In the city outside

this room he would never have noticed it, but after the perfumed flowers it was a bring-down, and now that the soft sunlight was off, the lawn was only CelloTurf again and it itched.

The next couple was already waiting in the entry room. Stan and Evanie nodded to them and pushed their checks into the locker slots. As they got dressed Stan said, "I'd really like to do this again some time."

"Zip me up, will you?"

"No, I mean it, Evanie."

She patted his shoulder absently and pushed the door open. They walked out into the city, and the heat and the stink smote them. Behind them the liquid-crystal sign glowed its message:

Harry's Place
30 Studsy Sex Spectaculars 30

The colors flowed into Super-Stud embracing the tenderest blond beauty who ever lived, with waving palms dissolving into mirrored walls behind them.

"Thanks, Stan. I'll see you."

He put out his hand to stop her. "I seriously mean I want to do it again, Evanie."

"But it's so expensive!"

"I've got a thousand dollars a week," he said proudly. "I can afford it now, what the hell?"

She was suddenly blinded with tears. "And how do you get it?" she sobbed. "No! Let go of my arm, Stan. I've got to go."

He called after her, sweet little rump jouncing under the hem of the work-mini as she hurried away, but she didn't look back. Perplexed—and, he realized, hungry— he pushed his way through the crowded hall to a fast-food. "Fuck her," he said to the cashier as he pushed his credit card into its slot, but it was only a money machine and did not reply.

* * *

Two hours later he was still sitting at the same table in the fast-food, but he had switched from food to drink. "I don't have to eat in a joint like this," he told the man across from him. The man had been sitting there for ten minutes, nursing a cup of imitation coffee and eying Stan's collection of empty glasses. He brightened up.

"Yeah, I could tell that by looking at you. You're used to better places, right, Mac?"

"I damn am."

"You can always tell somebody with, you know, some kind of status. It's the way you sit there, even."

"Right," said Stan. "Want a drink?"

The man looked at the flickering digits on the wall clock. "Well," he said, "I really ought to be getting along—" Which was doubtful; he was Welfare from clipped head to fabric shoes, nothing to do but wait for Thursday (payday), just the way Stan had been most of his life. Stan's face must have showed what he was thinking; the man said quickly, "Still, I wouldn't mind a beer."

Stan pushed his card into the cashier and read out the total glumly; after the beer, the readout showed he had $766.22 left in his account. Harry's Place wasn't cheap. "I just came from Harry's," he said. "You ever been there? Nice little screwery, if the company's right."

"I bet she was, huh?"

"You won that bet. Prettiest little thing you ever saw. I met her at . . . I met her where we both work."

"I had a job," the man said enviously. "What kind of work do you do?"

"Parts. What about your job?"

"Well, it was in personal service. I worked up in the penthouse areas when I was younger. Sort of general handyman. I used to go to places like Harry's all the time. Stud farms, casinos, travel—I've been skiing, two or three times." He knocked back the rest of his beer and pushed the empty container absentmindedly into the middle of

the table. "Yeah, you can have a pretty good life, when you have a job. What kind of parts do you mean?"

"All different ones." The forget-it shots were wearing off, the selective proteins that numbed the sense of boredom and made everything seem fresh and exciting, even sex, and Stan was rapidly tiring of his company. Funnily, he wasn't tiring of Evanie. In his not particularly adventurous life she was probably the five- or six-hundredth girl he'd screwed, and the fourth or fifth he had taken to Harry's, after he found out how to get a thousand dollars a week for practically nothing, but there was something about her that stuck in his mind. No, not in his mind; he could feel a crawling between his thighs when he thought of her, even with the forget-it wearing off and being in this crummy joint.

The Welfare man saw his next free beer wriggling off the hook. "Let me tell you what it's like, up in the high-rent district," he said. "You know they've got swimming pools bigger than this whole restaurant, water so clean you'd think it was perfume? Dances, with live orchestras?"

"I heard."

"It isn't the same, just hearing it or seeing it on the tube; you have to be there. Friend, the happiest days of my life were when I was up there. The women wore clothes that lit up, and turned peekaboo, and just hugged their little butts like skin. Just to look at them was enough! Almost enough. And half of them were just begging to get balled by the hired help, beds you wouldn't believe, all the grass and fine wine you could handle—"

"You talked me into it," Stan said cruelly. "I think I'll head up there for a visit now."

It wasn't exactly a lie, he told himself. He really could go up there, at least long enough to spend the rest of his thousand dollars in one of the restaurants looking out into the clouds over the ocean; and maybe he would.

* * *

Plenty of money in the balance, nothing to do. Stan wandered through the midlevel streets of the city, reminding himself that anything he saw he could buy if he wanted to. This was all Welfare country; not a soul in sight that had had a dime in capital or a dollar's pay in ten years. He wasted a few dollars in a game parlor, bought himself a new wristlet because it looked like something Evanie would appreciate, stopped to buy some pop-soy to give to a couple of nice-looking, hungry-looking kids but decided against it—you never knew when they might threaten to call the fuzz for molesting them if you didn't pay off. That wasn't his style; all he wanted to molest was a pretty lady. There was plenty of that around, too, and he cased the available material carefully without seeing anything that took his fancy.

What took his fancy was Evanie.

But what was the use of that, when she let him spend two and a half big bills in Harry's Place and then took off without even saying she'd see him again? Most girls appreciated that kind of thing a little more. That was half the best part of it, not just the fucking but taking her to a place your average working man couldn't afford more than twice a year and your Welfare stiff couldn't get inside the door of.

He found he was near an observation gallery, and pushed his card into the admissions turnstile—five dollars to look out the window!—and strolled out. Even there it was crowded, mostly couples and cops, the couples to make out in some place other than their dormitories and the cops to keep them from it.

He stood looking over Lower New York Bay through the smoggy clouds, without seeing much that interested him. The high walls of Jersey City were lighting up as it got dark, and far out past Sandy Hook he could see the lights of the offshore oil condominiums. It was the third time he had been there in three days, and it wasn't worth it. It was only worth it when you couldn't afford it; the reality was a waste of time.

All the things they used to talk about in the dorms, they were true enough. Having a job wasn't just getting a paycheck. Having a job was a thing to organize your life around. It was something to do. Having a job was thirty-two hours a week when you felt it mattered, some way or another, whether you were in one place or some different place.

Having a job was a lot better than being in parts, even though the pay there was all you could want.

Shortly before the end of the shift he went up to the Blue Balls office. The sign didn't say that, the sign said:

Associated Medical Services
of Greater New York
TransParts Division

but everyone knew it by the other name. Usually he didn't like to hang around there, but apart from being where he got his money, it was also where Evanie worked. The trouble with that was that he hadn't caught her last name.

Stan walked in through the door as though he had never been there before, and a receptionist smiled and said, "Good evening, sir. One of our account executives will be with you right away."

"I just wanted to ask you—"

"Yes, sir. It's company policy that our account executives give out all information. Here you are, Mr. Medway is ready to see you."

Pale, slim Mr. Medway in a sober scarlet jacket, smiling at the door, was waving him in. "Welcome to TransParts, sir. Please sit down. Would you care for a drink? Coffee? A Coke?"

"I just wanted to ask you something."

"Certainly, sir! But before that, let me congratulate you on your civic spirit. Whatever you decide—and remember, TransParts will not attempt to influence your

decision in any way—just the fact that you came here shows that you are an extraordinary person. Well. Let me tell you a little about us. TransParts supplies all of the surgical facilities in the Greater New York area with organs for transplant. Under Title Seven, Federal Statute 683, we are authorized to accept and process whole-body donations from any competent adult, and to reward the donor to the extent of fifty thousand dollars—assuming, of course, that the donor meets our rather rigid physical standards. But looking at you, sir, you seem the picture of health!"

"That wasn't what—"

"No outright sale, eh?" twinkled Mr. Medway, stroking his lightly graying sideburns. "I don't blame you for that! Well, I think I know what you would like. We can offer you one thousand dollars for what is, essentially, a fifty-to-one chance that you will walk out of this office with everything you had when you came in, *plus* our check for a thousand deposited direct to your credit account. The procedure? Simplicity itself. We bring you to a very comfortable room and present you with a tray containing fifty sealed bottles of a very fine liqueur. Each of them has something added. Forty-nine of them contain a mild sleeping potion; you fall asleep; eight hours later you wake up, you walk out. The fiftieth—well, sir, that's the gamble, eh? And you can come back and repeat this process every week if you like. Think of that! A guaranteed income, a thousand dollars a week for life! Why, we have clients who have been living off the fat of the land for *years*! If you'll let me have your credit card, for identification purposes—"

It was easier to do it than to argue. Stan handed it over, while Mr. Medway babbled on. "I'm sure you know, sir, that TransParts is officially licensed by the Federal government. We operate under the most rigid inspection possible. If you fear that there might be some—what shall I say? tinkering?—with the odds, let me tell you that our license would be pulled in a minute. We wouldn't dare! No, it's a fair draw and—"

He stopped, staring at the card reader.

He looked up at Stan, his expression ugly. "What the fuck, man? You're already on our books!"

"I know that."

"Then what the hell are you doing here?"

"I just wanted to ask you a question."

"Ask!"

"There's a girl," said Stan. "Her name's Evanie. I . . . wanted to get in touch with her. She works here."

Mr. Medway stared at him for a minute, then laughed. He tossed Stan's credit card back and punched a combination on his desk top. "Yeah," he said, reading. "She's in Post-Session Care, right? She's just about to go off duty. You can probably catch her at the employees' entrance."

The most astonishing thing about Evanie was, she still looked good. A little depressed, but good. When she caught sight of Stan her face flickered into a smile, then became sadder than ever.

"Hi, Evanie."

"Hey, Stan."

He put his hand on her shoulder, then pulled her to him and kissed her deep and long. He didn't let go, and she smiled up at him. "Don't you ever wear out, Stan?"

"I'm the picture of health. Want to do something, Evanie? We could go back and try out one of the other rooms at Harry's."

"Stan, it's crazy to waste your money like that."

"Why is it crazy? That's what I get it for, to spend it. If I run out, I go back and get some more."

"*Maybe* you get some more. Maybe you never come out again, and next week some guy on the two-hundred-and-fiftieth floor's wearing your balls."

He winced and backed away, and saw that she was near tears again. "Oh, Stan, I hate to think of you in there."

"Why me? You work there!"

"That's different, I know I'll be coming out at the end

of the day. You—do you know what they do to you in
there, when you lose, I mean?"

"For Christ's sake, Evanie, of course I know. It's an
organ bank. If I lose... if I lose that's the last I know,
right? I just don't wake up the next morning. And they
take me apart and heal sick people with my parts, heart
here, lungs there, anywhere somebody needs a transplant.
What's wrong with that?" He knew he was repeating what
the account executive had been saying, all the while he
was signing up, but he went on anyway. "My life might
save, I don't know, ten or twenty other lives, and that's
a fair rate of exchange. And meanwhile I'm off Welfare!
I've got a few dollars in my pocket, I can live like a human
being—"

"Stan," she said, "hold still."

"What are you doing?" She had taken something out
of her purse, was clipping it to his tunic.

"That's my ID badge, it'll get you past if they don't
look at it too closely. Me they know. I'm going to show
you what Blue Balls looks like from the inside."

He didn't have the heart for Harry's Place. But neither
of them wanted to go back to their dorms, so they wound
up in a cramped but not awful hotel room, rented, to the
desk clerk's surprise, for the whole night. It had a good-
sized bed, if nothing else. At first Stan didn't have the
heart for sex, either, or even for talking, but after a while
in the gentle dark with Evanie warm and tender beside
him, his spirits rose. They screwed and drowsed, whispered and explored each other, and drowsed again.

And when it was nearly time to get up and get out
Evanie said, "Stan, I really like you, and you turn me on
better than anybody else I ever knew."

"Me, too, Evanie. I wouldn't have believed it. Even
here, without the sets, without the forget-it, it's as good
as Harry's Place with anybody else."

"Don't say that, Stan, you didn't let me finish. It's no
good, Stan. I'm not going to see you again."

Fist to the solar plexus, when he hadn't been expecting an attack. He got his breath. "Evanie, that doesn't make sense."

"To me it makes sense. Every dollar you spend, it's a piece of your body. What did it cost you for the night, a hundred dollars? That brings you a hundred dollars closer to the time you go back to Blue Balls and take your chances again. I can't stand that, Stan, it'll drive me up the wall if I let it."

"I'm willing to take the chance."

"I'm not! Stan, don't you remember what I just showed you? The used-up stiffs with nothing left? You want to be like that? One leg, a head without the eyes or ears, plastic tubing where your gut used to be, pumping along on a heart-lung machine until somebody decides there's not enough left of you to sell and they pull the plug?"

Stan winced; he had been devoting a lot of his attention that whole night to trying to forget all that. "They weren't all like that," he protested. "Some of them looked just fine! Like they were only asleep."

"Asleep! Yeah, they keep some going—rare blood types, they just keep them on the machine to make blood to sell, for a while anyway. But they're not asleep. When you do it to a frog you call it 'pithing'; the brain's disconnected, there's nothing there but a vegetable. And even so, you didn't look too close, because they take off all the spare parts they can anyway. What's a blood factory need with a weenie, Stan? But some old guy'll pay plenty of money for it. You think I like it when I feel you inside me like that, thinking that same thing might be in me some other time but with some other guy on the other end of it?"

"Oh, hell, Evanie—"

"At least you're a man," she said morosely. "You see those pregnant women in the shops? They're making babies for somebody. Of course, they don't feel anything, because they're pithed, too. But I feel. I look at them and think about myself being there, after somebody has reached

way up inside me with a light pipe and a flexible forceps and pulled out my own ovum and thrown it away and stuck in some other woman's ovum. And then they fertilize it with sperm from her husband or her boy friend or whoever—" She pushed her pillow up and sat higher, looking down at him. "If you're the customer it's okay. You get the baby and you don't have to pay off in morning sickness or looking funny. Just in money. Daddy turns in a sperm sample, Mom picks out a nice-looking breeder female from the photograph album—of course, the picture shows her the way she used to be, not the way she is now. A couple quick squirts on the day shift and nine months later the hulk on the heart-lung machine squeezes out Junior for you."

"Evanie—"

"So I can't take it, Stan. If we had some real money, you know, enough for six months or so...if you had a job...But that's not the way it is. My job won't keep us both, it barely keeps me off Welfare. I don't want to go back to living on the fortieth floor."

"I don't want you to do that."

"And I know you can't get a job. Stan, I'm not blaming you. I'm just telling you what I can take, and this is past it."

"How did you get the job, Evanie?"

"I laid the right people, what did you think?"

"Oh." He scratched uncomfortably. "Do you suppose I—"

"Who are you going to screw, Mr. Medway? Any of the account execs, male *or* female? They don't need you, Stan. No offense. You're a real great guy, you know I think you are. But that was just luck, and a section chief who liked young chicks, and it won't happen again in a million years. Those guys in the upper brackets at Blue Balls, they don't just get salaries, they get a commission— for keeping you on the hook, Stan, for making sure you come in and take your bottle of fluid every week. They go to school for that, psychology, salesmanship; once

they've got the degree they're set for life, and they can
buy whatever they want. Even you, if they wanted you
bad enough, a lot cheaper than putting you on the payroll.
So this is it, Stan. I hope I never see you again, especially
at work."

He kept the room an extra day, the hell with the expense, and got a decent sleep, and followed it up with a
shower, clean clothes from the slot machines, and the
best meal he could find that didn't take more than half an
hour to eat. Half an hour was as long as he was sure his
courage would hold out; and then he took the transit elevator up to the Blue Balls office. "I want to talk to
Medway," he told the receptionist.

"Mr. Medway? I'm afraid he's with a client just now,
but one of our other account executives..."

"Medway. Tell him he's got a live one."

When Mr. Medway appeared, it took him a moment
to recognize Stan. "Oh, the one who was looking for the
girl. Didn't she work out? You want to pick another?"

"No, Mr. Medway, I want to make a deal. I want to
take twenty bottles, one after another. I walk out of here
with twenty thousand dollars or you get to keep the bod."

Medway sank back behind his desk, thumbs in his
armpits, looking at Stan. "You're a real gambler," he said
admiringly. "But you can't do that. It'd kill you. Twenty
is an overdose."

"I'll take that chance, Medway. I want the money. I
want to take it and..." he hesitated "...all right, I want
to take it and go to school and train for your job. I want
real money, Medway."

"Wow," said Medway softly. "I have to say I admire
your spirit. Well, you can't do it the way you say, but
TransParts is willing to roll the dice with any of its clients,
any stakes, just so it's a fair shot. How about this. You
get your choice of two bottles. One puts you to sleep for
the night, the other... that's a fifty-fifty chance, and what
you get if you win is twenty-five thousand dollars. Or if

you're really hot, you can take the long shot. The same
fifty bottles as always. Only this time only one of them
is just a sleeping pill. All the other forty-nine are too-bad-
Charlie. That's a forty-nine-to-one shot, according to the
arithmetic, but TransParts is willing to absorb the difference, so if you win that one, you walk away with fifty
thou. You can even get a hundred to one if you want it,
or a thousand. You name it. We'll set it up, just so the
arithmetic works out."

A thousand to one! My God, a million dollars! But to
have only one chance in a thousand of surviving... "I'll
take the twenty-five," he said.

"Good bet," nodded Medway. "When?"

"Right now."

Medway punched a combination into his desk top and
stood up. "Come on, they'll have it ready for you by the
time we get there." And so they did, the standard room
with its single bed and vase of flowers, and on the side-
board the little tray of bottles; but this time there were
only two on it.

You could spend the whole night arguing which is which,
Stan thought grayly, and reached out for the nearer. He
flipped off the top and drank it down. "Might as well get
a good night's sleep," he said, turning toward the bed.
"So long, Medway."

He didn't look around as the account executive went
out, and so he didn't see that someone had come in, until
she said, "I really liked you, Stan. I mean it."

He turned around, feet tingling in his pants legs.
"Evanie!"

"Go ahead, Stan, get into bed. You'll be feeling it in
a minute."

"I know." And he was, the same warm whirling that
he had felt every other time. That was good. But not really
good, he thought, the killer dose would feel the same going
down, he just wouldn't ever wake up. He tried a pleas-
antry. "I thought maybe you were coming to ... to ..."

The words got harder and harder to get out, but she

knew what he meant. "Not this time, sweetie," she said, drawing the cover over him. "I just came in because I wanted to tell you two things."

"Wh—" He couldn't even finish the "—at."

"That I really liked you. And that it wasn't anything personal, Stan. You see, I get a commission too."

THE WIZARD-MASTERS OF PENG-SHI
ANGLE

I mentioned in the introduction to this book that I had been greatly affected by a visit to China, and that an Oriental flavor might be discerned as a result. Well, here's the ginger-root-and-soy. What I didn't mention was that some of the science fiction now appearing in China was my own. Chinese friends gave me a copy of an anthology of Western science fiction, just published, which contained (they said) a story of mine. (I later learned it was "The Wizards of Pung's Corners", from an ancient issue of *Galaxy*.)

This interested me very much, not only for the obvious reasons but for two others. First, the reception "The Wizards of Pung's Corners" received in some quarters has always puzzled me. At least one scholarly dissertation on my work identified it unequivocally as a masterpiece and by all odds the finest story I had ever written. When someone tells me a story of mine is good, I seldom disagree, but the fact was that I barely remembered having written it. Second, it is an open secret that translation into Chinese may be very free. In fact, sometimes the byline on a translated story is

not "by John Smith, translated by Li Yongpo" but "by Li Yongpo, suggested by a story by John Smith." I wondered very ardently why this particular story of mine had been selected for Chinese publication—and even more I wondered to what degree it resembled the novelette I had written for Horace Gold a quarter of a century before.

Fortune dropped the key to the answer in my lap. The key's name was F. Gwynplaine MacIntyre (perhaps best known for his poetry in *Isaac Asimov's Science Fiction Magazine*), and he wasn't really in my lap but standing next to me at a cocktail party while I was bemoaning the fact that I couldn't read Chinese. Well, *I* can, said Froggy MacIntyre, and what's more I'll translate it back into English for you if you like. That is not the kind of offer I am able to turn down. I knew he would have to put far more work and intelligence into it than anything I could do in return could possibly justify—but I quelled my conscience and accepted his offer at once.

This is it. I thought it interesting enough to be worth a read (even for those who may already have read the previous, ah, masterpiece), and hope you agree. But it was not without its problems, and so I have asked MacIntyre to add a note of his own to say what they are—and why he no longer stands anywhere near me at cocktail parties.

INTRODUCTION TO THE TRANSLATION

I am not, I should say at the outset, the greatest authority on the Chinese language that the science-fiction field has ever produced. That would be Cordwainer Smith. I may not even be the second best: Charles G. Finney spent more time in China than I did. I do, how-

ever, have one excellent qualification for translating this
Chinese SF story into English. Here it is:

I have never read Frederik Pohl's story "The Wizards
of Pung's Corners" in its original English. I had never
even *heard* of it, in fact, until I had already translated
enough of the Chinese version back into English for
Fred to figure out which-the-hell one of his stories the
Chinese publishers had gotten hold of. (They didn't tell
him!) Thus, my translation into English of the Chinese
SF story "Péng-shǐ Jiǎo dí Wū Shǐ" is unprejudiced by
any previous knowledge of Frederik Pohl's English-
language version; I ain't never seen it. The story you're
about to read, therefore, is a direct translation of what
the Chinese SF readers saw . . . to the best of my fum-
ble-thumbed ability to translate it.

A few signposts to help you hack your way through
the verbal underbrush: Chinese, whether spoken or
written, is an extremely redundant language. So many
Chinese words have such similar pronunciation (which
makes Chinese the ideal language for pun lovers!) that
the Chinese like to tack several synonyms onto key
words to clarify their meaning. Where the English-
speaking writer would say "war," a Chinese writer would
say "battle-war fight-situation." What you or I would
describe as "green," the Chinese would identify as
"green-colored." In Chinese one must say "he nodded
his head", rather than the simpler and more elegant
"he nodded", because the Chinese verb *diǎn*, which
means "nod," also has at least seventeen other meanings depending on which noun it is appended to. Applied to the noun for "head" it means "nod," but applied
to the noun for "wine" it means "pour." Remove the
noun altogether, and the verb becomes ambiguous. So
Chinese authors—in a valiant attempt to prevent their
characters from nodding their wine and pouring their
heads—resort to redundant syntax. Don't ask me what
the Chinese would be for "he poured the wine over his
head and nodded." I have *tried* to remove most of the
unwieldy syntax from the following translation, but if
you trip over the odd oxymoron or dangling participle
here or there, don't pour any wine over my head. A
phrase that seems ungrammatical in English may be
perfectly correct in Chinese.

Ditto the punctuation. In recent years, Chinese publishers have made increasing use of English-style punctuation...but they don't use it in quite the same fashion as we do. I have kept the punctuation used in the Chinese version as intact as possible in this translation, changing it only where absolutely necessary. If I have used a semicolon where Fred Pohl's original story used a comma, or a colon where Fred used no punctuation at all...well, I did the best I could. Most of the punctuation appearing in my translation was taken intact from the Chinese version of the story.

Now we come to the wax tadpoles. In Chinese, most pictographs work overtime. Not only does every pictograph have one or more possible phonetic values (i.e., the way you would pronounce it), about ninety-five percent of the written characters in Chinese also have three or more dictionary meanings distinct from their phonetic values. Confusing? Well, consider the English-language symbol "I." We use it for its phonetic value, as a *letter* in words like "Ice," but it also has a specific meaning distinct from its phonetic value, as a *word*: the personal pronoun "I." Likewise, the symbol "A" does double duty: as a phonetic, in words like "Able," and for its meaning, the indefinite article "A." In Chinese, this conflict between the letter's phonetic value and the letter's specific meaning crops up *all the time*. The result? When Chinese writers translate an English-language name into Chinese—by employing Chinese pictographs that have phonetic values similar to the original English-language pronunciation of the name— they run the risk of using a combination of pictographs that link up to form a ludicrous—and sometimes downright pornographic—dictionary meaning. I call this the Wax Tadpole Principle. A few years ago, when the Coca-Cola Company first sold their product in mainland China, they marketed the soda in Coke bottles bearing a string of Chinese pictographs with the phonetic value *KO-KA-KOH-LA*. Unfortunately, those four pictographs have specific dictionary meanings unrelated to their phonetic values: *KO-KA-KOH-LA* in Chinese means "Bite the wax tadpole." See what we're up against?

The wax tadpole rears its ugly head again, not once but many times, in the story that you're about to

read . . . and the results may prove rather amusing. The main female character, for example, has a Chinese name that translates into English as "Horse-forest-grid-that-can-resemble-birdsnare." Another character mentions a popular breakfast cereal with a Chinese name that translates into English as "The son has approval to tie the Buddhist nun to the hermaphrodite." Wherever a proper name is introduced in the translation that follows, I've appended a footnote symbol (those little numbers up in the air) so that you can refer to the notes section following the story to get the precise translation. Some of the proper names in this story have translations that are, I think, quite chuckleworthy.

To give you the fullest possible comprehension of the linguistic subtleties in this Chinese text, I've included 88 footnotes explaining specific thorny points in the text.

Wherever I give the pronunciation of a Chinese word by transliterating it into English-language phonetics, the spelling and the diacritical marks are those used in the Hanyupinyin system, as developed by Professor Wu Jing-rong of the Foreign Languages Institute, Beijing.

This story should—I hope—give you all a pretty good idea of what Chinese SF fans are reading these days. I hope you enjoy reading it as much as I enjoyed translating it. Perhaps SF will provide a link between the Chinese and American cultures, and bring about better Sino-American relations. Until that day arrives, we'll all just have to bite the bullet.

Or, if no bullets are handy, we may have to pour Coca-Cola over our heads, nod, and then bite the wax tadpole.

Live long and prosper!

—F. GWYNPLAINE MacINTYRE
December, 1983

YEARS AGO THIS WAS THE SORT OF SITUATION THAT EX-
isted. Now pay attention. I won't repeat this.

There was an old man. Very evil. He was named Kē-
Gé-Lán,[1] and he drove in a lead automobile to Péng-shǐ
Angle. He was six chě[2] seven cùn[3] tall. He made many
people look up.

Why was this? Well, because a lead automobile had
not been seen before. Few people had seen a strange man
appear. This was not a normal situation. This is the way
Péng-shǐ Angle was years ago; it was a small place in the
wilderness, and didn't have people coming inside. The
place didn't have airplanes flying up above, or not for a
long period of time: but just before Kē-Gé-Lán the old
man arrived, there were airplanes. When this happened
the people became uncalm.

Kē-Gé-Lán the old man had bright black eyes, and he
wobbled. He got out of his automobile, and shut the door.
The sound of the door was not like the Volkswagen-
vehicle sounding kǎdōng, wasn't like the Buick[5]-vehicle
sounding kèyuè. It was only heavy. Because I've already
said it was very massive; it was made out of lead.

"Pardner!" In front of the Péng-shǐ Inn he called in a
big-sound voice. "Come take my baggage!"

Chá-Lǐ Fú-Lín-Kè[6] was the steward in there then—
right, the government official. Of course, he was merely
aged fifteen. He came out for Kē-Gé-Lán's baggage, he
had to circle four times round. The back of the automobile
had a big gap, and thick windows.

"Péng-shǐ Jiaǒ dí Wū Shī"
("The Wizard-Masters of Péng-shǐ Angle")
Original story written by FREDERIK POHL
Translated, from an unknown Chinese source,
back into English by F. Gwynplaine MacIntyre

While Chá-Lǐ hustle-hustled the baggage, Kē-Gé-Lán walked roundabout in circles. He wink-winked at Mrs. Chǔ-Jǐ-Wù-Dé[7], and watched young Kǎi-Xī Fú-Lín-Tè.[8] He nodded his head at the boys out front. He was truly a peculiar man, not half, acting as though he was the sort that belonged in there.

In front of the shop of Ān-Dí Gé-Lǎ-Mǐ-Sī,[9] Ān-Dí leaned back in his chair. He moved his feet away from the door, so that his yellow dog could get out. "This person seems to be decent enough," he told Jié-Kè Tài-Yī.[10] (That's right, the real Jié-Kè Tài-Yī.)

Jié-Kè Tài-Yī stood within the doorway; he looked unhappy. He had much more knowledge about the situation than the other people inside here. Now was not the time to reveal it, so he merely said: "We haven't many strangers in this place."

Ān-Dí shrugged, pushed his body down in the chair. It was most warm beneath the sun.

"That's enough, Jié-Kè," he said. "Such strangers as he should be inside here. The town is truly ready for sleep." He yawned while speaking.

Jié-Kè Tài-Yī didn't stay with him; he had to get home, because he knew a great deal about the situation.

Notwithstanding, Kē-Gé-Lán didn't hear them. If he had heard, he wouldn't be interested. Kē-Gé-Lán the old man was greatly able, not caring what people said of him, nor what was said of his sort. Otherwise he wouldn't have been able to be like that.

Thus, he entered the Péng-shǐ Inn. "I demand a suite of rooms, pardner!" He spoke in a large voice. "Want the best of all. Want one in which I can be very comfortable, truly secure."

"Good, sir. You are called—?"

"Kē-Gé-Lán, pardner! Āi-Dé-Suǒ-Ěr[11] T. Kē-Gé-Lán. There's a conceited name at both ends, because having them makes me conceited!"

"Of course, Mr. Kē-Gé-Lán. Coming right up. Now I'll look." He looked at his rooms list, even though he knew that except for Wēi-Ěr-Màn-Yī-Shǐ,[12] and Mr. Kǎ-

Péng-Tè[13] because his wife was angry, there weren't any people inside. He pushed out his lips. He spoke: "Oh, supremely good! The honeymoon suite is now empty, Mr. Kē-Gé-Lán. I'm certain you'll find it a very comfortable place. Of course, each day is costing eight-fifty.

"You say the honeymoon suite, pardner?" Kē-Gé-Lán like a swordsman took the pen from inside its pen-case. With a white head seeming like an old tiger he grinned.

This truly had reason for laughter, isn't that right? He had taken the honeymoon suite. That was indeed supremely laughworthy.

Unless people really got married, few of them had reason to take the Péng-shǐ Inn honeymoon suite. For Kē-Gé-Lán, you only had to look-to-see him to know that he was already many years from marriage—nowhere near it, he was years from marriage; being so tall, with bright eyes, not bending, yet he was unable to get married. He was already having age of eighty. You could see this by his wrinkled skin and hands.

The rooms clerk made a noise for Chá-Lǐ Fú-Lín-Kè. "We are pleased with your presence here, Mr. Kē-Gé-Lán," he said. "Chá-Lǐ will bring your baggage up. You are planning to stay long?"

Kē-Gé-Lán made a big laugh-sound. This was a calm and steady person laughing. "Right," he said. "Want to stay quite long."

Now, when Kē-Gé-Lán was alone in the honeymoon suite, what did he do?

Well, first he paid a ten-spot for the bringing of the bags. This surprised Chá-Lǐ Fú-Lín-Kè, to receive a tenner. He didn't generally encounter people doing such. He left, and Kē-Gé-Lán was delighted to close the door.

Kē-Gé-Lán was very happy.

He peered round, laughing like a wolf. He looked at the lavatory with its white enamel tiling. "Very good," he said in a quiet voice. He used the electric lights, switching them on, switching them off. "Supremely having interest," he said. "The hand must be used." He went into the drawing room, which had a nine-branched lamp with six

light bulbs, manufactured of the very best glass. Of the six only a couple were in the center. "Truly beautiful-good," Mr. Kē-Gé-Lán couldn't help laughing. "Yet it is very-extremely good."

Naturally, you know what he was thinking about. He was thinking of the big cavern-insides and the big machine-devices. He was thinking of the design-shift-testers[14] and the use-bomb-power-places. He thought of the self-holding-primary-mines and the connected dispersal channels. But now I'm in front of the situation. Now is not when these matters should be discussed. So none of you should ask.

Notwithstanding, the old man Kē-Gé-Lán looked roundabout, and he opened his own luggage.

He sat in front of a desk.

From inside his pocket he took a Kleenex,[15] and very fussily he picked up the blotter pad and dropped it.

He put the bag up on the not-have-cover desk, opened it, and put it against the wall.

You haven't seen a bag of such appearance! I insist that it looked like a sort of electrical worker's bag. Its back was a panel of Lucite plastic, with sparks and stars in its face. This looked bright-glitter-glitter. The front had a cathode-ray tube. Had a sweep-trace-device, a microphone, and a loudspeaker. All of this, having very much more. Why do I know all this? Of course, it's all written up in a book entitled 《Péng-shǐ Great Hall Eighteen Years》 made by V. P. Fú-Lín-Kè. Because Chá-Lǐ was eavesdropping and the door had a keyhole.

So the situation produced a bell-sound tinkle-tinkle, and the cathode-ray tube glimmered and lit up.

"Kē-Gé-Lán," the big old man said loudly. "Making contact. Let me speak a word with V. P.-Mǎ-Fēi-Dài."[16]

II

Now you already know what situations existed in Péng-shǐ Angle in those years.

Everybody knows the present situation, but back then it was small. Extremely-very small. Like the image of a fat old dame who is sitting on a rickety chair it is sitting on the Delaware[17] River riverbank-top.

The military commander "Scatter-in-All-Directions Move-Back Lord-of-Many" É-Sī-Tǎ-Bà-Lǔ-Kè[18] passed battle there beyond winter; he was a very peeved man and wrote to try to persuade the military commander Washington[19]; "I'm not getting any aid in this place, because the people are not behind this situation, and I haven't a person approaching me."

During the North-and-South War,[20] a small-small fight ensued in the primary marketplace. An officer of the Ninth Pennsylvania[21] Volunteers was pursued and the son of a merchant was hit in the head. (He'd been up on a horse and fell down. He'd been full of wine.)

You know that these were only small wars. They only inflicted small scars.

The big war Péng-shǐ Angle escaped.

Just to say, when the biggest-of-all war arrived, you see, Péng-shǐ Angle was watching from the fifty-meter demarcation-line, but they never had to do the job of a pass.

The cobalt bomb that hit the New Zé-Yǒu administrative district,[22] an east wind stopped it at the Delaware River.

History records that the radioactive dust that went through Philadelphia[23] went up the river forty miles. Then the air-machine spreading the radioactive dust was stopped by a pilot who wouldn't let it get past. (Péng-shǐ Angle was yet a mile farther on.)

The great city of Niǔ-Yāo-Xī[24] was surrounded by hydrogen bombs that almost reached Péng-shǐ Angle, but it was in the middle and the whole thing hadn't hit it.

Now are you knowing the situation? They hadn't got past our shield. But after the war we were abandoned.

But you know, that wasn't a bad sort of thing. I think you'll find this in the ancient books. Péng-shǐ Angle sensed that abandonment had very much favorability. The people

of Péng-shǐ Angle regretted the war, because it had killed
so many people. (Even though we won the war. Because
it wasn't as bad for us.) But even the worst-of-all sky has
collected itself a good face, and being surrounded at the
eight points of the compass by desolation had its advan-
tages.

Péng-shǐ Angle had a Nike[25] missile base, and they said
that they shot down the first helicopter that came, because
they thought the enemy were flying it. Perhaps they thought
rightly. But I promise that when the fifth 'copter came,
they no longer thought such things. And then there weren't
airplanes anymore. Outside Péng-shǐ Angle, I suppose,
the people had much to think about. They didn't deal with
Péng-shǐ Angle anymore.

And then Mr. Kē-Gé-Lán arrived.

After Kē-Gé-Lán had established communications—
because that's what the big bag really was, an electrical
communications device—he used it for a time. Chá-Lǐ's
forehead had a red impression for a couple of days, because he thought he could see inside the room, and his
head was pressed against the doorknob.

"Mr. Mǎ-Fēi-Dài?" Kē-Gé-Lán said using a loud voice,
while an attractive lady's face illuminated the apparatus.

"I am Mr. Mǎ-Fēi-Dài's bookkeeper," she pleasantly
said. "I see that you're there now already. Please to wait
a bit, and I'll give you Mr. Mǎ-Fēi-Dài."

Another face appeared on the screen; the image could
truly have been a blood brother to Kē-Gé-Lán. It was the
face of an old man who had the ability to let nobody stop
him, who knew what he wanted for himself, and for now
was able to obtain such. "Kē-Gé-Lán, pardner! Seeing
that you already got inside, I'm truly pleased!"

"It didn't cost even the effort to blow away a dust
speck, chief," Kē-Gé-Lán said. "I am now taking control
of operations. Money. This matter will require much
money."

"There is no difficulty?"

"There's none, chief. I can assure you of this. There won't be any difficulty." He grinned a grin, and took in one hand a small set of boxes inside one another. He opened a box, took out a small silver-blended-with-red-colored object. "I will be using this straightaway."

"What about the pool?"

"I have not yet looked, chief. But the pilots say they already released the material. You haven't had any opposition from the ground. These people used to shoot at every airplane they thought was coming, Now they're becoming vulnerable."

"That's as good as it could possibly be," V. P. Mǎ-Fēi-Dài in the small cathode-ray tube said. "Make this happen, Kē-Gé-Lán. Make this happen."

Now at the Xiào-Wān-Jiā-Nóng-Kè[26] National Bank, Mr. Lā-Fā-Jí[27] saw Kē-Gé-Lán enter, and he knew that an unpleasant situation was developing.

How do I know that? Well, this is in a book. This book is called 《Federation Budget that I Attained, and Adopted a Weight-Standard Law: A Study of Favorable Trade-Balance Strength,》 by Chancellor of the Exchequer (Retired) Wēi-Ěr-bǎi[28] É-dī-sī[29] Lā-Fā-Jí. Pretty much everything is inside books; you only have to know which book to look inside. But this is something that you young people must learn.

At any rate, Mr. Lā-Fā-Jí, who was only a minor official then, greeted the old man Kē-Gé-Lán. He was that sort of person. "Morning, sir!" he said. "Morning! Is the bank able to assist you?"

"We'll think of a way," Mr. Kē-Gé-Lán-*Xiānsheng* said.

"Certainly, sir! Certainly!" Mr. Lā-Fā-Jí was eager. "You'll want a bank account. Definitely! And want a savings account? Want a safety-deposit box? Most certainly! I suppose you require a Christmas Club account as well. You may be wanting an automobile loan, or want to use a mortgage, have a debt-consolidation loan, to make small—"

"I don't owe anybody," Kē-Gé-Lán said. "See here, what is your name—"

"Lā-Fā-Jí, sir! Wēi-Ěr-bǎi Lā-Fā-Jí. You call me what you like."

"Wēi-Lǎo,[30] this is my accreditation book." He put the contents of an envelope in front of Lā-Fā-Jí.

This banker look-looked and then frowned. He picked up a document. "Credit letter," he said. "It's been a long time since I saw such a thing. From the Danbury[31] administrative division of Connecticut,[32]? He shook-shook his head, and was upset. "These are all from outside, sir."

"I came from the outside."

"I understand." Lā-Fā-Jí put his voice heavily in the air after a bit. "Ah, sir I don't know. You wanted what?"

"I want 250,000 yuán, Wēi-Lǎo. Want it now. You will give to me quickly, what?"

Mr. Lā-Fā-Jí blinked.

Of course, you didn't know him. He was before your time. You can't know how this sort of request would affect him.

When I said that he blinked, I mean, pardner, that he really blinked. He blinked again, and it put him in a better mood. For a moment the veins had begun to bulge in his head; for a moment, he was about to speak. But he shut his mouth, and his veins calmed down.

You see, it was because Kē-Gé-Lán took the silver-color-and-red-color object out of his pocket. It shimmer-shimmered bright. He gave it a twist, and a squeeze, and it made a low pulsing sound. And yet that sound wasn't able to satisfy Mr. Kē-Gé-Lán.

"Wait a bit," he casually said, and he turned it a little, and squeezed it. "That's a good one," he said.

The sound was lower, but still it wasn't low enough to be able to satisfy Kē-Gé-Lán. He twisted it a little more, until the pulsing noise was so low that it couldn't be heard, and after that he nodded his head.

For not very much time there was silence.

And afterwards: "Want large banknotes?" Mr. Lā-Fā-Jí said. "Or better want small banknotes?" He got up in

a hurry, went to a cashier. "Give over 250,000 units! You there, Teng'ḿ Fèi-Ěr-Cǎi![33] Be quick. What? No, I don't care from where. If there isn't enough in the windows, go to the big safe. But bring me 250,000 currency units now!"

He sat down, gasping for air. "I very much regret this, sir," he said to Mr. Kē-Gé-Lán. "The state of the cashiers! I rather wish that the earlier ways would return."

"Perhaps they will return, friend," Kē-Gé-Lán said, grinning a big grin to himself. "Now," he said without being unkind, "I don't want you to keep speaking."

He waited, with his hand tap-tapping the deskfront. Until Teng'ḿ Fèi-Ěr-Cǎi and another cashier arrived with four large canvas sacks of banknotes, he did not have any interest in Mr. Lā-Fā-Jí. They put the banknotes on the desk and began to count them.

"Don't do it, don't bother," Kē-Gé-Lán cheerfully said, his black eyes glinting. "I trust you all." He lifted the sacks, nodded his head politely to Mr. Lā-Fā-Jí, and went out.

Ten seconds later, Mr. Lā-Fā-Jí shook his head around, rubbed his hand across his eyes, and looked at the couple-two cashiers. "What did—"

"You just gave him 250,000 units," Teng'ḿ Fèi-Ěr-Cǎi said. "You made me bring it from the big safe."

"Did I?"

"You did."

They could do no more than you-see-me, I-see-you.

Last-of-all Lā-Fā-Jí said: "It's been a while since I can recall that sort of thing in Péng-shǐ Angle."

III

Now I must tell you a part of the situation that had no pleasantness. This was involving a young lady named Mǎ-Lín Gé-Luó-Xiào-Kè.[34] I won't explain any of this to you all. Perhaps I oughtn't to bring up the matter, but it's part of our nation's history. And yet—

Ah, this is what occurred. Right, this is also in a book—a book entitled ⟨⟨Follow the Summons That Arrives,⟩⟩ by the knowledgeable celebrity. (And we know who "the knowledgeable celebrity" was, is it not so?)

She was not a bad girl. Not a bit of it. Or at least she didn't think herself a bad girl. She was the gaudiest, the sort of gaudiness that didn't give her a good place in life, and she wasn't smart. What she wanted was to be a television star.

But, of course that wasn't likely. Years ago in Péng-shǐ Angle, we didn't broadcast live television, there were only recorded images. Many widespread-appraisals[35] were left inside them, even though the already-gone broadcast-people's images were touting products that were no longer available anywhere, not to speak of in Péng-shǐ Angle. Mǎ-Lín's inspiration was the image of a television sales-woman named Betty Furness.[36] Mǎ-Lín strung up pictures of her taken from many tapes; put them up all over in her room.

At the time I'm talking about, Mǎ-Lín called herself a corporate secretary. Back then there weren't many people who wanted her services. (And afterwards, because there was other work to do, she had already given up that part of her trade.) But if anybody in Péng-shǐ Angle wanted somebody to help, writing letters or catching up on correspondence or such, they would go to Mǎ-Lín. But before this, she had never approached a stranger for work.

When the innkeeper told her that this Mr. Kē-Gé-Lán had arrived, and wanted to have a person to help him with some business, she was pleased with herself. She didn't know what the business was, but I must tell you that if she knew she would have helped him anyway. Of course any person expecting to be a television star would have helped.

She stopped in the Péng-shǐ Inn's lobby to change to new makeup. Chá-Lǐ Fú-Lín-Kè gave her a sort of look, even though he was not aged more than fifteen. She looked down at him, shook her head a toss, and went spectacularly upstairs.

She tap-tapped on the carved wooden door of Room 41
—that was the honeymoon suite; she was completely
aware of this—and she smiled at the tall old man with
bright eyes who opened the door for her.

"Mr. Kē-Gé-Lán? I am Miss Gé-Luó-Xiào-Kè, a corporate secretary. I'm told you wanted to summon me."

"Right," he said. "I did send for you. Come in."

He turned his body from her, and she came in and then
closed the door herself.

Kē-Gé-Lán was busy. He had already taken to pieces
the television set inside the room, on the floor.

He was thinking to mend the television somehow, Mǎ-
Lín felt-thought. This was most peculiar, Mǎ-Lín felt in
an obscure manner, because although she was not a truly
smart person, she knew that he wasn't a television repairman, nor any such a type of worker. She knew completely what he was. It already said on his card what he
was, that Mr. Lā-Fā-Jí had taken roundabout. He was a
place-study-and-go-build advisor.

Whatever that was known to be.

Mǎ-Lín was a very conscientious worker, and she knew
that a corporate secretary must be a worker with a conscientious heart. She said: "What is the trouble, Mr. Kē-
Gé-Lán?"

Unable to endure this, he raised his head. "I have not
been able to reach Danbury on this television."

"The Danbury administrative division of Connecticut?
Outside reach the television? Not so, sir. You aren't meant
to reach Danbury."

He stood up and looked at her. "Not meant to reach
Danbury." He thinking nod-nodded his head. "This 48-
cùn, 27-component color-constricted-path-out-strip device with open-wire airwave UHF-VHF hang-on-wall
television set isn't meant to reach the Danbury administrative division of Connecticut."

"That's how it is, sir."

"Á," he said, "this will really get a big laugh inside the
cave in Schenectady."[38]

Mǎ-Lín trying to help said: "It hasn't any sky-wire."[39]

Kē-Gé-Lán frowned, and corrected her. "Can't, not any way that can be. It must have a sky-wire. These wire-heads must have a use."

Mǎ-Lín very prettily shrug-a-shrugged.

He said: "Immediately after the war you wouldn't be able to reach Danbury at all. This I agree with. There was nuclear fission back then, answer-what? But now it is already not important. Danbury ought to be coming very clearly."

Mǎ-Lín said: "Not like this; after that. I once went with a lad named Dì-Mǐ Háo-Lán,[40] he had such a job, I mean to say he repaired televisions. A couple of years after the war, I was young, when they were able to get images from outside. But afterwards, they passed an article of law, Mr. Kē-Gé-Lán."

"An article of law?" His face was suddenly very fierce.

"Oh, yeah, I think so. Nonetheless, Dì-Mǐ had to remove the sky-wires from the television sets. He really did that. Afterwards they used television image-tapes; good, that was." She thought a thought. "He didn't tell me why." She spoke of her own will.

"I know the reason why." He plainly spoke.

"So, Mr. Kē-Gé-Lán, they only have those image-record-tapes. But if you think to watch anything, the steward will send it for you. They have very many of them. Dinah Shore[41] pieces, Jackie Gleason[42] pieces, and I remember they still have the doctor-medicine-program. Oh, and still have part of an old Western routine. You only need tell him what you wish brought."

Kē-Gé-Lán thought about that and said: "I understand." To himself, not to her, he said: "No wonder we couldn't get our heads in. Go-understand, we'll have a try-try."

"Why-what, Mr. Kē-Gé-Lán?"

"Not to worry about it, Miss Gé-Luó-Xiào-Kè. I am seeing this situation now. But it isn't pleasant."

He returned to confront the television set.

He wasn't a television repairman, he wasn't, but now he

knew something about the work involved, because he had the thing put back together in a quick interval. Oh, can't even say that much. But it wasn't in its original form. He had improved it. Even Mǎ-Lín was able to see this. Perhaps not advanced, yet changed from its original form; he had changed it.

"Better this?" he demanded, look-a-looking at her.

"You say how?"

"I mean to know, when looking at this image is there anything you have?"

"I regret it, Mr. Kē-Gé-Lán, but I don't much care to watch the first-stage-program.[43] You know how it is, it demands that I think too much."

Yet she obediently watch-looked the television.

He had already tuned the television to the recorded signal, that all the television sets in the Péng-shǐ Angle place were able to get. I think you don't know how we managed at that time, but there was an electrical tower that sent out its own unoriginal images, for people not wanting to look at the pieces. These were naturally by-gone objects. People didn't have anything new.

But Mǎ-Lín watch-looked, and it was funny, she began to make gé-gé-laugh[44] noises.

"Hey, Mr. Kē-Gé-Lán," she said, although he was just sitting there.

"This is good," he said, and he was pleased.

He had every reason to be pleased.

"Nevertheless," Mr. Kē-Gé-Lán said, "the priority matters receive priority. I want you to assist me."

"Very well, Mr. Kē-Gé-Lán," Mǎ-Lín said with a very smooth voice.

"I speak in reference to commerce. I want to hire some local people. I want you to help me find some local people, and to keep track of the records. Afterwards I'll need some raw materials. I'll need an office, and some work-rooms."

"Won't that require plenty-plenty money?"

Kē-Gé-Lán made a gé-gé-laugh sound.

"That, good," Mǎ-Lín said, satisfied. "Mr. Kē-Gé-Lán, I'm your person. I speak in reference to commerce. Can-you-can't-you tell me what sort of business you have?"

"I mean to make Péng-shǐ Angle stand up."

"Oh, that's as it should be, Mr. Kē-Gé-Lán. But, I mean how will this be done?"

"Auspicious-widespread-appraisal," the old man Kē-Gé-Lán said using the laugh of a goblin.

Silence. A fragment of silence.

Mǎ-Lín said in an air-voice: "I don't think they'll like this."

"Who?"

"The local people of great importance. They won't like this. You know, they won't like auspicious-widespread-appraisal. I mean to say that I favor you. I favor auspicious-widespread-appraisal. I enjoy it. However—"

"This isn't a matter of not liking it!" Kē-Gé-Lán using a fearsome voice spoke. "Our nation became this mighty by using it! It made us able to fight in a great war, and after that war it bound us into one large family again!"

"I understand this, Mr. Kē-Gé-Lán," she said. "Nevertheless—"

"Miss Gé-Luó-Xiào-Kè, I don't want to hear you say 'nevertheless.'" Unable to endure being vexed by this he spoke, "This isn't a subject for discussion. Think-a-think of the United States of America after the war. Maybe you don't remember. They didn't let you know the situation. But you know that the cities were all destroyed. The buildings were wrecked. It was only auspicious-wide-spread-appraisal that let us stand up—auspicious-wide-spread-appraisal, and the physical strength of go-study[45]; I wish to remind you of what a prominent scholar once remarked: 'Our purpose in go-study is to cause the customers to attain discontent.'"

Kē-Gé-Lán stopped for a bit, touched to the heart. "That was said by the automobile corporation person Chá-Lǐ F. Kǎi-té-Lín."[46] He said, "The most beautiful part of it, Miss Gé-Luó-Xiào-Kè, he said this during the twenties!

You think-a-think of this! He had such a thorough insight into the importance of scientific knowledge to us all. He had such a keen perception of the research and ingenuity of the United States!"

Mǎ-Lín said stammer-stammering: "This is truly most beautiful."

Kē-Gé-Lán nodded his head. "Naturally. You can see, your local people of great importance will be unable to have anything to do about this situation, whether they like it or not. We the people of the United States of America—we the genuine United States citizens—know that not having widespread-appraisal causes not having industry; and so we have made widespread-appraisal into a sort of very useful tool. Hey, you look, you look at this television!"

Mǎ-Lín looked, and presently she was *gé-gé*-laughing again. She quietly said: "Mr. Kē-Gé-Lán!"

"You see how it is? In case that isn't enough, you look, there is still forever the law backing us. We shall look-look, when the old bigshots of Péng-shǐ Angle contend with the physical strength of the total ground force of the Unites States of America!"

"I truly hope ten million legions won't leave to start a fight here, Mr. Kē-Gé-Lán."

"I don't think that's likely," he sincerely said. "Now we must work, good-what? Otherwise—" He had a look at his wristwatch, nodded his head—"It's important to say, we don't have to feel a need to hurry the matter this afternoon. You and I have an evening, how-about, the both of us have something to eat? And yet a drop of wine? And yet a bit of—"

"As you think proper, Mr. Kē-Gé-Lán.

Mǎ-Lín made for the telephone, but Mr. Kē-Gé-Lán stopped her. "Miss Gé-Luó-Xiào-Kè, I just now think a bit," he said, beginning to breathe heavily, "I will use the telephone. You sit there, and rest a bit. Look at the television."

IV

Now I must tell you all, about the great Jié-Kè Tài-Yī.

Truly, it was he. Jié-Kè Tài-Yī. The veritable father of the Second-Common-Mix-Nation.[47] Sit and listen, mustn't interrupt, because what I must tell you all is the sort of thing that you wouldn't have learnt in school.

That apple tree? No, that was purely an accident. You see, that could not have occurred. Because above the great street Madison,[48] an apple tree doesn't grow inside there, where Jié-Kè Tài-Yī was raised. Because Jié-Kè Tài-Yī wasn't the Second-Common-Mix-Nation's network-assembler. He couldn't be a leader because he had other work; he was employed in the Yóu-Sī-Dì[49] and Lǔ-Mǐ-Lún-Dì[50] announcement-of-appraisal corporation's S&L regiment, where he was household V.P.

It was so. He was an auspicious-widespread-appraisal man.

Mustn't cry. It was so, then. You see, before the war—oh, before the war—he had given up the work, and come to Péng-shí Angle, in order to retire.

Jié-Kè Tài-Yī kept his home at the Delaware River. He wasn't hygienic there. The hills surrounding Péng-shí Angle reached the rivulets of that area, and the radioactivity descended. However Jié-Kè Tài-Yī wasn't concerned by this, because he was already supremely old.

He was just as old as the old man Kē-Gé-Lán. Not only that, they had known each other during the time-duration they'd been with the corporation.

Jié-Kè Tài-Yī was tall; he wasn't able to match Kē-Gé-Lán on that score, but he was taller than six *chě*. In a manner of speaking, he resembled Kē-Gé-Lán. You've seen his photograph. The same sort of eyes, the same sort of fear-not-the-heavens, fear-not-the-Earth manner, and his voice was about as wide and deep. He could have

been an important man at Péng-shǐ Angle. They would have readily made him mayor. But he said he had arrived there in order to retire, and he retired; he said that the emergence of a large-scale earthquake would be required for him not to stay in there.

The inevitable outcome of this was the emergence of an earthquake.

First we see Ān-Dí Gé-Lǎ-Mǐ-Sī, as white as paper.

"Jié-Kè!" he said at the steps with his voice not having air, because all the way from his shop he'd come running.

Jié-Kè Tài-Yī took his feet off the porch. "Sit down, An-Dí," he said. "I believe that I know why you've come here."

"You know, Jié-Kè?"

"I think so." Jié-Kè Tài-Yī nodded his head. Oh, he was a handsome man. He said: "Airplanes are dropping a good deal of up-to-date henbane alkali into the pool, a strange man reaches this place driving a lead automobile. And we know the situation outside, is it not so? Right, this is the correct situation."

"Indeed, it is he," Ān-Dí Gé-Lǎ-Mǐ-Sī said petulantly, as he sat on the stairs, looking pale. "Because it's he, and we're incapable of taking action! This morning he came into our shop. He was leading Mǎ-Lín. We should have thought a bit about that girl, Jié-Kè. I knew that she would not have a favorable outcome—"

"What did he want?"

"Want what-did?[51] Jié-Kè, he had a writing tablet with a lead pencil; he wasn't asking for things but rather demanding—demanding—'breakfast food products,' he said. 'What sort of famous breakfast food products have you?' I told him. Oatmeal combined with maize fragments. Jié-Kè, he came through the air at me! 'Don't you people stock Cocoa Wèi-Zǐ?' he said, 'or Cuī-Zǐ, Yī-Zǐ, Ní-Zǐ, or Yī-Ní-Kě-Wèi-Zǐ?[52] What of Flavour Hóng-Ní,[53] or Plum Bran Dog,[54] or the small box with a handgun inside?' 'Don't-have, sir,' I said to him.

"But by that time he's having a tantrum. 'Potatoes?' he shouted at me. 'What about potatoes?' Oh, we had potatoes, they were inside. I told him this, he was very dissatisfied. 'You say potatoes that sprouted?' he said very loudly. 'Haven't you fabricated Potato Floss, Sī-Kē-Qí-òu-Jī-Mǐ-Qì Floss, or the Potato Chunks of Dàshū-Uncle Āi-Fú-Léi-Tè?' Then he showed me his calling card."

"I know," Jié-Kè Tài-Yī said, because now Gé-Lǎ-Mǐ-Sī had a bit of trouble speaking. "You needn't talk, if you don't think you should."

"Oh, I can tell it to you, Jié-Kè," Ān-Dí Gé-Lǎ-Mǐ-Sī strongly said. "This Mr. Kē-Gé-Lán he is an auspicious-widespread—"

"Steady on," Jié-Kè Tài-Yī said, standing, "you shouldn't make yourself do this. The situation is now unfortunate enough already. But it was correct to anticipate this. It is so, you had to anticipate this, Ān-Dí. We've had some good years, but we couldn't expect the good years to last forever."

"But what should we do?"

"Please stand up, Ān-Dí," Jié-Kè Tài-Yī said in a big voice. "Please come inside! You sit and pull yourself together. I will summon the others to join me."

"You seek trouble with him? But you should know, he has the entire United States of America ground force behind his shield."

Old Jié-Kè Tài-Yī nodded his head. "He's behind the shield, Ān-Dí," he said, although he had quite a pleased appearance.

Jié-Kè Tài-Yī's home was a sort of open-field house, with a sort of display inside. He was a great sort of man, was Jié-Kè Tài-Yī. You all know this, because you learnt it in school; perhaps you've been inside that house, but the house doesn't have that appearance now; I don't care what people say. The furniture inside hasn't the original form. Go have a look at the front—

Ah, yes, during the Great War, it's true, that was when

the radioactive dust flowed down from the mountains, so that nothing can blossom now. The locals stuck up some grass and trees and flowers. Flowers! I tell you, this has a peculiar shape. During his early years, Jié-Kè Tài-Yī had been a national-flower-commerce-place business-man. Hey, he didn't have a flower inside, not to speak of planting them himself.

But what do you care, that house was nice enough. He made Ān-Dí Gé-Lǎ-Mǐ-Sī a cup of wine, and had him sit down. He made a phone call, and asked five or six men to come see him. He wouldn't tell them what it was about. Didn't feel the need to set up a panic.

But there weren't many places where the people didn't already know. Coming in the lead was Dì-Mǐ Háo-Lán, he was the television workman, with Chá-Lǐ Fú-Lín-Kè riding on the back of his bicycle, held standing up. His voice with no air said: "Mr. Tài-Yī, they're already using the broadcast-wire. I don't know how they did it, but Kē-Gé-Lán is using our television broadcast hook-up. What he's broadcasting, Mr. Tài-Yī, is provoking emotions truly difficult to imagine!"

"It is so," Tài-Yī calmly said. "Don't feel trouble about this matter, Dì-Mǐ. I think I know what he's broadcasting.

He stood, going hum-hum, turned on the television. "Now it's broadcast the afternoon film festival time, answer-don't-answer? I think you left the broadcast record-image-tape running?"

"Of course, but he's making trouble with our broadcast!"

Tài-Yī nodded his head. "Let's all look-a-look."

The television picture seemed tilted, murky gray, then suddenly seemed to form an image.

"I remember this!" Chá-Lǐ Fú-Lín-Kè shouted. "This is my most-of-all favorite film, Dì-Mǐ!"

On the television screen, "Son-Named-Two"[55] was slowly moving on foot away from an evil man in a mask. "Son-Named-Two" tripped over a plank, and fell into a vat at his side. When he surfaced, he was stuck from head

to foot with putty mixed with mud-slurry, seeming bizarre
yet funny.

Tài-Yī stepped backwards. He spread the five fingers
of one hand in front of his own face, moved them up-and-
down up-and-down quickly while looking through them.

"Ah," he said, "so. Gentlemen, see for yourselves."

Ān-Dí Gé-Lǎ-Mǐ-Sī did the same sort of thing as big
old Tài-Yī did. He spread his fingers, and shook that hand
in front of his own eyes, as if protecting himself from the
bright television recorded-images. Up-and-down up-and-
down he shook-swayed his hand, using it to accomplish
a sort of stroboscope that blocked the unseen flash of
bright electric light.

Ah, yes indeed, it could be seen!

Not using the stroboscope, on the screen you'd see
lukewarm-faced Charley Chan[56] in his white-colored Panama straw hat. But using a stroboscope you'd see another
sort of image come. Without stopping the antique movie
there was another image also—every sequence flashing
for not much of a second, because it was supremely fast;
human consciousness couldn't grasp it. But, it struck the
human subconsciousness with much violent power.

Ān-Dí could not prevent his face from reddening.

"That—that gūgu,"[57] he stammer-spoke, feeling very
surprised. "The upper half of her body is without—"

"Naturally she is without them," Tài-Yī pleasantly said.
"That's imported to the subliminal consciousness, no?
Basic natural stimulation; you don't know you're seeing
it, but you hold it completely down in the subconscious.
No. You see held in her hand a box of Plum Bran Dog."

Chá-Lǐ Fú-Lín-Kè made a cough-cough sound. "Now
you come to mention it, Mr. Tài-Yī," he said, "I discover
that I've been thinking, right now to have a box of Plum
Bran Dog, and to eat it, ought to make the flavor very
beautiful!"

"Of course," Tài-Yī agreed. He cocked his eyebrows.
"Bright-buttocked women, right? But I think they should
have something to reach the female viewers also." He

was silent for a couple-two[41] moments, kept the others watching silently with him, and not stopping he shook the five fingers of his hand.

Not a moment later, his face reddened.

"Ah," he said with pleasure, "that is broadcast on account of the female viewers. You all see it there. It's subliminal wide-appraisal propaganda. It must have the key to stir up people's basic drives; it is flashed so quickly, it can be used so that people's brains will be unable to resist. So that while you're thinking of Plum Bran Dog, you're approaching the level of climax. Or what's more important, while you're thinking about the climax, you're beginning to think about Plum Bran Dog."

"Gosh, Mr. Tài-Yī, I often have those old thoughts about women."

"Everybody is like that," said Tài-Yī without ruffling his hair, while he nodded his head.

From outside there was a vigorous sound, and Wēi-Ěr-bǎi Lā-Fā-Jí from the Xiào-Wān-Jiā-Nóng-Kè National Bank came in. He was already pant-panting air, and looked extremely fearful.

"He just now did it again a time, he did it a time, Mr. Tài-Yī, sir! Mr. Kē-Gé-Lán came and demanded much money! He said that Péng-shǐ Angle must have a true net television pagoda. He said he's opening an additional office for the Yóu-Sī-Dì and Lǔ-Mǐ-Lún-Dì corporation, whoever those people are thought to be. He said he was going to make Péng-shǐ Angle return to the map, so he must have much money."

"You gave him that money?"

"I was unable to resist."

Jié-Kè Tài-Yī sensibly nodded his head. "Right, you were unable to resist. Even when we were children, when the corporation took charge and their people looked at you, while they had a finger on the trigger, you were still unable to resist. Water containing up-to-date henbane alkali, to make everybody in Péng-shǐ Angle more tame, not so strong and unyielding. I think that even though I

don't drink much water like some people, this will get to me. The television suitably has subliminal-widespread-appraisal, and for face-to-face meetings, a deep-sound thought-control-device is used. Lā-Fā-Jí, tell me, did you barely hear a buzz-buzz sound? I thought as much; right. They have something handy when they beckon to the child. Ah," he said, with a pleased sort of look, "the matter has sunk inextricably. We feel the need to fight."

"Fight?" Wēi-Ěr-bǎi Lā-Fā-Jí said like a whisper, because he was not a courageous man, notwithstanding that he afterwards became Chancellor of the Exchequer.

"Fight!" Jié-Kè Tài-Yī said in a low and deep voice.

Everyone in the place gazed at each other in speechless despair.

"We are a good hundred people," Jié-Kè Tài-Yī said, "and he is only one man. Right, we'll fight! We must distill drinking water. We must take that broadcast-device out of our television system. Dì-Mǐ should think of manufacturing a few electrical smell-probe devices, that he can use to look for the apparatus. We'll think of ways to block and break his mechanisms, we must destroy and extinguish them. That deep-sound equipment? Oh, yeah, he has to keep that at his side. We must subject him to a body-search. We can't get sentimental about this, mustn't, or our people won't be able to enjoy the good status they've had for generations!"

Wēi-Ěr-bǎi Lā-Fā-Jí made his throat clean. "Afterwards—"

"You can completely say 'afterwards,'" Jié-Kè Tài-Yī echoed. "Afterwards the United States Cavalry come vigorously down from the high mountains, to support him. So, however, gentlemen, as you now already know for yourselves, the true appearance of the situation is that we must enter the field of warfare."

And in fact they did, although you would be unable to say that they felt pleased about the matter of war.

V

Now I shall tell you all a tale, of the conditions outside Péng-shĭ Angle at that time.

The face of the lunar sphere is not more distant-remote from us. Oh, you are simply unable to imagine, truly unable to imagine. I don't know if I'm able to tell the matter clearly to you all, but it's all set down in a textbook; if you're willing, you can read it ... a textbook written by an important person, a military leader wrote it, who afterwards became a general (but that was much after this matter, and in a different army) and he was named T. Huá-lái-Shì[58] Kāng-Méi-Ēn.[59]

That textbook? Well, that textbook was entitled ⟨⟨The Finish of the Start.⟩⟩ It is the first scroll in a twelve-scroll set of memoirs. Those memoirs are entitled: ⟨⟨Follow Tài-Yí: The Seizure-by-Force Boundary-Struggle.⟩⟩

War had been approaching, war with a larger and larger threat; eventually it threatened everything, as the ultrasonic radiation devices went beyond hysteria and attained the level of terror. But the ⟨⟨Epoch⟩⟩ publication said that there was time for the public to think-enter wrong-wrong[60] about the situation.

The experts thought of a separation plan. Break up the cities, scatter-separate, diffuse the population and industry, so that for even the greatest bomb they should be a target so small as not to be worth mentioning.

But dispersal intensified a tremendous weakness—they needed many more freight trains, many more cargo ships, many more transport aircraft, moving forward raw material and moving out finished products not connected to each other, according to the duty roster. Well, they weren't easy to attack and destroy, but they made it easier to completely cut off the traffic-thread of supply.

The decision-people said not to adopt a dispersal method but rather to excavate air-raid shelters. But not merely

air-raid shelters—the factories must dig for ore-sand, drill to fetch oil, and extract cooling elements combined with heated air—cause them not to rely upon cargo that might never arrive, nor even to be able to talk about this (because the war would be continuous for so much time; it might be for a second, it might be for an unbearable eternity) that the workmen would be unable to stay down belowground, nor to rely on the ability of brains to reach the image-making boards and go-study laboratories and matter-assemble boards, because the brains might go the way to death, or be turned into something that couldn't be recognized as brains.

Well, the underground factories designed for themselves very completely, designed in a never-stopping always-curving rise.

Just as we and our machines appeared to be facing an enemy, with every advancing step we needed to grow more skillful, more clever, more swift than the enemy race. Faced with the matter of our having fewer and fewer soldiers, to rely on the pure inference-gathering that, with war every day continuing to descend, more and more many people were slaughtered, and only fewer and fewer remained to manufacture the slaughter-people military-devices. Against this, to ensure that the factories could not be captured nor subjected to danger, they couldn't hesitate to stand watch over these factories and guard their money and valuables against evil—to stand guard against every sort of mechanism, every sort of restraint-equipment, exploding-thing and die-light that men were able to devise—and later the machines would dominate everything. The machines would never stop speeding up production—producing more and more quickly, able to more and more powerfully slaughter people.

Another step in the descent—these fortress-type factories hung up hooks to each other, so that the factories that it was difficult to think of defending, in the difficult-to-think-of event that they should sink, would when faced with destruction or extinguishment send out a signal,

maintaining the original mission and giving this assignment to the nearest other factory—so that the surviving factories would share the responsibility for the work, increase production speed, advance another step towards ending life, while there were yet fewer guardians operating still more kill-people-devices.

And they had a last-of-all plan—to arrange for the machines to supply good things, housing, clothing and means of transport to a nation of people recovering from nobody-knew-what sort of bomb, bacteria, poisonous gas—if only the war were to continue to descend, no matter what sort of military device you could think of—the outcome could not be escaped.

Naturally, the machines were equipped with the components necessary for a peace signal: that is, the free air itself. Never ceasing to take surveys of the atmospheric layers, the machines producing war-goods would change to produce peace-goods-materials.

And such indeed was made.

Yet, how could it have been known, that the machines would be unable to distinguish between wartime and peacetime?

Here was Dǐ-Tè-Lü[61]: ten-times-ten-thousand *yingmǔ* of uninhabited desolate land, windows covered by curtains, walls broken to bits. Looking down from above, the walls of the city. But underground—ah, the pulse of activity could be seen beating quickly! The rumble-rumble opening-and-contraction of the raw material transport-channels, pulling in raw material and ore-sand, belch-belch-producing finished automobiles. Transport-channels looking like spiderwebs extended to the iron-ore bedrock beneath the lakes. Row upon row of barges sailed forth from the water-mud shipyards like the submarine base at Luò-Lǐ-Áng,[62] and without men to draw their sails the submarines swam the lakes and canals; going to their product drop-off locations, the submarines surfaced carrying glittering brand-new Buick-nameplate and Plymouth-nameplate automobiles.

What made them the latest style?

Why, reliance on industrial planning! Because the old style underwent a change of appearance. The '61 flow-body-move model moved over for the '62 8-type ultra-flow-body-move model; double-bright headlamps became triple-bright; white-ring wheel-belts became pine-blue-colored and then moved back to black wheel-belts.

It was a matter of planning efficiency.

What the founding ancestors learnt of production was basically like this: what you build doesn't matter; it only matters to have people want to buy it. Don't worry about humanity's powers of judgment. They are a worthless sort. Powers of judgment are unable to transport manu-factured products, unable to push commerce. Rather you should depend on the man-and-monkey habit of curiosity.

Of course, curiosity depends on keeping secrets.

So, generations of automobile manufacturers tested many of the latest devices, produced by workmen who promised to keep their mouths shut. There was no atomic bomb explosion method kept so excessively secret. All of Dì-Tě-Lü repeated their safeguard procedures: Every year when it was time for the latest style, the streets were filled with canvas-covered mystery-playthings; people discussed this—oh, right—they couldn't help but laugh; this was most funny; yet while they were delighted, they felt queer; it was perfectly correct to make a joke of the mystery, but behind the joke the people wished to own the new-model automobiles themselves.

Then the manufacturers put up their ears. Ah, so that's how it is. Curiosity, no? So they rented a secret com-partment, to design brand-new freezing equipment, then made a big fanfare revealing this. Yessiree, Bob! The electric iceboxes were immediately snatched up. Right, it was like madness.

The United States radio corporation had no choice but to accept the lesson, and use it themselves to add a flour-ish; when the Vinyl record-image-device was made, it was good for continuous use, was colored, extremely up-to-

date. They designed it secretly, and then, the very last-of-all flourish, they deliberately revealed the secret; this was the clever touch that the Manhattan[63] corporation hadn't learnt—the secret that concealed the true secret. Because the Vinyl-image program was only a sort of smokescreen; it was the ultimate sort of security measure; the Vinyl-image campaign-program was only a cover for the program imported underneath.

This transported manufactured goods. But the whole affair had its limits. Mankind itself cannot keep a secret.

So be it; some anonymous bigshot said; we will all let humanity perish-drop! Let a machine design the look of the new models! Attach a design component. Cause the design-shift-tester-devices and the randomly-select-devices to proceed with the reform in a fashion exceeding man's ability to imagine. Give the factories self-automation; conceal them underground; provide them with a sort of procedure to make them able to weave new procedures for themselves. Truth to say, why shouldn't it be like this? As Kē-Gé-Lán had come to quote Chá-Lǐ F. Kǎi-té-Lín: "Our purpose in go-study is to cause the customers to attain discontent," and machines can confirm the occurrence of this as well as any sort of man. Truth to say, they can do it better than a man.

So, the whole world was a place filled with quartz-stone caves, which sent forth many mysteries without stopping. The war gave industry a very good start, beginning with the method of dispersal, and then, thanks to bomb-avoid, the factories were concealed in rock; now security procedures rendered the factories a self-contained system. Products flowed out in a wild huge unstopping wave.

Yet they were unable to stop coming down. It wasn't possible to get inside the caves to deactivate the machines, nor even to slow them down. The people whom it was originally thought would consume the products were for the greatest part already nonexistent; the products emerging in a quick unstopping flow had to be con-

sumed. The auspicious-widespread-appraisal people had
to market the products, and in this respect they were very
skillful.

This was the situation outside: an extremely-very busy,
extremely-very big place. Don't hesitate to count the very
big destruction received during the Great War.

I can't tell you how very busy, nor how very big; I'm
only able to tell you all a very little of that situation. There
was a building, covering many *yingmǔ*, known as the
Five-Angled Skyscraper. Of course it had five sides: a
side for the Army, a side for the Navy, a side for the Air
Force, a side for the Marine Corps, and it had a side for
the business office of the Yóu-Sī-Dì and Lǔ-Mǐ-Lún-Dì
auspicious-widespread-appraisal corporation.

So, here was this great building the Five-Angled-
Skyscraper, which was the center of the United States in
every respect. (There was also this locality known as "Go-
Parliament,"[64] but that system is not very important. In
fact it wasn't important at the time.)

And here was this military leader Kāng-Méi-Ēn, in his
red-colored uniform, the uniform with epaulets, and from
his waist hangs a small ornate gold-plated double-edged
sword. He was in the Yóu-Sī-Dì and Lǔ-Mǐ-Lún-Dì corporation's waiting room, watching television. He'd already been waiting in there for an hour, and eventually
the people summoned him.

He went in.

Don't any of you try to imagine the sort of frame of
mind he had when he entered that pigskin-wall-protected
room. You can't guess. But you should know that he was
convinced this room held the key that would open his way
to an infinite road; he was convinced of this beyond any
doubt, and as it afterwards unfolded, he was right about
this.

"Major," an old man said not at all politely; this man
was remarkably like Kē-Gé-Lán, remarkably like Jié-Kè
Tài-Yī, because they were all very much the same sort
of man, these charcoal-colored white people[65] of the first

flow-great-study social class. "Major, he is conversing with us long-distance. It's just the sort of situation we feared. And there have been difficulties."

"Yeah, right, *xiānsheng!*"

Major Kāng-Méi-Ēn had a stiff-straight body posture, very much of soldierly bearing, because he had worked as an army officer for fifteen years, and this was his first opportunity to take part in battle. He had escaped the Great War—oh, yeah the entire ground force had escaped the Great War; the war ended so quickly, that the troops on maneuvers weren't able to get to it—and warfare hadn't come since that time. Except under certain specially designated conditions, it wasn't safe to fight. But perhaps those conditions were being provided now, he thought. And if he could lead a go-on-journey force, and could do a remarkable job, then a thing like that ought to have big say for the career of a major today!

And so he stood in stiff-straight posture, fully vigilant, standing with his vision shooting in four directions. His straw hat was held under one arm, and one hand was on the sword-handle of his sword, and he looked extremely ferocious. *Hǎi*, that's to be expected. The image being received on the television inside that pigskin-wall-protected boardroom would make every honest army officer extremely ferocious. The government authorities of the United States had been made to look the fool!

"L.S.," said the image of the face and chest of the old man on the copy-image screen, "they have stood up to me! They have taken my broadcast-device from me, cleared away my sprinkle-release-medicines, taken away my deep-sound-fixture. All I have left is this transmitter-lid!"

This Kē-Gé-Lán whose image was being seen in the room was no longer so gentle and cultivated; he seemed very agitated, and extremely angry.

"Truly interesting," comment-said Mr. Mǎ-Fēi-Dài whose underlings of the comparatively intimate sort called him "L.S." "They hadn't taken that transmitter-lid too.

They should have known that you would contact us, and that we would retaliate."

"But they wanted me to get in touch with you!" that voice from the kinescope shout-said. "I explained this matter to them, L.S. They are becoming like mad. They think war should arrive."

After a bit more talk, L.S. Mǎ-Fēi-Dài turned off the television.

"We'll give them what they want, right, Major?" he said, his own form standing stiff-bolt-upright like a poker.

"We'll do just that, sir!" the major said, and he saluted and turned his body round to leave. By then he could already feel the eagles on his shoulder-epaulets—and who could know what lies ahead or say, but that there may be five-pointed stars!

The first retaliatory journey began at once; the people of Péng-shǐ Angle should have expected them to adopt such measures afterwards, could have expected it—and in reality they got it.

I've already told you all, that there hadn't been warfare for a period of time, although many-many people still prepared for warfare as for them it was the first-rate priority. You all must feel that outside Péng-shǐ Angle this matter seemingly had no contradictory nature.

First the Great War had caused people, no matter what, from adopting any fierce manner. The old style of warfare—that is to say warfare using guided missiles and radioactive material and atomic cannon—was already most supremely costly and caused people not to deploy it. Only great fortune was able to prevent the sudden development that this globe would be able to wipe itself thoroughly clean, and provide perishment-fall for the people, to have nothing any more complex than the *jǐsuǒdòngwù*[66] develop, and that world only good for single-cell creatures to gradually start anew. The present situation wasn't like that.

First of all, atomic explosives had received severe restriction. The entire world had approximately twenty or

thirty nations possessing the hydrogen bomb or more advanced military devices, and every one of those nations had men on duty twenty-four hours of every day, with their fingers ready to press the knob; except that whichever nation would dare to first use atomic weapons again, they would press down those knobs and thoroughly clean-perish-fall the Earth. So this was not viable.

And airplanes, for the same reason, lost a large part of their function-use. The satellites equipped with round-round look-at-bright eyeballs kept watch on every nook of the world day and night without stopping, so that you wouldn't dare throw so much as a dynamite bomb, because perhaps one myopic person keeping watch on the satellites as they moved about the Earth's face might mistake that ordinary bomb for a nuclear bomb—and thereby press those knobs.

In this such fashion, there only remained the infantry to resort to.

However that mustn't be just an infantry! An arrangement of twenty-three men, they possessed the firepower of the entire Napoleon[67] army group. A group was made up of approximately two hundred and fifty men; it can be confirmed that the First World big-War could be won by relying on them.

Portable weapons produced dozens of reality-slivers of iron-and-steel mesh, bullets that flew and hit so swiftly that you couldn't help but aim at a target and the bullet-hole would cut it in half. If everybody's eye could see the locality, the rifle bullets could fly to it. If the eye met up with black sky, or dense fog, or because the hills blocked eyesight, whether the eye could see or not, then the infrared ray-aim-device, the radar and pulse-bright interfere-type observe-devices could take the place of you and me and hit that target, like as if it were nearly as much as ten *mǎ*[68]-units away from you in broad daylight.

This was right to say, that these were the most advanced weapons in all the world. In fact the weapons that this infantry put up were of such a modern sort that while

one half of a military company was still busy studying
how to use them, the other half had already stepped back
and found them unable to be used again. In the event of
having a 13-model double-belted-uranium-drill white-of-
the-eye move-all-weather aiming-device, who would then
want a 12-model type?

Truth to say, that was the number-one triumph of the
era; in fact, the design-quick discard-as-useless and high-
speed turnaround plan of the farthest-back-original television set or automobile from Dì-Tĕ-Lü slowly came to
expand its aspect to include carbines and rocket cannon.

This scene was utterly wonderful, and utterly terrifying.

And so, battlewards, or towards whatever disaster could
occur, people approached the state of heroism.

Major Kāng-Méi-En (this is said in his writings) led an
entire military company, altogether two hundred and fifty-
two men, and started towards Péng-shǐ Angle. Aircraft
brought them to the Lehigh[69] province, that had been
covered with radiation-ray burn-fragments, but the
scorched earth was once again lacking dangerous qualities. Inside there they changed over to automobiles and
continued to advance.

Major Kāng-Méi-Ēn was an extremely calm and cool-
headed man. The sandy soil all round Péng-shǐ Angle still
possessed radioactivity, but it did not present any ques-
tionability. Because his army division's equipment was
very-extremely complete and advanced. Kē-Gé-Lán could
use a shield, but the United States Army could easily
outshield him; Kē-Gé-Lán drove an automobile made of
lead, but this go-on-journey force used for their travel
iridium metal-cast[70] vehicles, with appropriate gamma-ray
protect-screen equipment on top.

Each group had its own half-track lead-move-transport
vehicle. Not only did each man have his own portable
weapon; the top of each vehicle was equipped with a
105-millimeter big cannon. The big cannon on top had

shoot-by-itself attachments and auto-controlled insurance interlock. Hydraulic brackets supported the big cannon's ten-thousand-direction orient-plate. Radar sought its target. Auto-controlled digit computers collected data about the direction in which their target was going to fly.

In the personnel-transport-vehicle up front, Major Kāng-Méi-Ēn sent down the last-of-all command to his rank-and-file soldiers:

"This is war approaching, brethren! The decision of when to fight has now already arrived! For a long period of time you've all drilled for battle, and now you're already personally on the scene. I don't know what Destiny will bring us inside there—" in saying this he waved an arm to touch the morning in the direction of Péng-shǐ Angle, and this posture was conveyed into each move-transport-vehicle in the entire motorcade, via the on-the-spot reflected stereoscoping multicolor image—"but come victory or defeat, and I know we'll have a victory, I want each of you men to know that you've all joined the best military company, that has joined the best regiment, that has joined the best fight-in-the-open-country infantry group, that has joined the best division—"

Just then, from the 105-mm big cannon on the leading personnel transport vehicle, there arose a rumble-rumble sound, because the radar equipment had already found its target all by itself, while the cannon fired at a moving thing it had seen, and this cannon dwarfed the sound of the major, so that he couldn't extend his tribute to the large military force, the division headquarters, the army group and the Supreme High Command.

The Battle of Péng-shǐ Angle had begun.

VI

Now the first target was struck, but it wasn't any person.

It was only one end of a milk cow, and just about due

for mating again. It shouldn't have gone up to the softball field, but it already had, and since it was facing straight into the direction in which the military division advanced to attack the small town, it made the highest-of-all high sacrifice. Of course it didn't know that it had made this sacrifice.

Major Kāng-Méi-Ēn spoke to his deputy officer with an angry voice: "Lái-Fèi-Cí!⁷ The artillerymen must tie up all the safety-insurance of our big cannon. The men can't give way to receiving this sort of situation." To see that old milk cow get turned into hamburger, to see it covered with meat-sauce, was something people shouldn't have to see. Best to tie up those big cannon, at any rate, until we could see whether Péng-shǐ Angle was really ready for the first battle.

So Major Kāng-Méi-Ēn made the army vehicles stop-stay, and told the personnel to dismount them. They were now already past the radioactive region that really had danger.

The battle regiment accomplished an extremely good-looking spread-apart; they moved very-extremely quickly, and were very-extremely good-looking. From the top of the old gather-cathedral pagoda in Péng-shǐ Angle, Jié-Kè Tài-Yī and Ān-Dí Gé-Lǎ-Mǐ-Sī gazed into the distance through a telescope, and I ought to tell you, Gé-Lǎ-Mǐ-Sī wanted to stop resting on the bottom of a big eruption. But Jié-Kè Tài-Yī only hum-hummed, and nodded his head.

Major Kāng-Méi-Ēn issued an order, and each man in the battle-line began digging trenches. These men had swamp, these men had mud; moreover the men had to dig into hard-hard rock-stone, and some of them—most-near-away-from where the first target was—only had to dig through a thin slice of hamburger and meat-sauce. This had no consequence, because they didn't use the Second World big-War type of dig-trench shovel; they used self-digging devices that could dig into anything no matter what; and not only that, but when they dug the

trenches their insides were lined with a very attractive porcelain-type gloss. This was indeed supremely mighty.

And yet, in another respect—

Ah, you see, this was the situation. Twenty-six personnel transport vehicles had delivered them into this place. Each vehicle had its own driver, had a have-use-driver,[72] had an urgent-situation have-use-driver, and had a place-repair-workman. It had its own radar and electrical-set-up-equipment repair-worker, its own radar and electrical-set-up-equipment repair-worker assistant. It had four large artillerymen, and had a place-contact-officer and a get-in-touch-with-commanding-officer-contact to get in touch with the government officials.

Yeah, right, of course, they had a need for that many personnel. Without having them, the military division wouldn't be able to deal with anything.

But these men added to the others already resulted in two hundred and eighty-two men.

There was also the fight-in-the-open-country kitchen, that had a kitchen staff of forty-seven altogether, and also had a go-political-supervise-getalong-and-food-study committee, the connect-parts-together-regiment with a soldiers'-pay-and-provisions group, and a military-police squad; as well as the meteorology group: you should see it as they set up the teletype machine and the fan-shaped-receive-device, and see the contact-go-up-to-sky-empty-release-air-balloon-shapes: you would feel very proud. The war hospital had eighty-one hygienicists and attendants, nine medical officers with independent medical administration mechanisms; the specific-type-of-service group, which placed a three-dimensional square[73] above the fronts of the personnel vehicles, busily erected the movie screen, and formed the first handball match among the unequal-value personnel group. The four follow-army-clergymen had their own assistants, plus also they had the moral-culture-doctrine, not-know-opinion and get-ready-to-shake division of the brain trust; the government records official and eight dispatch trainees: they were

boldly taking magnetic-tape recorders from one foxhole to another foxhole, wanting to take down notes and measure footprints as history took shape, as it was said, wanting to take down notes and firsthand impressions of something that hadn't occurred yet. Plus also Canada, Mexico, Uruguay, the Scandinavian[74] Federation, and the Soviet Union had all sent military observers with their orderlies and aides-de-camp: and of course people came from ⟨⟨Star-and-Strip,⟩⟩[75] ⟨⟨New York Times,⟩⟩ ⟨⟨Christian Scientific Knowledge Protect-Report,⟩⟩[76] ⟨⟨Sī-Kè-Lǐ-Pǔ-Sī—Huò-Huá-Dé[77] Alliance-Report,⟩⟩ five image-wire corporations, eight television nets, one record-film-strip corporation, and one hundred twenty-seven news bureaus with hear-the-news war correspondents.

Of course this was organized as a refined-simple war group. So each reporter had only one hear-the-news officer.

And yet...

This sort of thing left just-enough-only forty-six men in the battle line.

Upstairs at the top of the old gather-cathedral, Ān-Dí Gé-Lǎ-Mǐ-Sī put on a long face and spoke: "Look-a-look at them, Jié-Kè! I don't know; perhaps allowing widespread-appraisal to return to Péng-shǐ Angle wouldn't be a bad matter. You look now, it was a carnival-grounds life before the war, but—"

"Wait-a-wait," Jié-Kè Tài-Yī spoke peacefully, and went hum-hum inside.

They weren't able to see it very well, yet the battle line was now in chaos. They had faced the knowledge that the safety-insurance of their fight-in-the-open cannon had been tied up, and that the complete fire-strength of the military division consisted of forty-six carbines. Yeah, right, this wasn't bad; but no matter what is said, ten days before the go-on-journey force was outfitted, then had all been equipped with E-Z fire-strength revolve-turn carbines. But some of those men in the regiment didn't have

an intimate knowledge of the new-model weapons yet.

All up the firing line this sort of situation developed:

"Shān'ḿ,"[78] one person shouted to the private in the foxhole alongside. "Shañ'ḿ, hear me speak, I don't know how to make this what-is-it carbine work. When that what-is-it blue light goes high, is-it-right-isn't-it-right to say that the what-is-it safety-insurance is already disengaged?"

"That what-is-it is completely unknown to me," Shañ'ḿ replied back, his eyebrows cocked as he looked at the multicolored, bright paper-sealed instruction manual. That instruction manual had the extremely move-people title ⟨⟨Repeat New Gain Good-Fit and Tranquility Five-Step Supernatural Eye Technique.⟩⟩ "Do you see what it says up front? This is what: 'When the Supernatural Eye has entered the not-move condition, it only takes the positive failsafe[79] move-work, and thereby assures the Jiffi-Kleen[80] carbine of strong ejection with release, notwithstanding when used with the shoulder-sit-stay-cushions."

"You say what, Shañ'ḿ?"

"I said that the what-is-it is something that I cannot understand," Shañ'ḿ said, and threw the instruction manual into the uninhabited strip of land in front of him.

But afterwards he regretted that, and crawled out to bring it back, because even though nobody was able to use it, and it had nothing to do with the mud and earth all around Péng-shǐ Angle, inside that instruction book were glossy photographs of female bright starshines with the pieces put together[81]—because when the underground factories produced military devices they also produced instruction books. Of course they felt they had to do this sort of thing, as they were very good at making instruction books; as the charts became complicated, they used more photographs. Those car-vehicle images would make people shout to look at them.

A few minutes afterwards: "They don't seem to be doing anything in there," Ān-Dí Gé-Lǎ-Mǐ-Sī vague-vaguely said, while he watched from above in the high pagoda.

"Right, they aren't doing anything, Ān-Dí. That-what, we cannot remain sitting in this place. Come, and we'll return to the situation to look-a-look."

Ān-Dí Gé-Lǎ-Mǐ-Sī didn't want to come, but Jié-Kè Tài-Yī couldn't very well be overruled, so they went down the twisting stairs, and met Péng-shǐ Angle's fourteen-member volunteer army, those were all that had come, and went over to that softball field.

Twenty-six personnel move-transport-vehicles made an electrical noise arise of its own accord, and the cannon-pagodas of their 105-mm cannon turned to aim at that stand-alone army.

Forty-six rifle hands, interspersing talk with curses, tried to make the new image of their À-Kè-Yī[82]A.C. blue-thread aim-band cross the blue-colored horizon true-view-sector appear-emerging in the screens sealed up into their off-model radar.

And that Major Kāng-Méi-Ēn, emitting shouts when he saw this, sway-looked a set of documents in the face of his deputy officer. "What sort of seventy-eight varieties of pickled mess is this?" he insisted, because a soldier remains a soldier no matter how much height[83] he has. "When the enemy-people are coming straight towards us, I can't withdraw the men from the firing line!"

"The army so orders, sir." that deputy officer said while maintaining his composure. He had obtained a doctorate in military affairs, and he knew which person's orders had what sort of significance to whom. "The turn-forces strategy wasn't my idea, sir. Why don't you handle this with the Five-Angled Skyscraper?"

"But, Lái-Fèi-Cí, you fool you, I'm not in touch with the Five-Angled Skyscraper! Those what-are-they reporters have already squeezed the television channels! Now you insist that I withdraw every rifleman facing the line, and let them have a rest in holiday-camp for three weeks—"

"No, sir," that deputy officer set him straight, finger-showing the orders while speaking. "Only twenty days is

right, sir, including round-trip travel time. But you would do best to act promptly, sir, I can only see it this way. This order is written 'Urgent Dispatch.' "

Ah, but Major Kāng-Méi-Ēn was not a blockhead. No matter what they said about him afterwards. He had studied the tragic downfall of von Paulus[84] at Stalingrad,[85] he had studied how Lee[86] with the support of Heaven's good fortune had escaped from Gettysburg, and he knew what might befall a far-journey force within an enemy-people's area, if they happened to be afraid of the situation. Even a very big sort of far-journey force. And you must remember, this far-journey force of his was quite small.

He remembered that as you lose daylight, everything in that place becomes your enemy; many more of the Nazi Sixth Army died unnatural deaths of frost-cold combined with dysentery than slaughter-died from the Soviet people; when Lee withdrew the bumping of the carts sent more wounded-and-sick men to loss than did the great cannon of Meade.[87] So he could only have no choice but to be in accordance with such means as were made.

"Now retreat!" he big-shout-spoke. "We must withdraw at once to back inside the warehouse."

Withdraw-return-repeat and reorganize troops; isn't this good? But the situation wasn't so simple.

The soldier-vehicles moved backwards, appearing like a flotilla going in a big roundabout. Those vehicle-machine-soldiers had learnt to drill in this fashion. But one move-soldier-vehicle got tangled up with the specific-type-of-service-group's movie screen, and as a result collided with another vehicle, and three other vehicles found themselves piled up among the advance-structural-components of the fight-in-the-open hospital with no way out. Five of the vehicles that had assumed the burden of extra assignments, using their rear axles to drive the table dynamos, were within fifteen minutes completely unable to get out, as a result of having become penned up among it all.

The final situation was that the twenty-six vehicles had

only four among them able to move out. And it was very apparent of course that those weren't enough, so this wasn't simply a retreat; this was simply first-rate disaster.

"Now there is only one resort," Major Kāng-Méi-Ēn ponder-looked from the center of the fragmented chaos, his face trickling the tears of a hero. "But how much I hope that I had not thought to try to make a reason to change myself from lieutenant to major!"[88]

This was such: Jié-Kè Tài-Yī accepted Kāng-Méi-Ēn's surrender. Jié-Kè Tài-Yī's countenance did not have an iota of amazement. But I can't say anything of the sort about the people among the stand-alone volunteer army.

"Don't want this, Major, you may keep your double-edged sword," Jié-Kè Tài-Yī said mildly, "and the officers your army has among it may retain their accurate-flat-trajectory nothing-jump power-tote weapons."

"Thank-thank you, sir," the major sob-spoke, and stagger-stagger-walked ahead and went inside the army officers' club that the link-section-assemble-division hadn't stopped building yet.

Jié-Kè Tài-Yī looked behind the image of his back, with a peculiar pondering sort of expression.

Lā-Fā-Jí, brandishing a walking-stick made from a thirty-inch root grown from a peach tree—this was the only weapon he could find at the time—mutter-mutter spoke: "This is a first-rate great victory! Now I guess they won't get the general idea to come provoke us again!"

Jié-Kè Tài-Yī had not a word to say.

"You don't deem such a thing as this, Jié-Kè? That they won't be bold enough to come in here again now?"

Jié-Kè Tài-Yī gazed at him lukewarmishly, as if getting ready to reply to his question, but suddenly turned to Chá-Lǐ Fú-Lín-Kè. "Chá-Lǐ, listen to me. Do-you-don't-you have a prop-up-pistol squared away?"

"Right, Mr. Tài-Yī. Also have a twenty-two millimeter rifle. Want me to get hold of them?"

"Ah, right, I think such as this." Jié-Kè Tài-Yī watched

that young man run away. He used his hand to cover his own eyes. Afterwards he said: "Ān-Dí, do a bit of something for us. Have that major give our group a military prisoner to take charge of, who knows the road to the place of the Five-Angled Skyscraper."

A bit of time later, Chá-Lǐ returned with that prop-up-pistol and that twenty-two-millimeter rifle; as for later matters, they naturally joined the scope of history.

NOTES

1. Wherever a proper name appears in the manuscript, the Chinese translator has used Chinese pictographs bearing a phonetic similarity to the original name. Since most of the pictographs in Chinese have both a phonetic value and a specific meaning, each character's name in this story translates into a phrase or sentence in Chinese. In these notes I will give the Chinese translation of each proper name as it appears in the text. The pictographs forming the name *Kē-Gé-Lán* (?Coughlin?) would translate as "curriculum-grid-orchid."

2. The *chě* is a chinese unit of length corresponding roughly to one-third of a meter.

3. A *cùn* is one-tenth of a *chě* (see Note 2), or roughly one-third of a decimeter. It is worth noting that while many Americans and Britons are still resisting the metric system, the Chinese have been using a decimal-based system of measurement for several centuries.

4. The Chinese phonetic approximation of Volkswagen is *Fó-Kè-Sī-Wǎ-Gēn*. It would translate as "The Buddha can whinny and shingle the root."

5. *Bì-Kè* is apparently the Chinese phonetic approximation for Buick. *Bì-Kè* would translate as "Able to finish."

6. *Chá-Lǐ Fú-Lín-Kè* (?Charley Flink?) would translate as "The forest cannot examine the texture."

7. *Chǔ-Ji-Wù-Dé* would translate as "The five-odd ugly virtues."

8. *Kǎi-Xī Fú-Lín-Tè* (?Casey Flint?) would translate as "Triumphant strains of the West in no particular forest."

9. *Ān-Dí Gé-Lǎ-Mǐ-Sī* (?Andy Grames?) would translate as "Pull this rice grid for tranquil enlightenment."

10. *Jié-Kè Tài-Yī* (?Jack Tie?) would translate as "The ultimate hermaphrodite can be outstanding."

11. *Āi-Dé-Suǒ-Ěr* would translate as "your large rope's dusty morals."

12. *Wēi-Ěr-Màn-Yī-Shǐ* would translate as "the impressive strength of your one graceful pig."

13. *Kǎ-Péng-Tè*: As mentioned in Note 1 (*q.v.*), *Péng* is a common Chinese surname. *Kǎ-Péng-Tè* would therefore translate as "Intercept the particular Péng."

14. "Design-shift-testers." When an English-language term has no existing translation into Chinese, the practice is to use however many Chinese words as may be necessary to convey the general sense of the English term. The Chinese pictographs appearing in the text at this point translate as "design-shift-testers." Throughout this text, the appearance of a long string of words all joined together by hyphens indicates a series of Chinese pictographs strung together to describe an object or concept for which there is not yet any word for in Chinese.

15. *Kè-li-Níq-Kè-Sī* is a Chinese phonetic representation of "Kleenex." The pictographs used here would translate as "This diligent *li* can have ability." The pictograph *li* is one of the comparatively rare Chinese characters that has a phonetic value only, with no specific meaning.

16. *Mǎ-Fēi-Dài* would translate as "Lead the evil horse."

17. *Dì-Lā-Huá*, a phonetic approximation of "Delaware," would translate as "Pull the magnificent Earth."

18. *É-Sī-Tǎ-Bà-Lǔ-Kè* would translate as "This pagoda-cloth can be stupid, eh?" in which the pictograph having the phonetic value *É* is an interjection.

19. *Huá-Shèng-Dùn*: the pictographs used here would translate as "Magnificent flourishing hesitation."

20. "The North-and-South War." I have translated this phrase literally, but it obviously refers to the American Civil War.

21. *Pēn-Xī-Fǎ-Ní-Yà* would translate as "spurt-sunset inferior-mud-law."

22. "New *Zé-Yǒu*" (the Chinese pictograph for "new" plus two characters possessing the phonetic value "Zé-Yǒu") is apparently the Chinese translator's attempt to render the name of some geographic or political district in the U.S. *Zé-Yǒu* would translate as "October pool."

23. *Fèi-lǎ-Dé-Ěr-Fěi-Yǎ*, would translate as "*lǎ* morals fees of your

humble mute." *Lǎ* is a Chinese pictograph having only a phonetic value, with no specific meaning.

24. *Niŭ-Yāo-Xī* would translate as "Weigh the western button," and to judge by the context it appears to be a phonetic rendering of "New York City." But why would the Chinese translator render the word "new" phonetically in *this* case and translate it directly into the proper Chinese character for "new" in the passage for "New *Zé-Yǒu*"? (*Cf.* Note 22.) There is apparently an inconsistency here on the part of the Chinese translator.

25. *Nài-Kè*: the Chinese pictographs having the phonetic value *Nài-Kè* would translate as "can-be-apple."

26. *Xiào-Wān-Jiā-Nóng-Ké*: Apparently a Chinese phonetic approximation of some American proper name that I am unable to determine. The pictographs used here would translate as "Agriculture can also resemble curvature."

27. *Lā-Fā-Jí* (?Lafarge?) would translate as "Pull the fortunate emission."

28. *Wēi-Ěr-bǎi* would translate as "your impressive strength *bǎi*," in which the pictograph having the phonetic value *bǎi* possesses no dictionary meaning.

29. *É-dī-sī*: apparently a phonetic representation of some English-language name.

30. *Wēi-Lǎo* would translate as "old impressive strength."

31. *Dān-bǎi-Lǐ* would translate as "scattered red *bǎi*," with *bǎi* being a pure phonetic. See Note 48.

32. *Kāng-Niè-Dí-Kè*: the entire phrase would translate as "to dye Dí's well-being black scrupulously." Judging from the context, it is apparent that this entire passage (see also Note 47) means "Danbury, Connecticut."

33. *Teng'm Fèi-Ěr-Cǎi* would translate as "boiling water '*m*, your vegetable expenses." The phonetic character '*m* has no dictionary meaning.

34. *Mǎ-Lín Gé-Luó-Xiào-Kè* would translate as "Horse-forest grid-that-can-resemble-birdsnare."

35. "Widespread-appraisals." Because the advertising profession and its excesses form a consistent theme in Frederik Pohl's SF during the period in which this story was written, the 1950s, I suspect that the Chinese pictographs "widespread-appraisal" are a crude approximation for "advertising" or some similar word or phrase in the original English-language text.

36. *Bèi-Dì Fú-Nèi-Sī. Bèi* is an uncommon Chinese surname; the entire group of pictographs would translate as "Bèi's stamen is not within this."

37. *Xiǎojiě*: Chinese title of respect for an unmarried female who is younger than the speaker, roughly equivalent to the English-language "Miss." *Xiǎojiě* would translate literally as "little elder-

sister."

38. *Sī-Kè-Nè-Kè-Tǎ-Dì*: the pictographs employed here would translate as "This pagoda can be able to stop the Earth."

39. "Sky-wire." Literal translation of, presumably, "aerial" or "antenna."

40. *Dì-Mǐ Háo-Lán* would translate as "rice-stamen good-orchid."

41. *Dài-nuó Shāo-Ěr-Sī*: the pictograph *nuó* is a pure phonetic with no meaning; the other characters would translate as "This trifle of yours is black eyebrow-paint."

42. *Jié-Qī Gé-Lì-Sen-Sī*: the pictographs used here would translate as "prominent-base this sharp grid is full of trees."

43. "First-stage-program." I don't know what English-language phrase the Chinese writer was attempting to translate here. The pictograph employed here refers to a "stage" in the theatrical sense rather than "stage" in the meaning of a level.

44. "*Gé-gé*-laugh noises." An onomatopoeic invention. Our English-language word "giggle" would be almost a precise equivalent.

45. "Go-study." Mark research, perhaps?

46. *Kǎi-té-Lín* would translate as "Triumphant strains of the *té* forest." The pictograph *té* is a phonetic with no meaning.

47. "Second-Common-Mix-Nation." Alternate translation: "second people's-republic."

48. *Méi-Dí-Xùn* would translate as "Dí abdicates from favor," in which *Dí* is a Chinese surname.

49. *Yóu-Sī-Dì*: apparently a phonetic rendering of an American proper name. The pictographs employed here would translate as "This prominence of the Earth."

50. *Lǔ-Mǐ-Lún-Dì*: apparently a phonetic rendering of an American proper name. The pictographs would translate as "stupid rice feudal ethics of the Earth."

51. "Want what-did?" This interrogative fragment has no subect and cannot be translated more completely.

52. "Cocoa *Wèi-Zǐ*": apparently a brand name for a breakfast cereal. The pictographs possessing the phonetic value *Wèi-Zǐ* would literally translate as "Tie the son together"; *Cuī-Zǐ* would translate literally as "The son hurries"; *Yī-Zǐ* would translate literally as "The son is a hermaphrodite"; *Ní-Zǐ* would translate literally as "The son is a Buddhist nun"; *Yī-Ní-Kě-Wèi-Zǐ* would translate literally as "The son has approval to tie the Buddhist nun to the hermaphrodite." Whew!

53. "Flavor *Hóng-Ní*." The phonetic value *Hóng-Ní*, would translate roughly as "Taste the red Buddhist nun."

54. "Plum Bran Dog." Why would a breakfast food name translate into Chinese as "Plum Bran Dog"? Perhaps the English-language name was "Plum Bran *Chow*," and the Chinese translator read this as "chow" in the sense of a chow dog rather than in the

sense of food. Another possibility: the Chinese pictographs for "Plum Bran Dog" would be pronounced *Méi Kāng Gǒu*. Perhaps in the original English-language version the cereal was called "Muck 'n' Goo" or some similarly appetizing name, and the Chinese translator rendered this phonetically as *Méi Kāng Gǒu*, which is Chinese for "Plum Bran Dog."

55. "Son-Named-Two." Based on the context of the subsequent paragraphs, this appears to refer to Charlie Chan's Number Two Son.

56. "*Chá-Lǐ Qián*," Earl Derr Biggers's Hawaiian detective of Chinese ancestry, Charlie Chan. Biggers, when naming his character, may not have realized that "Chan" is in fact not a Chinese surname at all; Chinese-Americans surnamed Chan have usually undergone an Anglicization somewhere along the line. *Qián*, a legitimate Chinese surname, is also the word for a type of Chinese copper coin. The nearest English-language equivalent would be the surname "Penny."

57. *Gūgu*. In Chinese folk etymology, the *gūgu* would be a slang term for a young unmarried female with whom one is not on intimate terms . . . but would like to be.

58. *Huá-lái-Shì* would translate as "the magnificent bachelor *lái*," in which the pictograph *lái* is a phonetic with no dictionary meaning.

59. *Kāng-Méi-Ēn* would translate as "the well-being of the graceful plum."

60. "Think-enter wrong-wrong." I have translated this phrase as literally as possible because I cannot determine its correct English-language meaning.

61. *Dǐ-Tè-Lǜ* would translate literally as "bottom-special-law."

62. *Luò-Lǐ-Áng*. The Chinese pictograph employed here for the phonetic value *Luò* is the name of a Chinese river. *Luò-Lǐ-Áng* would translate as "inside the highwaters of the river Luo."

63. *Màn-Hǎ-Dùn* would translate roughly as "the graceful pause of exhalation."

64. From the context, the phrase appearing here seems to refer to the United States Congress. But there seems to be some confusion: the pictographs appearing at this point in the text, *guó-huìchū*, would translate as "go-Parliament," whereas the orthodox Chinese word for the U.S. Congress is *guóhuìměi*, which would translate as "beautiful Parliament." This arises from the Chinese name for the United States, *Měiguó*, which means "beautiful nation." Perhaps the Chinese, not being as enamored of the United States as they used to be, are phasing out use of the adjective "beautiful" to describe the United States. This would explain the translator's decision to use *guóhuìchū* rather than the more conventional *guóhuìměi* here.

65. "Charcoal-colored white people." In other words, even though the people themselves are white (i.e., Caucasian), they are covered with some charcoal-colored substance or clad in charcoal-colored material. Charcoal-gray flannel suits, probably.

66. *Jǐsuǒdòngwù* has two possible translations: "chordate animal" or "notochord-creature." At this point in the Chinese text there appears a footnote symbol, and at the bottom of that page is a footnote in Chinese which I translate as "living thing that has evolve-changed a rudimentary vertebrate body, principally of the marine class."

67. *Ná-Pò-Lún*. The pictographs employed would translate as "The logical sequence has been held and broken."

68. *Mǎ*: a Chinese word denoting a system of measurement or calibration, but it does not indicate what sort of quantity (volume, temperature, distance, time) is being measured. *Mǎ* would translate into English as "unit," but it does not denote any specific measurement standard.

69. *Lì-Hā-Yī* would translate literally as "the sharp exhalation of the hermaphrodite."

70. "Iridium metal-cast vehicles." This appears to mean that the vehicles are iridium-*plated* rather than *made* of iridium.

71. *Lái-Fèi-Cí* would translate literally as "the expense of thatching *lái*," in which the pictograph *lái* is a phonetic with no meaning.

72. "A have-use-driver." This appears to mean an auxiliary or backup driver.

73. "A three-dimensional square." I have translated this phrase as literally as possible, but I am unable to figure out precisely what it refers to. A cube? A geometric figure that is two-dimensional and three-dimensional simultaneously? Some sort of geodesic paradox? I don't know.

74. *Sī-Kān-de-Nà-Wéi-Yà*: The entire string of pictographs would translate as "This *de* can receive and tie together that which is inferior."

75. This is a reference to the G.I. publication *Stars and Stripes*.

76. The *Christian Science Monitor*.

77. *Sī-Kè-Lǐ-Pǔ-Sī* would translate literally as "these insides can be this universal." *Huò-Huá-Dé* would translate literally as "sudden magnificent virtue." The entire string of characters should translate as "the Scripps-Howard News Syndicate," with all except the last three pictographs being employed as phonetic characters rather than determinatives.

78. *Shān-'m*: The phonetic character *'m* has no dictionary meaning. *Shān* would translate as "mountain."

79. *Fèi-Ér-Sài-Fú*: The pictographs would translate literally as "Don't squeeze your expenses in."

80. *Yī-Fú–Kè-Lín*: The four pictographs are apparently a phonetic

approximation of something like Jiffi-Kleen. *Yī-Fú–Kè-Lín* would translate literally as "Neither he nor she can be the forest."

81. "Female bright starshines with all the pieces put together." From the contest this phrase probably means something like "starlets with attractive builds" or "well-stacked starlets."

82. *À-Kè-Yī*: apparently a phonetic representation of a word that I cannot determine. The pictographs would roughly translate as "One can say '*ah*.'"

83. I have translated this phrase literally; a more appropriate but less literal translation can be obtained by substituting "rank" for "height."

84. *Féng Bō-Lēi-Sī*: *Féng* is a fairly common surname in Chinese, and the pictographs used here for the phonetic values *Bō-Lēi-Sī* would translate as "Tie this wave up tightly."

85. *Sī-Dà-Lín-Gé-Lēi-de*: The pictographs would translate roughly as "Tie up tightly this orchard."

86. The Chinese pictograph for "plum," which would be pronounced *Lǐ*, is used here to refer to General Robert E. Lee.

87. *Mǐ-Dé*: The pictographs employed here would translate literally as "rice-virtue."

88. Has the Chinese translator made an error here? Why would the character speaking think to pass directly from the rank of lieutenant to major, bypassing a captaincy? I have checked my translation carefully against the possibility that I myself may have made a mistake here, but this does not appear to be the case. The ranks described at this point within the Chinese text, *shàngwèi* and *shàoxiào*, would translate respectively as "lieutenant" and "major."

ABOUT THE AUTHOR

Frederik Pohl has been about everything one can be in the world of science fiction: fan (a founder of the fabled Futurians), book and magazine editor, agent, and, above all, writer. As editor of *Galaxy* in the 1960s, he helped set the tone for a decade of SF—his own memorable stories such as *The Space Merchants* (in collaboration with Cyril Kornbluth). His latest novel is *The Cool War*. He has also written *The Way the Future Was*, a memoir of his forty-five years in science fiction. Frederik Pohl was born in Brooklyn, New York, in 1919, and now lives in Schaumbury, Illinois, with his wife, Elizabeth Anne Hull.